DEATH CULT

ALSO BY JANUARY BAIN

DEATH CULT

AN ANNE HALE PI THRILLER
BOOK 4

JANUARY BAIN

**ROUGH
EDGES
PRESS**

Death Cult
Paperback Edition
Copyright © 2024 January Bain

Rough Edges Press
An Imprint of Wolfpack Publishing
1707 E. Diana Street
Tampa, FL 33610

roughedgespress.com

Paperback ISBN 978-1-68549-520-6
eBook ISBN 978-1-68549-738-5
LCCN: 2024946119

For Don

DEATH CULT

ONE

PRESENT DAY, ANCHOR, ALASKA

> You must die. If you come back, then you
> share with all of us what you learn. If
> you don't, you've been chosen to move
> on from this plane. Reincarnation will
> be your route to salvation.
>
> ~Mother

I have to tell somebody. He glanced furtively over at the occupant of the bed to the left of him, listening, wondering if he'd waited long enough. It was the middle of the night; snores and other disgusting human sounds echoed all around, but by now everyone in the crowded men's dormitory should have been fast asleep. His chief concern was the brother to his left who was always getting up to use the bathroom at the most inconvenient hour. Not like he hadn't heard about it often enough, grumblings about the state of his prostate interrupting his every meal. The last thing he wanted was to be questioned by the old man who would no doubt tattletale on him first chance he got. The snitch had been up not twenty minutes ago, but his regular, even breathing made it appear he'd gone straight back to sleep. He had to chance it. The press of time was eating at him, the ticking of an unseen clock a constant reminder that soon it would be too late.

He pushed back the blanket before pulling out the small bag he'd hidden under the covers. It contained enough food and water to get him by until he could make it to the highway and civilization. He picked up his boots from the floor to avoid wasting time putting them on, and then began to creep along the wooden planked floor, cautiously avoiding the creaky board near the corner of his bed.

Thankfully the brother didn't challenge him as he crept past his cot. Only the old man had permission to visit the bathroom at night due to his medical condition. But the geezer was, in reality, the least of his concerns. The watchmen would be on patrol, ostensibly on the lookout for an intruder, but knowing what he'd learned two days ago it was more than likely to keep those inside prisoners. He swallowed at the sudden dryness in his throat, sweat trickling down his spine.

He did have a plan to take care of them and keep them off his trail, but he worried as much if it would work as whether he had the courage to follow through. He patted his pocket, making sure the book of matches was still there. He'd gone to great trouble to acquire them, sneaking into the supply room and snatching them up when no one was looking. Then keeping them hidden for this moment.

Outside the large wooden structure built to resemble a Quonset hut in shape and home to more than a hundred men, he paused to pull on his boots. The cold turned his breath to fine ice crystals, frosting the air around him. It would have been far better to run in summer, but by then it would be too late. He needed to warn someone of what was going on, but first he had to get away. First Call had about done him in, though when he'd risen up and been baptized a new member, he'd felt pride at being chosen. What was planned now was far worse. How could they do that? Over two hundred people lived in a state of such belief here, an urgent need to make the world a better place. And willing to give up everything to do so. Family. Friends. Wealth. The depth of the betrayal sliced him to the bone, crushed his spirit to dust. She couldn't be allowed to get away with it. He had to do something. Share his burden with others. Find someone who would know what to do.

He started across the compound. He'd left a warm jacket in the men's shower room, stashed above one of the ceiling tiles. He headed there, keeping a sharp look out for the watchmen, his boots crunching on the icy snow making him cringe in apprehension of getting caught and hauled before the community. Or worse yet, silenced forever. He began to pray to his God. *Please make me invisible. If you let me get away, I promise to do good all the rest of my days.* He'd been so certain that coming here was the answer to all his prayers. His need to feel connected to his fellow humans who wanted the same things he longed for with every fiber of his being. To make a difference for the betterment of a world he was certain had lost its way. How could he have been so wrong? He'd landed in the exact opposite kind of place.

A hellhole. One where they wanted to use everyone to get what they coveted. Money and power.

He slipped inside the shower room and retrieved his jacket, thankful to pull it on to ward against the bone-chilling cold. He had many miles to go before he could consider himself safe from her wrath. He zipped it up but left his gloves in his pocket for now. He'd need the dexterity for what he planned to do next.

But as he approached the main house where she lived, he couldn't even bear to think of her in the word she insisted on, his courage began to fail him even as he tried to prop himself up thinking what kind of parent does such vile things to their flock? No. He had put an end to this. He crept along the side of the sturdy structure, no doubt kept warmer than the men's or women's dorm. Of course, it was a much smaller dwelling to heat. The firewood needed to keep the woodstoves alive in this camp took a great deal of people power. Everyone chipped in, cutting wood for days on end to supply the community's needs. The simple act of doing for all was what sustained him during the difficult trials of learning how to acquire such homesteading skills from the more experienced members.

A sudden noise woke him from the zombie-like trance he'd fallen into. He froze in his tracks. What was it? Was someone coming? No sound or movement followed the alert. He gathered what little remained of his courage and headed for the giant woodpile where he'd stashed the gas can earlier. Much as he didn't want to do it after all the work it took to create the stash, he needed a diversion. He reassured himself with the reminder that soon they would leave anyway and not need the fuel.

With shaking hands, he picked up the red-painted metal container and began splashing the wood with the gasoline. The powerful odor set him back on his heels and he dropped the can before moving a few yards away to be safe from flashback. He understood the unseen fumes would spread out like a nuclear bomb along the ground and burn anything within its reach.

It took him a few tries, but finally he lit a match, setting the entire package alight. He prayed no one could see the burst of flame. He threw the fireball at the wood and ran as fast as he could in the opposite direction, toward the outside perimeter fence, praying for salvation with every step.

No sooner was he a few hundred feet away from the woodpile when it caught fire in a loud whooshing sound behind him. He looked back over his shoulder to see blue flames crawling all over the cut-to-size timber. The wood was seasoned, left sitting for a year, and perfectly ready to burn at its best. And it did. Roaring to life like a hungry beast.

He kept running, his legs pumping, his body fine-tuned from the time he'd spent in the gym preparing to move to Alaska in good physical condition at least, if unskilled in the way of survivalists. He was no sooner at the outside perimeter when shouts erupted in the distance as the fire was spotted by someone.

Good. Keep them busy while he escaped. Sure, he felt some guilt, but even more, he felt relief at knowing he was doing the right thing. They would thank him in the end, he'd bet on it. Once they knew what he had found out. What their game plan was. How evil the top echelon was and their plans for Sister Joan sickened him to the core. He heard the slight noise of a twig snapping nearby. Had someone followed him? A terrible pain on the back of his head erupted before the world tilted dizzily. He fell to the ground and everything went black.

TWO

A commotion in the outer office drew Anna's attention. What else was the universe going to toss into the mix this morning? The day had not started off well. She'd been woken up from a deep sleep by what was becoming a weekly terror, never knowing when it was going to strike. Over and over, finding her beloved sister Tia at the bottom of the deep, dark grave, her body encased in a white shroud. He'd dressed them in wedding dresses, the Black Rose Killer. Each time she hoped to find her in time. It never happened. Every time she found her; she was already dead; cold and still as marble. Nothing like the precocious, loving sister she'd been raised with when the Pace family adopted her as a teenager. The pain was as real and visceral as when it first happened. She swallowed against the bile thoughts of the nightmare brought on, trying to push past it. What she wouldn't do for a drink, but day drinking was out of the question. One would lead to two and she knew it would be too easy to fall into that bottomless pit.

Then Kelly Smith, the young girl she'd rescued from

the clutches of Cullen Cross, a.k.a. Jack the Ripper, had called from college. Upset. She was worried about a new friend, Tabitha Owens, deciding to abandon her design degree after a video surfaced of a sexual nature involving the friend and two members of the football team. She wanted Anna to drop everything and stop her from leaving, whatever it took. *Lock her up and throw the key away* were her exact words. Apparently, the young girl was talking about joining a group of like-minded individuals who wanted to make the world a better place. It didn't sound awful or that the girl was in any immediate danger, but more like her friend was making a decision Kelly didn't approve of.

When Anna had patiently explained people are allowed to make their own choices in life, that no one could stop the girl from leaving, her ward had erupted into a tirade of curses and tears. Since her mom had died at the hands of a ruthless killer, she'd been oscillating between extreme moods. Anna understood. It would take time to absorb the shock, time to learn to cope better. But Kelly had insisted she wasn't wasting another moment in Anchor and had jumped in with both feet to the college scene. After deciding on the Fashion Institute of Technology in New York or FIT, she'd even created the competitive portfolio for an application required in less than six weeks, the three garments she'd constructed backed up with ample photos and sketches. Anna admired her drive and zeal, though worried she wasn't ready to fly away so soon. But the girl had hung in there and was nearing the end of the school year, her exams only a matter of weeks away, and then she might be talked into coming home for the spring and summer.

But even her promise of removing the damaging video from social media had not pacified Kelly. It bothered Anna. Maybe she should fly down there again? She'd made the commitment to visit once a month and was only a week away from a scheduled visit anyway. She didn't want this incident to derail Kelly's chances of obtaining her own degree in design by being distracted at this crucial moment. Yes, she'd head down to New York City on the next flight out of Anchor.

Her private office door flew open as Anna brought up the phone number for Anchor Airlines. A young woman of no more than eighteen or nineteen came rushing in with a determined, don't-even-think-of-stopping-me, look on her face.

"I'm sorry for barging in like this, but I need your help. My sister's involved with a crazy group. She needs rescuing!"

Anna got up and approached her. Her wide-eyes and desperate look made Anna's heart squeeze with sympathy. "Are you okay? Let me get you some water." She steered the now crying young woman to a seat near her desk. She poured her a glassful and handed it to her. The girl drank half of it. Hiccuped.

"Now, let's slow down and you can tell me what happened, okay?"

The girl agreed with a nod, her lower lip trembling.

"What's your name?"

"Emily Stubbs. I flew up here all the way from New York City. Cost a bundle and now it's all wasted if I can't get my sister to go home with me." The girl had a slight lisp when she spoke. An attractive girl except for the redness around her eyes, with thick brown hair and blue eyes, a strikingly pale complexion.

"Nice to meet you, Emily. I'm Anna." Anna sat down at her desk and opened a computer document to begin taking notes.

Drinking the water appeared to have calmed the young girl down. "I saw your sign when I was driving down the street about to turn in my rental car and leave Anchor—I'm only here to find my sister—when I knew I should stop. That you could help me. I know your name's Anna Hale. Everyone knows you. You figured out the Jack the Ripper case. Saved that young girl from being butchered. I saw it on the news." Emily shuddered at her own description.

"Me and a few others. It's always a team effort."

"You look like a lone wolf to me."

The girl's abrupt words took her by surprise, the tears having dried up. Anna liked the new sign out front designed by her partner, Charlie, who ran the office, of three prominent wolves with others lurking behind ready to assist. Wolf Pack Justice. A tight membership of her adopted brother, Detective Josh Pace, his friend and now hers, a fellow soldier from the sandbox, Tom Jackson. And sometimes, Zeke Law, the new owner of the Yellowbird Motel, who had been invaluable during the investigation to bring the Ripper to justice. She avoided thinking about the recent case whenever possible. It had taken a heavy toll, driving her to her knees at time. Most cases were like that, always more than expected heading in. Good thing. Otherwise, no sane person would chance it. *Helps to be a little crazy, running with the wolves.*

"Trust me, it takes a team of like-minded individuals to solve cases. What can I do for you, Emily?

"I need to find my sister, Faith. My mom's sick. She had problems in the past and now she needs a new liver. Faith's a blood match for her. Our best bet to save our mom."

"Does Faith know anything about this? Your mom being sick?"

Emily averted her eyes. "I guess. But she doesn't understand how bad she is. I just need to see her. Explain how sick she's gotten. If Faith doesn't come with me now—"

She left the words unspoken.

"Where is your sister living?"

"At a place called Ironwood. She joined a group. Circle of Friends. Sounds like a cult to me. You have to hand over all your stuff and work on the farm. I can't imagine why Faith thinks it's a good idea. She was always talking about someone she called Mother with a capital M before she vanished off social media about three months ago. *Mother this, Mother that.* Like she doesn't have a real mom she should be worrying about." The scathing tone that accompanied the spiel was jarring. Emily was mercurial in her moods. A trait she shared with Kelly.

"Why did Faith run away?" There was a lot more to this story than she was sharing. For the young girl to have ended up at the commune located at Ironwood, she must have been desperate for something more in her life. And that something pushed her into joining the cultlike compound at the end of the world. Push/pull factors were always at play in life's decisions.

"Our mom used to be an alcoholic and a druggie, *okay.* Faith couldn't take it anymore, so she left us all in the lurch as soon as she could. But Mom's not drinking or using now. She's sober." Emily came across on the defensive side. Anna understood. Hard to admit family secrets when most people would prefer to keep them buried. Alcoholism and drug use had ruined many a life. Memories of her own drunken bully of a stepdad were quashed as soon as they arose. Anna refused to go there today.

"How long has she been gone?"

"I'm not sure but must be close to a year and a half now." Emily wouldn't meet her eyes. Again.

"And you're only now looking for her." She said the words without judgment. But where was she when Faith first set out, probably feeling lost and alone? And what pushed her out of the nest?

"Does it matter? Does it mean you wouldn't help me? Help my mom?"

"No. But it does mean you might have to prepare yourself for Faith's refusal if she won't leave. It's not illegal to work on a farm, raising food." It sounded to Anna like the commune up at Ironwood had changed considerably in the past year or two. Last she knew, they were a tight-knit band of like-thinkers who didn't open its doors to new members. Had they applied for official church status with the state? One of the many things she'd need to check on.

"But it's not like Faith to do something like that. They must have done *something* to her to make her turn her back on her family, brainwashed her maybe? Please, I just need to see her. I know I can convince her to come home with me. She's a good person. She once cut off all her beautiful long hair, her best feature, to give to charity to make a wig when a friend at school got cancer. That's the kind of person she is. Naïve and way too giving."

"Did she have any money? Was she coming into an inheritance, maybe?"

"*Phttt*, our family was the poster child for poor growing up. Always scrounging for everything. You ever see that Netflix series, *Shameless*? That was us. Mostly still are. Faith's the oldest of my three siblings, so any money she earned, she turned over to our mom. Why?"

"Well, it means she didn't need to buy her way in.

Circle of Friends must have taken her in for another reason. Which also means we can't prove fraud or her being taken advantage of. How old is Faith?"

"Twenty-one."

"Well past the age of majority," Anna murmured. "What has she said about this so-called Mother?"

"She's beautiful and kind and loving. She seems infatuated by the woman. Like she's in love or something. Scary shit. Couldn't you go and ask to see her? You're a private investigator. They'll let you in. Tell Faith what I've told you? About Mom? I'm sorry, I don't have any money left to pay you. I used it all up getting here."

Anna waved off the money issue. "Don't worry about that. But I don't think being a PI will help on this occasion. In fact, might be more of a hindrance if anything untoward is going on there." *Unless I go undercover?* She didn't say the words aloud; she needed more information first. "I take it you've already tried to see her?"

Emily chewed on an already too-short fingernail. Anna noticed most were bitten to the quick. Emily may have ignored the plight of her sister, but she was worried about her mom. "Yeah, didn't do me any good. They turned me away at the gate. I drove up there yesterday. Assholes. They wouldn't even pass along a note to her. One big tall guy in particular acted all superior. He has a scar running down the right side of his face. Kind of a scary looking. But he said in no uncertain terms it was *hallowed*, privately owned land and I wasn't welcomed there. Like they were really something special and I was nothing but garbage for not believing in their cause. Well, family first, then we'll talk. Faith *has* to come home with me. It's her God-given duty to help." The fire in Emily's eyes suggested the meet n greet with the Circle of Friends had not gone well. Probably fireworks on both sides.

Anna worried that Faith only wanted to use her sister because she needed something, not bothering to contact her until now. But the young woman could make up her own mind once she knew the real deal. She was family. They at least had the right to ask her. If indeed she was happy at the commune and didn't want to leave, there was no way to coerce her. Anna would need evidence of abuse to get the law to step in otherwise. A wellness check. Of course, she could break the girl out herself if she was being held against her will. Assemble the team and go in guns blazing if necessary. Or more likely a night mission to help Faith escape. Too many unknowns to call it at this point.

"Do you have a photo of your sister?"

Emily pulled out her iPhone. "Yeah, I have one."

Anna took the electronic device and studied the image of a young girl, similar enough in coloring to Emily. She could see the family resemblance, but with sad, sad deep blue eyes that penetrated her defenses. With her head cocked to the side and her large blue eyes looking up shyly at the camera through thick eyelashes, the image was vaguely reminiscent of Lady Dianna. Pretty girl, she appeared thinner than the sibling.

"I'll need printed copies of this image. How long ago was it taken?"

Emily shrugged. "About two years ago, before she took off."

"What kind of work was your sister doing before she left?"

Again, the averted eyes. Her body language spoke volumes of things Emily didn't want to share with her.

"Whatever she had to. Babysitting, running a small daycare, stuff she could do from home."

"No job outside the house?"

"She left school in the eighth grade to help out. Mom always says life's a better learning experience than school could ever be. But Faith—she's smart. Reads a lot. Always talking of making the world a better place. She has to come home now. Mom just needs a piece of her liver, for heaven's sake, not the whole damn thing!"

Hmm. "Okay, leave me with this and I'll look into it."

"Today?" Emily leaned forward, her expression eager. Anna had planned on going to New York. Maybe she could delay seeing Kelly for a day or two? The idea didn't sit well though.

"I need to do some research to do and I have something else pressing I must deal with first. But I promise you I will get to this as soon as I can. Are you staying in town?"

"I hadn't intended to. It's expensive and I need to get home. My sister Carly Jo and brother Mason aren't that good with Mom, so I got a friend watching out for her. Do I need to stay here if you're going to go and get her anyway?"

Anna would literally move heaven and earth to get to one of her siblings, to see them safe. She tamped down her thoughts on it and gave Emily a free pass. *For now.* "No. I'll contact you. I just need your address and phone number."

"Great." Emily got to her feet after rattling off the information, ready to flee. "Aw, thanks for this. I owe you one."

"Pay it forward," Anna said.

"Yeah, sure. Whatever you think." The girl dashed from her office, sailing right by Charlie's desk.

You don't want to know what I think. Though it was easy enough to check out Emily's story. The tricky part was breeching the defenses of the compound to get the opportunity to speak with Faith. Going straight at this thing, her usual modus operandi, was likely to backfire. A little undercover recon might be more the ticket. Anna had money. She could easily buy her way in. Or at least make them think that was what she was doing. All cults love a new member with plenty of cash to spare, right?

THREE

ONE YEAR AGO, LAS VEGAS, NEVADA

The opportunity to acquire one more chess piece to destroy the queen presented itself in the most unlikely of places. The messenger leaned forward in the theater chair, watching the stage show intently. Just thinking of it made the humming increase dramatically in their brain until they couldn't hear anything of the outside world. They fought the urge to press their hands over their ears in efforts to dull the sensation.

Enough. Focus. Observe how the sleight of hand is brilliantly done. It would take an expert to see the artistry behind the magic. The voice soothed, calming the raging waters as it always did. Suddenly, a revelation in a flash of intense inspiration arrived like an epiphany from heaven. Yes. It would work splendidly.

The best plans did involve the long game. Patience was essential. Wasn't revenge always best served cold? It was the thinking of popular culture which didn't mean it was automatically suspect, but this time the hell unleashed would be monumental. Enough to signal the final collapse, leaving only the mastermind to rule the perfect oasis existing in a world of chaos. Armageddon couldn't come soon enough.

The audience erupted in a wild round of applause, signaling the end of the evening's entertainment. The messenger rose to their feet and joined the wave of humanity exiting the building. At the last second, they veered right and headed for the backstage area. No time like the present to begin things. They would make it more than worthwhile for the grifter to listen to their proposal. All the facts that mattered had been collected in a private dossier over the past few weeks. But the one fact that stood out was the driving passion of the possible collaborator, explaining why they had chosen this particular person: their intense need to be important beyond measure since their time wandering in the hot desert sun. Provide it, and it would ensure they'd be eating out of their hand in no time.

The messenger walked confidently past security, laying off a few bills through their own sleight of hand to allow access to the dressing room kept separate for the evening's headliner. At the proper door, they knocked and waited for a response.

The door opened almost immediately. Guarded, heavily made-up eyes greeted theirs. "What do you want?"

"The same things you do. A brand-new beginning. A chance to shine brightest in this world. To be remembered. And to unleash hell on humans destroying our planet as we speak."

"What the fuck are you talking about?"

But they could see they had aroused their interest. The slight widening of the eyes, the flare of their nostrils. The pupils had even enlarged, making their eyes appear midnight blue.

Time to begin.

FOUR

PRESENT DAY, ANCHOR, ALASKA

"The world is ending and people are too blind to see. Can they not read the signs? Wars, broken borders, economic chaos, plague, a planet strewn with filth and garbage."

Mother paused for effect, letting the words sink in. She was backlit by the setting sun, a figure dressed all in white, standing regal as any queen from antiquity on the raised platform, the sight overwhelming to those assembled before her. Sister Beatrix blinked rapidly, her eyes burning from the tasks of the day as she watched along with the family. Maybe she should have kept her sunglasses instead of offering them to a fellow member? The person she'd lent them to was nowhere to be seen today. Where was Brother Lazar? He hadn't turned up for work in two days. Maybe he was in the medical wing due to the recent fire? A couple of people had been burned fighting it, trying to save their winter fuel source to no avail. Now everyone they could spare from other duties was employed in cutting down more trees and preparing them for the woodstoves that kept the dormitories warm and heated the main house where Mother lived with Brother Adam.

"Our time is coming. Rest assured. We will be together and let no man try to separate us. Until then, we must trust our true path. The path leading to enlightenment. The righteous shall overcome. But to reach that exalted pinnacle, we must abandon our human egos, our frailties, for they will keep us separated from each other upon arrival. Husband from wife, parents from children, brother from sister, friend from neighbor. Only giving up all earthly things, can we hope to become our best selves and not go blindly into the good night, forever doomed to wander in the dark alone. *No fear. We are the chosen.*"

"*No fear. We are the chosen,*" Sister Beatrix mouthed the words along with the others, right on cue. Exhausted from physical labor from sunup until well past sundown, hungry to the bone from lack of supper, she stood in line, swaying back and forth as she fought the desperate urge to lie down and sleep. *Five minutes is all I ask.* Her mind drifted on a soft, white cloud—

Another member, Sister Erbin, dug her sharp elbow into Beatrix's side. She hissed, "Stay awake. Mother sees all."

Sister Beatrix pinched the tender inner skin of her underarm in an effort to stay the course. Soon there would be stew and bread, a glass of wine. *You have to stay awake,* she admonished herself. Enlightenment came at a cost. She was told this right from the start. No one tried to pull the wool over her head. But it was higher than she'd realized a year ago when she'd begged for the chance to become part of the chosen, knowing she had no riches to offer having grown up so damn poor she'd often gone hungry, her alcoholic mom lurching from one crisis to another. Why did she have children anyway? She suppressed the images of the men she'd had to endure to make enough money to pay rent, to avoid having her family made homeless. Her mom always asked her for the favor, saying it would be the last time she'd ever have to do it. Liar. Always guilty of filth, and forever sinning against her own family, using most of the proceeds to feed her own addiction, leaving little for shelter and food.

But the true Mother had taken her in anyway, blessed all her earthly sins away. She'd offered compassion when she'd wandered in from the wilderness, accepted her as one of their own lost sheep. Explained that one must wear down the ego and the body for wisdom to have a fertile field in which to grow. Not that she didn't want to do her part, grow food for the many, help pack the plastic doves for market. Mostly she wanted to learn a better way forward away from oppression and a world allowing such atrocities they sickened her to the core. But the cost, exhaustion and lack of calories, was taking its toll. How can one eat knowing so many are going hungry? She knew that it was a personal choice, not unknown among others in their group, but one that made her feel far more virtuous than those who partook freely of all they were offered.

However lately, when she'd caught sight of her reflection in the shower room mirror that she normally avoided worried about being considered vain, she'd been shocked at how sharp the bones in her face were, how brittle her hair. She'd never thought of herself as pretty, just ordinary looking, but now she offered little beauty to the world. She must try harder, learn to shine from within as Mother said. Then she would be beautiful, her shining soul prepared to join with others. She saw the beauty in the faces surrounding her on a daily basis, the zeal to become a better human being. She must learn to emulate them more. Become a better person. Take a bit more time with her appearance. It wasn't discouraged to stay clean, well-groomed. Others managed to look presentable, eating and sleeping more than she allowed herself. If only she wasn't so tired all the time. Maybe she had something else wrong with her? Something medical? She was too young to be tired so much of the time. Perhaps she needed to see the nurse.

Mother drew herself up higher now, a commanding figure standing alone on the platform. Surreal. Dressed in her favorite color white, her thick waves of platinum hair cascading down around her shoulders, she was radiant, so perfect on the outside like someone out of a dream, an angel. Beautiful and poised, as Beatrix longed to be and sensed she may never get close to being other than living here at Ironwood among friends of the faithful. But she dreamed of being like Mother who always smelled of exotic roses, making everyone want to cling to her and never let go.

Mother raised her arms and the wide sleeves of her flowing dress fluttered open, giving even more of an impression she was an angel descended to earth. "I have an announcement. We are ever closer to achieving the perfect number. With the arrival of Sister Joan in a matter of hours, we have need of only one more member to reach our full compliment. Then we will be ready and will be shown what to do. *No fear. We are the chosen.*"

"*No fear. We are the chosen,*" a chorus erupted all around, confirming the good news. Two hundred and twenty-two was the magic number to complete their flock. The number promised they were at the right place, right time for moving forward. Would she be personally ready for such an amazing gift by overcoming all her fears? A gift of eternal life among the stars, free of human bonds, was scary and wonderful all at the same time. And what would that look like?

Beatrix tamped down the all-too-human fear at what would happen at the moment of ascension. It couldn't be more frightening though, she comforted herself, than First Call. The day of her baptism was as stark in her mind as if it had happened only minutes ago. The drink that Mother had served her, its milky sweetness comforting. Her loving hands braiding her long hair to keep it out of the way. Then the shock of icy cold water rushing to close over her head, lungs burning from lack of oxygen, the terrifying fear of not measuring up, of giving in to the terror. She had resisted the panic at first, telling her body to relax, that of course she would be chosen. Hadn't Mother promised it, whispering it in her ear the vision of her rising to join with them only moments before the ordeal had begun? It had made her feel special, eased her worry. But each passing second had felt like an eternity. She discovered she didn't want to die, and it overcame her resolve to stay calm, to accept her fate. She remembered to her shame striking out, trying to escape, but only for a second or two. Then the wondrous relief at being saved, pulled up and into the loving arms of Mother.

"Rise, Sister Beatrix, and join with the chosen. Never more will you walk alone, blind in the desert. Instead, you will be surrounded by an oasis of love and acceptance. We are your sisters. Your brothers. Have no fear. We are the chosen," Mother said, a smile lighting her beautiful face. It filled her with a resolve to stay strong, to follow in her footsteps.

Now the new wannabee, Sister Joan, would soon undergo the same ordeal, either rising to be with them, or going back to be recycled, not worthy as yet. Beatrix was proud she had passed the test. Someone as poor as her, arriving at the compound broke and hungry. It had all been more than worth it though, undergoing the transformation. Yes, a few souls had been lost to reincarnation though she had never seen it happen or had any idea where their human shells were buried. Since she'd arrived, all those answering First Call had risen from the water, alive and well, excited they had been chosen. But it was whispered all the material goods in the world could not save a soul. That those handful of souls not chosen to become friends had been rich, signing all their possessions over to Mother. Those who joined with her had to do so for the betterment of the group. Everyone partook equally, an arrangement everyone agreed was fair.

To her mind, most rich people were evil anyway, hording their funds. Never giving a shit about the *peasants, the undesirables.* Made sense they had to be recycled. What did she care? She was chosen. But even as she thought the words, she felt shame for her uncharitable idea. Maybe the new person had never been in her thread-bare boots, hungry and willing to do anything to fill the painful ache, born lucky, rich, unaccountable to others for her very survival, but still she was a fellow human being who was looking to improve herself. She could only hope that Sister Joan would rise to join with them, her soul not to be taken for recycling. Then her guilt at disliking the rich would be eased.

Crystal Vanderbilt pulled up the beloved image of Mother on her iPhone, running her forefinger over the beautiful face. She'd lost her own mother at birth and knew in her heart everyone blamed her for her untimely death, though it was only her sister Sara who had spoken the words aloud. Sara, who had shared the explosive news on her fourth birthday, screaming at her and pounding her pretty birthday cake to mush before being hauled away by her nanny, but not before sharing her view that if Crystal had never been born, her mom would still be alive. The sharp pinches and knocking her to the ground every chance her sister got when no one else was looking made sense after that revelation.

She brushed the tears away. Now she had a fresh start. And a new name to go with it. Sister Joan. Like Joan of Arc. The name and idea behind the legend pleased her. Suggested a true place of acceptance within the Circle of Friends, hers for the asking.

She glanced over at the two monogrammed suitcases stuffed with cash stacked on the front seat of the SUV. Money to aid those in greater need than herself. Her family certainly hadn't earned it. Money created more money, multiplying indefinitely with an endless supply available, meant to be used for more than lavish parties. Or buying the rights to have their names immortalized on buildings.

Why was her family so blind to the need existing all around? Hidden away in a mansion as isolating as an underground bunker with fancy bodyguards and tight notch security, making certain they could not see what was right in front of their faces. That was how. Completely out-of-touch and seeming proud of the few charity events they hosted, giving as much to their rich friends in party favors as they donated. But if she raised one objection, said one word about how she saw it, she was laughed at, called idealistic and a dreamer. *No, Virginia, there's no Santa Claus.* Something her sister had also informed her of the year she turned four.

Her cell phone pinged. A line of text appeared reminding her of a therapist appointment for later in the day. Ha! So not going to happen. She deleted the words with prejudice. She'd already thrown away the crutch of meds prescribed to make her a freakin' zombie, having quit taking them weeks ago. Now she was flying high, naturally. And when she got to Mother, she'd be washed off all her sins, leaving her past behind.

FIVE

"Damn it! Is that a person?" Detective Josh Pace braked hard, the police SUV fishtailing slightly before coming to a dead stop in the middle of the gravel road. A dusty snow cloud rose instantly, obscuring his view. He was driving back from the Crowder homestead after investigating a theft of a homemade quilt stolen off a clothesline. He'd taken all the time necessary to calm down the owner and creator who'd been up in arms about it. It had gone missing along with various food items from the springhouse and a coffee can filled with household money. Now, his mind elsewhere, he'd nearly run over an individual lying prone on the roadway. In his defense, the sun was in his eyes, making it difficult to see. And it was unexpected to see a human being lying in the middle of the road, but he was grateful he'd avoided hitting them.

Josh placed the vehicle in park and jumped out, choking from the fine particles suspended in the air, reminding him he needed to get his asthma prescription refilled. He bent down and lay two fingers against the man's throat to check if he was still alive. A faint thread-like pulse gave him hope.

He quickly called it in on the radio, giving his location to dispatch and advising them of the incident. He was only ten miles north of Anchor and could get him back to town before the ambulance could show up but was hesitant to move the man if he was injured.

The man was wrapped in something, with only his head and shoulders out, facing toward Josh. He recognized the blanket immediately. The stolen quilt from the photo May Crowder had just shown him. It was dusty and dirty but looked salvageable without any visible rips. The tears in May's eyes as she explained she had just finished making it for her young granddaughter came to mind. She'd left it on the line to air it out before sending it off to her so it would smell of fresh air and sunshine. All her hard work down the drain had upset the sixty-something woman. And rightly so, it was a beautiful piece of Americana. A log-cabin design.

The motif of the quilt resembled one in Anna Hale's guest rooms, bringing her beautiful face to mind. He closed his eyes. *Anna.* He had been so close many times to telling her how he felt about her, having been in love with her for years. Hell, he'd even promised himself after she'd rescued him from the nightmare of a coffin death at the hands of the Black Rose Killer, to tell her how he felt about her. To take the chance. If only he didn't value their friendship so much, he would cross that line in a heartbeat. But what if she felt the same and they had been wasting time by not being together?

Well, he wasn't much of a prize, that was one problem. The other being she had vowed often enough that she would never marry, not wanting to be held accountable to anyone for her actions. She was a driven woman.

As passionate about justice as any lawman he'd met. But they both shared that ideal. And he would never stand in her way, only help her on her journey. No one else knew her well enough to promise her that. But was it enough? Lately, a part of him was realizing how quickly his life was being lived. When he saw a happy family with children, more and more he wanted the same.

He finished up the task of making the unconscious man as comfortable as possible, praying the EMS team would be on the scene soon and wishing there was more he could do.

A low moan from the victim stirred him to action, to speak soothingly in an effort to keep him calm. "Hey, man, I'm here with you. You're going to be okay. I've called for an ambulance. It will be here soon. Just relax. You're safe now. Help is on the way."

The man looked terrified at the moment he opened his eyes and stared up at Josh. Then just as suddenly, his eyes went blank, like all life had been wiped from within. Josh quickly checked his pulse again. The faint beats had ceased.

He immediately went into crisis mode. He began CPR, pushing hard and quick at the victim's chest as he'd been taught. A hundred compressions a minute, two inches deep into the middle of the chest.

"Stay with me," he urged the man.

Within minutes, he heard the faint sounds of a siren. He didn't stop his actions until he felt another presence at his side.

"I'll take over now, Detective," the female paramedic said.

Josh got out of her way and plunked down a short distance from the victim. He wiped the sweat from his face and took a moment to catch his breath. Another emergency responder joined the first one, a male, and they went about their job, checking the man's vitals and giving him oxygen before loading him in the back of the ambulance.

"You did good, Josh. He's stable now," the first paramedic said. She gave him a wide smile along with the use of his first name. It was then he realized they had gone to the same high school together. A daredevil and rebellious teenager, Lola Marcom had been in a grade lower than himself. Her graduating class would have voted her most likely to *need* assistance from medical personnel, not be the one providing it.

"Lola Marcom. Surprised to see you here." She looked good, like she'd gotten her shit together since graduating Anchor Regional Comprehensive School, or more commonly called ARCS, they'd both attended. Even in the uniform, he could see she was in excellent shape, with a trim figure. Her long white-blond hair was tied up in a ponytail, exposing the slim column of her throat where he could see the rapid beating of her pulse. Her scent was lightly floral, not off-putting at all. Her makeup was lightly applied, something he appreciated, not like in high school during her Goth period. She was much prettier now.

"I know, right!" She laughed, a good hearty laugh suggesting she didn't take herself too seriously. The movement caused her ponytail to bounce around, catching the sunlight.

"Are you seeing anyone at the moment?" She raised one well-groomed eyebrow. One thing Lola hadn't changed about herself. She was still direct.

"No." With Anna always being the one in his thoughts, he hadn't done much dating. Other women paled in comparison alongside her. But he wasn't a monk either. A man has needs.

"Good. Here's my card if you'd care to go out some-time?" She handed it to him. "Gotta run. Give me a call or I'll call you. We got some catching up to do, Detective Josh Pace."

She made it sound like a threat or a call to action. Josh watched Lola trot over to the ambulance and jump into the driver's seat. A hand wave and the vehicle took off in a cloud of dust. He glanced at her card and turned it over. She'd added her personal cell number and a smiley face with tiny horns drawn on. He had to grin.

SIX

"Welcome to Circle of Friends," Mother said, holding out her arms in greeting. "Our home is your home, child."

Crystal Vanderbilt rushed to embrace her idol. She had dreamed of this moment every mile of the way on the endless drive up from Manhattan. Then waiting impatiently at the gate with demands to see her pass, every second of the wait an eternity before finally getting to meet Mother in person. And Mother didn't let her down, embracing her like a long-lost daughter. The scent of roses filled her up as she clung to the warm, vital woman. She didn't want to *ever* let go.

"I'm so happy to be here! To meet you in person!" Crystal knew she was gushing but found herself unable to stop. Her heart was hammering, and she felt light-headed from such a wave of intense emotion she could scarcely breathe, her body humming with excessive energy.

Then Mother took her chin and stared deep into her eyes, like she could see into her very soul. The light-colored irises reminding her of the ocean overwhelmed all her senses even as her own eyes opened wider, unable to look away. She'd never seen a more beautiful woman. A halo of platinum waves caught the surreal light of the setting sun. She was perfect in person, an angel descended from above. Everything one could want in a mother.

"We are happy you can join with us. Think of us as family, the brothers and sisters you never had. You are safe here. See this time moving forward as an opportunity to become a better person. To live on this planet lightly, giving back more than you receive. That's the ticket to happiness, living your true self, unencumbered by doubts. Or false vanity. Together we can make our stand together and live free of society's restrictions. When you answer First Call, your name shall be Sister Joan, giving rise to a new saint. Do you accept First Call?"

Crystal swallowed, barely able to breathe. *First Call.* She understood the importance of being baptized. To be rising again as a true member of the Circle of Friends. She couldn't let her fear stand in the way now. Not when that was why she was here—to overcome fear, the taint of her birth, and rise above everything that had gone before.

"Yes, I do." The words came out on a mere whisper. A prayer. It was a heady moment, far heavier than expected. A moment vibrating with expectation and exhilaration. She trampled on any other voice in her head, saying the defensive mantra that had kept her from succumbing to the abyss since as far back as she could remember. *Don't let them grind you down.* To that now, she added a new challenge: *Live free in this moment.*

Mother finally broke their locked gaze. She squeezed

her shoulders with affection, nodding. Crystal took a steadying breath. Yes. Everything would be fine.

"*No fear. We are the chosen,*" Mother said, the glow around her brightening with her words. Her aura mesmerized Crystal.

She repeated Mother's words, curtseyed—as it felt right—and gestured at the vehicle she'd arrived in. "I brought something along to help. It's in the front seat. I hope that's okay. Of course, the vehicle is now yours."

"Each gives according to their means," Mother said with a calm, beatified expression on her face. "Whatever you bring to us, all are welcomed and equal here, from the humblest beggar to the daughter of a rich man."

Crystal nodded. Equal footing was all she asked for. To not be judged for things out of her control. No one can choose where they are born, what generation they are raised in, or even how others decided how they will see and treat you. For the chance to be something more than a rich man's daughter, reviled for being rich. For being the cause of her mom's death. Sure, she was fawned over by some for having money. But that was not what she wanted in life, needing to pull her own weight. Find her place under the stars and make a difference in this world that looked more and more to her as if it had gone completely mad.

At Ironwood she could hide out, refocus, and discover things about herself. Important things. It had not been a decision undertaken lightly. She'd thought long and hard about coming here, to the end of the world. She'd read all their literature online, liking the messages that aligned with her own thinking. So what if some of their chat were AI-generated? It was still what the group stood for. And their views aligned precisely with the way she wished the world actually was. About being true to yourself, stripping away life's artifice and embracing the spirit of sharing and giving. She'd even zoomed and spoke face-to-face with Mother on a number of occasions, pouring out her heart and asking her endless questions. The always patient answers from her had given her hope for a better existence, for someone really hearing what she had to say. Yes, she would embrace this priceless opportunity with all her being and accept this new world. Become a better person. *No fear. We are the chosen.*

SEVEN

Anna booted up her laptop. Time to check out Ironwood's online presence. She keyed in specific search parameters and up popped the group's main website. The expansive header for Circle of Friends was resplendent with a woman all in white against a sky-colored background, her spectacular platinum hair cascading around her shoulders while she held a white dove outstretched toward the viewer in the palm of her hands. *Mother*, of course. The woman somewhat resembled Doctor Molly, the many layers of photo tampering making the woman look like a living deity with surreal light-colored irises and backlit hair, an old trick from movie studio days when they wanted their stars to come across as beautiful. A wig and contacts? Plastic surgery? Or maybe she had a sister, insanity having run amuck in the Strobel bloodline? Afterall, it had produced Elvis Strobel, the Black Rose Killer. And Anna wouldn't trust the good doctor so far as telling her the correct time of day. But no, this woman wasn't the lost therapist never quite off her radar.

But an even more alarming fact became apparent after a short while of navigating through the slick professional website. They were using artificial intelligence in a form of chat speak to an amazing degree for a so-called charity organization with religious oversight. Anna tested it, keying in answers to questions like she was searching for meaning in life and getting back very specific responses in real time catered to her inquires that felt exactly like a real conversation with a human being. A great deal of sophistication and time had gone into building the software to its very specific needs. Far as she was concerned, it was entirely too Orwellian, too similar to thought control and newspeak, and not that far from an unnamed country where its policy of the reward system encouraged a specific type of behavior. Step out of line at one's peril. Want a mortgage? Toe the party line. Want a decent paying job? Toe the party line. What would they make of Anna and her thirst for justice? She'd have to do a one-eighty to even begin to fit in. And no one told Anna Hale what to do.

When she answered a seemingly innocent question with a response indicating she was quite unconcerned about slaving away to buy her daily bread, it took her to a new portal, one that promised her the opportunity to speak to Mother in real time. Obviously, they favored the rich, no different than any other business or political sphere. She shut down the idea of a chat at the moment with extreme prejudice. If some of them had access to the internet or television, they might remember her. And the business she was in. Her face had been pasted all over the news when her team broke the Jack the Ripper case a few months back.

Even more concerned now, she backed out of the site. She pounded her fists on the desk in a fit of unusual temper. *Damn AI to hell!* It was beyond evil to use it to persuade vulnerable people using such an insidious method. More precisely, damn the people who created it for such nefarious means. Sure, AI offered a better quality of life for some with medical innovations, but it came with built-in job losses no economist could promise would make human beings' lives better in the long run. Too many people now on the planet needing a decent opportunity to work and provide for their family, to have legions of robots taking away their wages. Plus, AI offered too many opportunities for corruption by a totalitarian despot far beyond what any lawmaker could imagine at the moment. Wholesale willy-nilly expansion of the technology without a thorough ethical evaluation for the common good needed to be reined in or results promised disaster. Social inequality being a glaring concern along with privacy rights. She had to agree with the pope on that official stance. Just thinking about the fallout gave Anna an instant headache.

She sat back and began to plan her next steps, staring at the landscape painting she'd bought to liven up her office. It was of a mountain scene with pristine snow glittering under a noonday sun. Nature was her cathedral and allowed her to think more clearly. How to gain access to Ironwood? They hadn't let Emily Stubbs in but they'd let her sister Faith in. How did members know each other? Code word? Hand signal? Some kind of mark? Christians used a fish back in the day. Mother had a dove in her hand. Hmm, that was a possibility.

Okay. Nothing else for it but to actually join up now and go through the hoops. But not before crafting a disguise. And for that she needed to go home and work from her war room.

She closed down her laptop and headed into the reception area. "Charlie, I'm going home to work."

"Has Josh called you?" Charlie looked up from her own keyboard to give her a speculative look. Charlie always knew *everything* going on in Anchor. A more perfect office manager and business partner she could not imagine.

"No. What's up?"

"He found a man lying unconscious in the middle of the road while driving back from the Crowder homestead. The guy had stolen one of May's quilts of all things. One she'd made for her granddaughter. Like the ones you bought for your guest rooms. The guy sure wasn't living in high cotton to steal from a clothesline!"

The saying meant the victim was poor. It was Charlie unleashing her Southern heritage. Anna hid a smile. "Is he okay?"

"He's awake, at times, but unable to speak. Apparently, the porch light's on but no one's home. Doctor says he has amnesia, the worst kind, brought on by some kind of extreme trauma."

"Dissociative amnesia," Anna said. "Far rarer than the other types. Means he's lost his identity. May not even recognize himself in the mirror. Tragic. Something really bad must have happened to him or he saw something horrible. Any physical injuries?"

"A severe concussion and he's a bit underweight, but otherwise unhurt. Lucky thing Josh didn't run him over. Hard to see this time of year with the sun always glaring in your eyes."

Anna sent Josh a quick text asking where he was. When the answer came back almost immediately, she made a quick decision. Her plate was filling up rapidly today, but she'd have to deal with it. Problem with the business so often was a convergence of energy, when everything happened at once, like the universe was testing her. She accepted it, not believing in chaos but a rhyme and reason for everything. This too would likely fold into the mix and create something far bigger than it at first appeared. "I'm heading over to the hospital."

"I'll keep this justice ship on course. And make sure Friday and Diva are looked after." Charlie nodded at the pair laying down and watching them from the corner sofa. The pair were inseparable, always looking for the other when one was out of sight.

"You always do. I don't say thanks nearly enough for all you do."

"You're just preachin' to the choir now, boss." Charlie grinned, making Anna shake her head. She was incorrigible. And entirely irreplaceable, a true original.

Anna bundled up in her parka and pulled on thick woolen gloves before heading out to her truck. It might be almost April, but it was damn cold with most likely a few more snowstorms expected. Spring couldn't get here soon enough. The old burns on her neck always throbbed when exposed to the cold and she pulled her scarf tighter to compensate. She glanced around her town, noting a van parked diagonally across the street with the discrete logo of a dove on its driver's side door. Twenty to one it belonged to Ironwood. Instead of getting into her truck, Anna took a quick detour and jogged across the main drag, keeping a sharp lookout for traffic.

The van appeared empty, though it was difficult to be certain, the tinted windows far darker than most states allowed. Perhaps someone was hiding in the back? The vehicle was parked in front of Lucky's café. Anna took a chance and headed inside. Maybe the occupants had come to town for food and supplies? A chance to consume something different than lentils and lettuce. They may well be self-sufficient as advertised on their website, but they still needed some things, like extra hair conditioner and makeup for Mother if nothing else. She made a face thinking of the wonderous beatified image online of the matriarch directing this crew however she wanted.

Anna pushed open the door to the café and looked around at the array of customers lined up. Lucky's served what everyone craved—cheeseburgers and fries. The best in Alaska, their business tagline nailed it, *you want healthy, eat someplace else.* Alaskans didn't accept fools gladly but would rather speak plainly and honestly. They valued the courage to confront a challenge head-on, loyalty and hospitality being their sounding boards. No wonder she enjoyed the closest thing to frontier living the United States possessed with its underlying moral code tied to the American dream. Alaska was still a western outpost in many ways, rough-hewn people filled with self-determination and rugged individualism looking to bring order and justice to their lives without being swamped by too many restrictions. Black hats and white hats were more obvious on the landscape of the midnight sun. It suited Anna just fine.

She unzipped her parka and sat down at the one empty stool left along the counter. All the booths were filled and she took a moment to check out the occupants. The most likely suspects were in a booth toward the back of the restaurant. Two men chowing down on cheeseburgers like it was their last meal stood out, one because he had the zealot look down to a tee and the other for his prison warden demeanor. He had to be the guard that turned Emily away from her description of a scar running down the right side of his face.

After ordering a coffee from the waitress who shook her head at the inquiry if she knew the pair, she got up and walked past the booth, stopping at the corkboard. It was used by community members to post about things for sale, rent or to give away. She ignored the men, wanting to listen in. She pulled a phone number off a sheet for the relator and held it in her hand as she pretended to punch in the number into her cell phone. The two men were finished eating, their plates damned near licked clean. Mr. Menace was downing the last of his coffee, his jacket pushed up on the forearms like he was some kind of macho guy, giving her a good view of his thick, hairy wrists.

"It's Sister Joan something," the younger zealot said with complete conviction, his eyes lighting up at whatever image was dancing across his fevered brain. "I sure hope she does good at First Call."

"*Phttt*, I've seen better," Mr. Menace said. "But she's got something better than looks." He rubbed his fingers over his thumb in the universal sign for loaded with cash.

"Mother doesn't care about that." Zealot looked horrified, like his idol was being pelted by rotten tomatoes.

Mr. Menace glanced over at Anna, his eyes narrowing with suspicion.

She spoke into her phone. "Good morning." She studiously looked at the posting board and ignored the two men. "I see you have a place to rent, out on Cariboo Drive. Is it still available?" she asked. She ran a finger down the advertisement like she was nervous or desperate.

"Anything else in that price range?" she pushed out her bottom lip and gave a soft sigh.

"Okay, well, I thought I'd check." She hung up on the non-call and walked away to the counter, leaving cash for the coffee and a generous tip. She had one answer now. But what the hell was First Call?

EIGHT

Josh looked up from talking to the doctor to spy Anna striding into the hospital room. Their eyes locked for a moment over the patient lying prone in the hospital bed, and he could see the wheels spinning in her brilliant mind. She was here about more than the victim he'd found unconscious in the middle of the road on her mind. Most likely hot on the trail of a new case.

Not that the traumatized man he'd thankfully not run over had anything to say that would help the law discover what had led to his collapse, at least not yet. The doctor couldn't promise anything, but the man was awake at times, albeit briefly. So far, he'd been unable to share anything about himself or what happened to him that left him lying in the middle of the damn road. God, the poor bastard didn't even appear to know who he was. Would he recognize himself in the mirror eventually? It was one of the worst side effects of dissociative amnesia, losing one's identity, if indeed that was what he would be diagnosed with.

"Do you know this man, Anna?" Dr. Barr asked as Anna walked up and joined them.

"No, I don't recognize him. He has no ID on him?"

"Nothing. All we got is a tattoo to go by."

"A tattoo. What kind of design?" Something in Anna's demeanor told Josh she was in possession of some intel.

"A dove. On his inner wrist," Josh answered for the doctor.

"Interesting. How's he doing?"

"Only time will tell. I'll call you if things change," Dr. Barr said. "Anna, good to see you." He left the room.

"What's going on?" Josh asked.

"Had a visitor at the office this morning." She quickly filled him in on the facts Emily Stubbs had shared. How desperate she was to find her sister to save her mom's life.

"Anna. Tell me you're not going to do what I think you are?"

She shrugged. "Somebody has to find out what's going on there. The AI they're using to recruit new members—scary shit. Top of the line and very specific. Useless for any other application without a whole new set of parameters. Weird time in history; AI is so clever and yet amazingly stupid at the same time. It can beat a human at chess while the building burns down around them, unaware of the big picture. Can't see it ever surpassing humans, at least not in my lifetime."

"No computer could ever equal the great Anna Hale in any lifetime, the most unique individual I know," Josh said, a twinkle in his eyes. "I defy it to even try. Passion cannot be programmed, the intrinsic part that gives humans the drive to bridge the gap in their reasoning to use all the parts to create a whole, no matter what it takes. AI is light years away from achieving it, if ever."

The hospital door swung open again, and in walked Lola Marcom, the paramedic and classmate he'd met out near the Crowder home. Her mere presence instantly charged the air. Hell, her card was still in his pocket, nearly burning a hole clear through it as the two women took each other's measure in less than a heartbeat. Maybe he knew Anna too well. They were bonded by something so strong, a shared vision of how life was to be lived. Even as he wondered if Anna took it too far at times, put herself into danger too easily. Like this new idea of pretending to join with the Circle of Friends at Ironwood.

"Josh," Lola said. She advanced to stand by his side, placing a hand on his forearm. "Fancy seeing you twice in one day. I must be living right. How's our patient doing?" She asked like it really mattered to her how the yet-to-be-named young man was faring. He liked that in her. More people should live in aid of helping others instead of always focusing on themselves twenty-four seven. They'd be far happier achieving a more balanced life, though Anna seemed to take it to an extreme, unable to balance any personal time with her passion of saving others. Why couldn't she see that it was possible to have both? Josh dreamed of late of having a life with more balance, more order knowing what the day was going to be like or at least some days. To not always be on the case and have no time for friends and family.

"He's unable to communicate who he is but the doctor said his physical condition, other than being badly dehydrated and malnourished, was improving. He's awake off and on, more off."

"Good. He needs to rest."

"Lola, I haven't seen you in quite some time," Anna

said, entering the discussion. "Where have you been hiding yourself?"

Lola grinned and removed her hand from his arm. "Anna Hale as I live and breathe. I see you grew into your nickname."

Anna raised her eyebrows at the woman.

"Wolf woman, that's what my group of friends called you. And it's your business name now, right?"

"Not just wolf woman anymore. Wolf *Pack* Justice."

Anna gave Josh a certain look.

He cleared his throat. "Yes, more of us are wanting to see justice done."

Lola's brow creased into a frown as if trying to understand. "But you do that as a lawman, right? With the Anchor Police Department. Not like Anna. It's two entirely separate things."

She made it sound that his occupation was far superior in scope than Anna's. Anna chose to ignore Lola, leaving the answer up to him. She moved to the patient's bedside and pulled out her cell phone, snapping a photo of the guy's inner wrist while Josh shifted from one foot to the other.

"Oh, I get it. It's because you are brother and sister. Nice of you, helping out your sister." Lola was all smiles as she jumped into answer her own query with an answer she appeared to fully appreciate.

"*Adopted* brother and sister. We lived apart for years until I was taken in by Cindy and Alex after my mom was murdered," Anna said. She finished her task and slid her phone back into her pocket.

"Yes, of course, terrible thing about your mom. But it stands to reason you both feel family loyalty, right?"

"Anna will always be family," Josh said.

"Besties," Lola said.

Josh was afraid to look at Anna. She had to be rolling her eyes at the choice of word. But he found it endearing, though on second thought, he quashed the idea. Besties meant no hope of love and passion, only best friends for life.

"Well, I should run. But a few of us are meeting up after work at O'Brien's. Join us if want. We do it every Friday night. Consider it your personal invite anytime you care for some laughs. Oh, and you too, Anna."

Lola squeezed his forearm one last time, reminding him of the tiny pair of horns she'd drawn on the smiley face for fun. The woman did have some intriguing devilment driving her, even while she had become a productive member of society involved with important work. And she wasn't afraid to be a woman, which he appreciated.

"Call me anytime you're looking for company. I'm just a phone call away, Detective."

Anna didn't say a word, but they both watched the perky paramedic exit. Josh couldn't help but notice the extra swing to Lola's shapely hips. How she managed to look so good in such an unattractive uniform was anyone's guess. Maybe it was a matter of attitude. Okay. Time to get back to business. He'd decide later if he should take Lola up on the invite. It probably meant nothing. She might be a woman who liked to flirt more than anything, enjoying leading guys on for fun. He had no problem with it; sometimes life was too serious to be taken seriously. Anyway, it was too early to tell what her deal was. But yes, he was intrigued and just might swing by O'Brien's for a beer. It had been a while since he'd chosen fun, always emersed in a current case or solving some cold crime. He could use some companionship. And a bit of flirting never hurt anyone, or at least anyone not otherwise involved with a partner. Would he wish it different, hell yeah.

"Why did you photograph the tattoo?" he asked, forcing his mind back to the present. Dreaming wouldn't get him anywhere with Anna.

"I'm ninety-nine percent certain it's my ticket to gain entry to Ironwood. You know, you should go to O'Brien's." Anna didn't look at him as she offered up the advice. "You need companionship. Some friends to have a laugh with."

"You should come too."

She snorted. "That invite wasn't for me, big guy. It was only meant for you. And don't be surprised if it's just the two of you, because the others couldn't make it with some convenient excuse."

Josh shook his head, though he knew it would be a sign of Lola's intent as well as Anna did. "No, she wouldn't do that. It's just friends meeting for drinks."

"You don't know women. I'd advise stocking up on condoms. Economy-sized box is your best bet."

Josh felt stymied, not certain of how to answer the charge. Sometimes Anna was too astute. Too direct. If just once she'd soften up a bit, not be so driven to only work with no play. But was she confirming they would never have anything more than what they had at the moment? Some part of him had always hoped, slim as it was, one day in the future they'd be a couple. Anna was saying the exact opposite. Hell, even telling him to go for it with another woman. Seemed like the nail in the coffin to him.

"Maybe I will."

An uncomfortable silence followed. Thankfully an orderly came bustling into the room, announcing, "I need some time with my patient. Alone."

They moved into the hallway and Josh turned to speak with Anna, tamping down the unexpected pain. She may not need more, but he knew he did. It wasn't too late for him to marry and have a family. Maybe it was time to give up the torch he'd been carrying for her all his life? It wouldn't be easy, but if he wanted a life, it might be the only way forward. "Don't go up to Ironwood just yet, okay? I want to check some leads first. Maybe it won't even be necessary."

"Don't see any other way to get the real intel." Anna paused. "But okay, I need to head to New York to see Kelly. She called this morning all upset about a friend."

"Nothing serious, I hope?" He congratulated himself on how calmly he was able to speak when she had just torn away his last shred of hope for them to ever have a future together. Funny, they could talk about all kinds of shit about how they felt about life and choices and death, but they couldn't talk about this. Other than her standard line about never going to marry. He had no choice but to follow her lead.

"Usual shit. Somebody posted photos online to get back at somebody else. It never ends."

"No, it doesn't, does it." He cleared his throat, feeling the need for some fresh air. "Keep me informed about Kelly. I've got to head back to the office." He strode away without waiting for her answer. Enough was enough.

NINE

Anna stood still for a moment after Josh took his sudden departure staring at nothing while others bustled down the hallway. Something had just happened between them. Something more than her being jealous of the easy way Lola Marcom had sashayed into the hospital room and tied Josh in knots with her little performance. She felt some distance had developed between them and the realization made her uncomfortable, knowing she was the main cause, not Lola.

What was Josh looking for? They never talked about the really personal stuff. Well other than her standard line, when she said she was going to go this life alone, dedicating it to helping those in need of the kind of help they couldn't get elsewhere. Plus, her personal drive to provide justice. But Josh never said he was going to forgo being a husband and father. He'd make a great father. His having had a good one to model after was a testament to the fact.

Until now it had all been speculation. But they were getting older. At some point the opportunity for him to marry and have children would be too late. She ignored the sudden squeeze to her stomach as she realized the same could be said about her. If she couldn't see herself doing those things with him, marriage and family, if indeed that was what he wanted, then she had to step aside for someone who desired the same things he did. But did it have to be someone like Lola Macom? The woman had rubbed her the wrong way, acting all coy around Josh and cock teasing him. Highly inappropriate in a hospital setting. Anna wasn't a prude, but she didn't appreciate the woman's obvious lustful interest in Josh with her standing right there. *Besties*, yuck.

Damn it. She needed to pull herself together and accept the inevitability of someone, if not Lola, turning Josh's head one day. But then why did it bother her so much? She never meant to be a dog in the manager, not respecting those with the deplorable stance if they couldn't have someone, no one else could. *So yeah, suck it up, Anna.* Josh deserved a good life. However he wanted it to unfold. She needed to get back to work. Only solution for it.

———

She started moving and didn't stop until she'd advised Charlie of her plans, kept her appointment at the tattoo parlor, and had packed light for a couple of days in New York City. In short order, she was at the airport waiting on the small plane. When the roar of the twin engines alerted her takeoff was imminent, she braced for the surge, then watched the ground drop away as the airliner rose into the dreary gray-tinged skies and they flew out over the nearly invisible mountain peaks. The drab color and discombobulation of the day reflected her somber mood all too well, adding to a feeling she was leaving something very important behind, something she might regret one day.

"Can I get you something?" the flight attendant asked, waking her from her dismal premonition. She needed to fight such thoughts with every fiber of her being. Life. It was meant to be lived. Lives were meant to be saved. Only way to give it meaning. There could be no better reason for her way of dealing with things the way she did than past experiences, dismal as they were. They'd made her into the person she was today. Willing to step up to do things others would more sensibly shy away from.

"Yes, an orange juice, please." It would be too easy to get drunk. She wished she had a seatmate to distract her, but the plane was flying with a few empty seats and the one next to hers remained unfilled.

She toasted herself with a glass of juice and began to plan, staring out unseeing at the darkening skies. She absently ran a thumb over the fresh tattoo on her wrist still covered with a thin layer of plastic to keep it moist. If she didn't like the dove tattoo later after the case was resolved, she'd either have it lasered off or changed to something else. She didn't have time to get temporary ones created and couldn't be bothered with the hassle of application. It was just a prop in the game anyway. And a lot less painful than a bullet hole. Or a fire.

"Ladies and gentlemen, this is your captain speaking. Please keep your seatbelt securely locked and your seats in the upright position. Be advised we may experience some turbulence today. Remain calm and in your seats at all times."

Anna's seat belt was already in place. She was all too aware that some turbulence could not be predicted and always kept the seat belt buckled. She finished the last swallow of her juice and handed the cup back to the flight attendant. No flying missiles would be in order as well. All around her people were complying and doing likewise.

The deep whine of the turbine engines as they moved through the air drew her attention and she braced her arms on the seat rests, listening and waiting. She disliked things out of her control. Hadn't today been tough enough without the current threat? They were still flying over Alaska having only left the airport a few minutes ago. The fact that they were over a mountainous region did nothing to calm her nerves.

A sudden bucking of the aircraft, followed immediately by a plummeting drop in altitude sent Anna's stomach reeling in hot pursuit. She pressed her lips tight together as those around her screamed or moaned or cried out, the sound of retching and the stench of vomit tainting the air. A series of bumps and slams kept her holding on tightly to the seat rests, the jarring far worse than a carnival ride. Some older people were groaning in pain as their joints were pushed to their limit.

Then a shift in the pitch of the engines alerted her to more trouble as the lights in the cabin dimmed. Electrical problems? The roller-coaster ride hit high gear. Anna had to work harder at convincing herself it was extremely rare for turbulence alone to cause a plane to crash. More suspect was pilot error, mechanical failure, or sabotage. Not so reassuring, but she acknowledged the statistic that though there was approximately one chance in sixteen million of crashing in an airplane, still extremely rare compared to one in every hundred and fourteen car trips. The weather though, as she turned her head to glance out the window, was worsening by the second, the skies ominous. A wild streak of lightning made her jump half out of her skin. She grimaced, working hard not to allow any sound to escape her lips.

The baby's loud wails from a nearby seat escalated, cranking up the tension. Anna's heart squeezed, wishing she could do something to help or reassure the frantic mother. She'd made note of all the passengers earlier, counting heads. Thirty-seven people and four crew members on today's flight.

Then the worse drop of all occurred, the aircraft plunging into freefall. *Oh, dear Lord, I know I haven't always been the best person I could be, but if we live through this, I promise to try harder.* She knew it was the common call of anyone thinking they might die soon, but it was all she had.

The faces of her family rose in her mind. A happier moment when they'd all been alive and enjoying a special occasion together, the twins, Mia and Tia's graduation from high school. The family had reservations at the Anchor Inn, but the weather had been so foul, electric had gone out in the town and they ended up having to stay home to celebrate. Everyone had pitched in. Candlelight was optional as the house had been supplied with an excellent backup generator by Alex Pace, but it had seemed more fitting and added a romantic component to the dinner. The twins had looked so beautiful in their dresses. And Josh, he'd looked like the proverbial big brother, making them laugh by sharing stories of college. Anna remembered it all as vividly as if it had happened yesterday, how handsome he'd looked and how much he had cared. Josh hadn't changed a bit over the years, as dedicated to family as ever. She had to accept that he would want a family of his own one day. Hell, he deserved it. *Please let him get the best life possible.*

Another wild, painful downward lurch forced her mind back into the present. She pried her eyes open to peer through the window once more, but the view outside the aircraft shocked her. Stunned her senses. They had lost so much elevation and the top of a snowy mountain peak loomed far too close, like she could reach out and touch it. Beautiful. And beyond terrifying. She held her breath. Was this it? The end of a life barely lived?

TEN

Josh was on the phone with Tom Jackson, longtime friend, and the newest member of Wolf Pack Justice, when he caught sight of a familiar figure out of the corner of his eye sashaying their way toward him, a wide smile of greeting on her full lips.

Lola.

Twenty to one she'd come to entice him to head over for drinks at O'Brien's. She was in street clothes now and carrying a jacket. The clingy style of dress she wore suggested she had the goods and was proud of it. Josh had to admit it, he enjoyed a woman unafraid to express her femininity when the occasion warranted it. It was Friday night in Anchor, Alaska, after all. If she couldn't enjoy herself after working hard all week, it was a sorry state of affairs.

"Tom, do me a favor. Drop by O'Brien's tonight. I need a wingman."

Dead silence on the phone for a sec. "Okay." Tom cleared his throat. "Soon as I finish up my report for Anna."

Maybe his spur-of-the-moment decision to involve Tom was a mistake? Inadvertently he'd just given his buddy the ammunition needed to pursue Anna himself. Josh was aware his buddy was attracted to her but had kept himself in check, knowing of Josh's prior claim to her affections. But then neither of them had a real chance with her no matter how they felt about her, not until she got over the idea that because she was so heavily involved in pursuing justice, she had no time for anything else. Other people managed to juggle work and home, but Anna seemed reluctant to even try. He was equal parts angry at her and sad. Hell yeah, a few beers were in order. And some damn fun for a change.

"Gotta go." Josh hung up on the call and greeted Lola with a nod, deciding to play it cool. Maybe give the guys a bit of fun for a change. "Nice dress by the way, but I'm going to have to ask you to leave."

"Why is that?" she asked, adopting a posture with hands on her hips and a defiant dare in her eyes he knew had to be drawing the attention of every man in the squad room as she stood near the corner of his desk. Lola was beyond hot.

"Because you're making everyone here look bad in comparison." Sure, it was an old line, but it was still fun to practice a bit of harmless flirting.

She laughed at his words, a warm belly laugh that came from deep inside and no doubt improved the morale all the members of the force in attendance. He saw Browne sitting and gaping at the pair of them, not even pretending to mind his own damn business.

"I came by in hopes of enticing you to O'Brien's. It's the twenty-first century, last I checked, so it's our turn to take the full initiative. Go after what we want."

"If by our turn, you mean women asking men out, I'm

all for it, no matter what century. By the way, you'd better be careful wearing a red dress around this crew."

"Why's that?" She cocked a perfectly groomed eyebrow at him and tossed her shiny blonde hair allowing it to cascade over one shoulder, drawing attention how silky the long strands were. Shit, sexy as Hades. She perched on the corner of his desk, revealing a side slit in the fabric. Now it was his turn to gape with his mouth open. He shut it just as quickly. *Play it cool, Josh.*

"Everyone's taser is now set to stun. And some of these guys need to stop, drop and roll to put out the fire." He cleared his throat.

She laughed again and stood up, running her hands down the front of her dress to smooth the fabric. "Ready, Detective?"

"If he's not, I am," a lone voice called out from the back of the room.

Lola acknowledged the compliment with a small smile and nodded at Josh. "I'll be waiting at O'Brien's and I'm buying." Nice she was giving him the option then. His respect for her grew. And she was bringing out a side of him he'd long forgotten even existed. Sure, he kibitzed with the guys, but almost never with the opposite sex. His torch for Anna was always there, keeping him walking the line. But she had told him in no uncertain words that it could never be, no matter how much he wished it or wanted it.

He watched Lola head on back out of the squad room, her retreating figure studied by every man in the room. Exactly as she intended. She was a stunner, no doubt about it. Problem was, even thinking of another woman gave him a bad case of guilt. Maybe he needed to get over it? Life. Too damn short in his opinion. By the time you learned how to be yourself, figured out what you wanted, time was pushing you to decide on a path before it was too late. Because if he didn't make a commitment soon to having a wife and family, chances for the future he envisioned would become impossible and pass him by. All his buddies were married now, most with one or two children, or one on the way.

"Hell, Pace, what's stopping you from escorting her right now?" Browne asked, his face almost comical with disbelief.

"I need to finish this report. Then I'll head on out."

Browne shook his head. "Any woman coming on to me like that, I'm going to be after her like white on rice. Take it from a veteran, those kinds of opportunities come by once in a lifetime, if then, buddy. A gorgeous gal showing interest is what most men dream about."

"Keep dreaming, Browne, and your old lady's going to chew you a new one," one of the detectives hooted. "But hell yeah, give me her number and I'm following her out of here like a puppy dog. *This gun's for hire*, like the song says."

"And on that note, I'll see you guys Monday, and hopefully not before," Josh said, picking up his jacket from the back of his chair and slipping it on before read-justing his belt and gun holster. He zipped up his coat and pulled on his gloves.

"But seriously, buddy, don't blow it," Browne said in a lower tone of voice meant just for him. "You're not getting any younger."

Josh grimaced. What was it about the energy today? All this talk about getting older and losing opportuni-ties was annoying. But Browne was just being himself, wanting to instill his wisdom in the detective he'd mentored since Josh had joined the force a year ago. He tamped down his anger. Or was it guilt? "None of us are. But I appreciate the sentiment. Enjoy your weekend."

"The wife's extended family are coming in from Seattle. Envision a horde of locusts of biblical proportions and you know how my weekend's going to play out. Consider yourself lucky."

Josh strode from the room, keen to get away for a change. Everything he'd learned about Lola was increasing his interest in getting to know her better. Perhaps tonight he'd find the time to speak with her one-on-one and see if they had something in common more than a wild spark of lust, though that wasn't exactly nothing. But if he was going to see a woman, there had to be more to it than physical attraction, there had to be a shared vision. Hell, he was getting ahead of himself here.

He unlocked his personal vehicle with a press on the key fob, a trusty half ton like most drove in Anchor, and turned his sights on O'Brien's. Beer and a hot woman awaited.

ELEVEN

Anna was holding on desperately to the seat rests. Somehow the pilot navigated over the deadly mountain tops by the slimmest of margin before descending into the valley below. No new cockpit announcements to passengers and crew as the pilots were no doubt far too involved with preventing a crash, fighting to keep the aircraft airborne. They were likely frantically searching for a place to land. She already knew the safety drill, and she leaned forward without being told into the fetal position, tucking her head down so her chin was near her chest to avoid having her neck snap back. Her feet flat on the floor in the brace position, as ready as she could be. Others nearby followed her actions. Seconds later, one of the stewardesses came on the intercom, announcing the proper protocols for landing, her professional voice hiding most of her fear of what was about to happen.

Then the plane lost power, the void making the aircraft hang in the sky, as if waiting for the hand of God to reach out and grab it. If only...

The final plunge to earth filled the air with screams. Curses. And prayers. Anna held on, wishing she could fly. See her family one last time. Hug Zoe, Charlie, Friday, and Diva. Tell Josh she had always loved him. She comforted herself with the knowledge he must know on some level how deep her love of him went. All the way to forever and back.

Impact was a bit lighter than expected, though the airplane bounced a few times through a skiff of snow drifts before coming to a final halt. By some miracle it remained intact, the pilot and co-pilot having pulled off the feat, avoiding trees and landing on a flat stretch of land. It appeared to be an unmanned runway for a small aircraft, plowed not too long ago. People cried and moaned all around her, trying to regain their senses. A wave of vertigo swept over her. She forced herself to take stock. She was alive, unhurt in her seat. Time to exit in case of fire, the next threat to human existence.

The two flight attendants were already up and out of their seats, instructing the passengers to move and leave their luggage behind. Anna always chose a seat over the wing of the plane whenever possible, and this time she was only five seats from the nearest exit. She knew enough to wear sturdy, natural fabric and good boots. She even had her unzipped parka on with warm gloves shoved in the pockets along with a woolen scarf and hat. She followed the small stream of people milling in the aisle to await her turn on the slide.

The air had never smelled sweeter when Anna arrived safely on God's green earth a couple of minutes later. Or more like into six inches of snow, the land all around the airplane a white expanse of snow-covered valley, the outline of the runway just visible. The view demonstrated just how lucky they'd been with the high-peaked mountains cradling them in the one spot they could have landed. The snow was powder, not tightly packed, and she sunk in to her lower calves. Not a problem for her with her high boots and warmly lined pants, but anyone in dress shoes was going to suffer. At least there was little wind in the valley and the temperature was a bit above freezing. Though with nightfall fast approaching that would change. Hopefully a rescue crew was on its way. She hurried a safe distance away from the plane before she pulled the woolen hat from her pocket and tugged it on over her ponytail and yanked on the warm gloves.

"Could you help me?"

Still regaining her senses and feeling a surge of euphoria at being alive, she turned toward the young woman asking the question. She was carrying a baby that looked about six months old, the mother's face expressing helplessness. She looked panicked and desperate, her face tear-streaked. The baby was crying pitifully.

"Of course. What can I do?" Anna switched into high gear.

"Could you hold him? His name is Henry. I have to change his diaper, but I left the bag on the plane. I gotta go back and get his stuff. His formula and his diapers and his rash cream..." Her voice trailed off.

Anna took the infant from the woman. He was all wrapped up with just his little face peeking out. He was blue in the face from crying. She understood. A part of her wanted to cry too, but it would be more from relief than anything. She looked up at the plane. Everyone appeared to be off the aircraft. A couple of people were holding their heads like they'd suffered a concussion, but no one looked critically injured. The crew were working to assess everyone's condition and no doubt someone was calling for help.

"I don't know if they will allow anyone back in for a while. Maybe ask that flight attendant over there?"

Anna pointed the woman out. The woman rushed off to confront the crew member and she looked down at the baby who had finally stopped crying and was now gazing up at her in wonder. His color was better now, pink. She rocked him a bit, not used to babies, but thought it was the thing to do. He seemed to like it and actually smiled at Anna, his toothless gums a surprise. The quick change in emotions startled her. How quickly can a baby forget? And when do they start to smile, she wondered, enjoying the sensation of holding him. The people around her were busy converging into small groups or wandering around the crash site, most of them busy on their phones trying to reach loved ones. She needed to make some calls too, to let everyone know what happened, so they wouldn't worry. Kelly would be waiting to hear from her in New York.

She kept rocking Henry as she waited for the mother to come back. She'd had very little experience with babies, other than a few babysitting gigs as a teenager, preferring to do outside chores to inside ones. She just knew they were a lot of work, but she was even more worried about something happening to her and leaving the child motherless. But holding the little bundle made her feel an emotion she hadn't felt before. A need to nurture another human being.

She was half relieved and half disappointed when the mother came bustling back to take the child off her hands, having gotten a few supplies from the stewardess who must have gone out of their way for the desperate mother to locate the items.

"Thanks for holding him. They said it could be a while so I need to fix Henry up. He's got a worrisome rash."

"Let me help you get him situated," Anna volunteered. "You'll need to lay him down to change him, right?" She looked around, wondering how to manage the feat.

"I have a blanket we can lay on the snow. He needs a change so badly. Rather potent at the moment." The woman grimaced to let her know what the deal was. It had to be bad for his tender skin to neglect a change with the rash she'd mentioned.

"Right." Anna worked to clear a spot for the woman using her gloved hands to push the powdery snow away a few feet and to act like a windbreak. She laid the blanket down on the ground and assisted the woman in changing Henry's diaper. The woman did it quickly and efficiently to keep the baby from getting any colder than necessary, before bundling him up snugly again. Henry took it rather stoically, his short sturdy body reminiscent of a possible future as a pugnacious prize fighter. His tiny fists beat at the air putting his personal stamp on the image.

"Thanks, my name is Jo, by the way." The young woman rocked Henry as she spoke. Anna glanced down at her footwear and was reassured to discover her wearing thick boots and clothing. Jo was on the ball.

"I'm Anna. Nice to meet you." The incongruous words made her snort a laugh. "Well, maybe not exactly like this."

"But we're alive." Jo hugged her baby tighter, her eyes filled with wonder. "I wasn't so sure there for a bit."

"Will you be okay if I check to see if anyone else needs anything? And find out what's going on?" Anna glanced around to see what the deal was as she asked her question. Thankfully most people were dressed well enough, though some would be in trouble soon with the wrong kind of footwear. Hopefully the plane would be declared safe soon and they'd be able to reload everyone.

"I'm fine. Go. Maybe check to see if help is on the way?"

"I'll be right back with answers." Anna strode away to join the larger group of crew members and half the passengers. No fire had erupted on the plane as yet, so there was every hope it wasn't going to happen.

She pulled out her phone and checked for bars. None. She wrote out a text to Josh and Zoe anyway, hoping to send it through soon.

Before she could even ask her questions of the crew, the sounds of incoming snowmobiles erupted and everyone turned silent. They were more than welcomed. Anna glanced toward the loud piercing engine noises and saw a group of four black machines eating up the distance to the aircraft, coming in from the northwest.

"Hallelujah," one passenger said, a wide grin splitting his face.

"I hear you, brother," another said, clasping his hands together in a prayer like fashion.

As they drew closer, Anna noticed a large logo applied to the front hood of the speeding machines. An image of a dove, same as the one she'd just had tattooed to her inner wrist. Her heart rate sped up. Since when had the northern commune of Ironwood acquired such resources? And what were they doing scouting so far afield?

TWELVE

The low, friendly roar of O'Brien's on a Friday night in Anchor greeted as Josh when he opened the front door. Along with the scent of warm, steamy bodies fueled by hormones and camaraderie.

"Hey, Detective." Christopher Browne, his partner's son, stood in the entrance leading to the main section with all the tables and long, mahogany bar.

"Chris. How's business?" The young man, barely out of his teens, rented a tattoo parlor in town called Odessey. His father was not exactly pleased but knew enough to let his children choose their own path.

"I tattooed your sister Anna this afternoon. She show you? A pretty white and blue logo of a dove on her inner wrist. I tried to talk her into expanding it a bit, add some extra shadowing or maybe a banner with Wolf Pack Justice on it. But she had a picture on her phone and said it had to be *exactly* the same." Chris shrugged. "Maybe you'd like one too? Got a special on this week for families."

Josh held back a stream of expletives and nearly bit

his own tongue in the process. What was she thinking, permanently marking her flesh with a cult tattoo? She was obviously headed undercover. A fucking dangerous thing to do. His gut ached with the idea of her heading into the fray once more. Joining a cult was no walk in the park. People like that were volatile, often the leader's paranoia about anyone not sharing a similar belief matched their warped view of the world. He knew far too much about Jonestown and Waco to ever take such affiliations lightly. In his pursuit of knowledge, his own personal brand of epistemology philosophy, the need to separate justified belief from opinion was embedded in his mission statement: *how* do we know. Both he and Anna shared that need to pursue the truth of crimes, to bring justice to the victim or victims, comparing stories of what might have happened to arrive at what did occur. But only Anna stepped out onto the furthest reaches of the thinnest branches to obtain the knowledge. One day the branch might break and he worried if he would make it in time to catch her before she fell. That was his deepest truth. His deepest fear.

"What's wrong, Josh?" Chris asked with a frown.

"Nothing. It's fine."

"You not into tattoos?"

"It's not that. I've heard you do good work. I'll pass along your sale information. So, I hear the relatives are breeching the castle walls this weekend. Your dad filled me in."

Chris shrugged. "Good time to head out of town myself. I'm going skiing with a few friends. Catch you on the other side. And don't forget about the deal."

"Not likely," Josh said, tongue firmly lodged in his cheek. He sent a quick text to Anna asking her what the hell she was thinking branding herself with a cult logo, then waited a few seconds to see if she would answer. Nothing.

He slipped his phone back in his pocket and headed into O'Brien's main area. If he got a tattoo beyond the one from being in the military, it would be of a broken heart. First, he lost his father Alex, his sister Tia, and then his mom, Cindy. If Anna didn't slow down, she'd be adding herself to that tragic list. The thought was unthinkable, and he took a deep breath in an effort to clear his mind of the fucking torture.

Lola caught sight of him before he noticed her. He caught the movement as she waved eagerly from a round table she occupied with a few others from work, her grin of greeting a balm to his bruised ego.

"Hey, PIC, glad you could join us," she said. She patted an empty seat beside her. "Sit. We were just talking about you and the new case of amnesia guy."

"PIC?" he asked, intrigued. He nodded at the one man and woman already seated at the table, recognizing two paramedics who worked alongside Lola. Susan and Ray were an engaged couple, planning to marry in a couple of months.

"Yeah. Partner in crime. Seems to fit since we met by finding that guy on the road." She ran a finger down his sleeve. "And looks like I have a hankering to PIC you."

He half-choked back a laugh, unsure of the new moniker. "I like your brand of subtlety, Miss Lola. As Charlie would say, you're as cute as a button and as subtle as a bull in a China shop. I think I'll call you Signal. Seems like a good strong name for you from the vibes I'm getting."

She grinned wider. "Sig and PIC. I like it."

"It'll look good on a business card." He carried on the banter.

"That'll be a start." She grinned wickedly.

"You got chutzpah, Sig, gotta give you that."

"Wanna dance? I need to claim my stomping grounds, judging by all the looks in our direction. I take it you don't get out much, PIC?"

"No. Not enough." He got to his feet, removed his jacket before placing it on the back of his chair, and then offered Lola his hand. "I've got a hankering for the two-step, if I can remember how."

"Don't matter anyhow. I just want to see how you move."

When he swung Lola into his arms, he was surprised by the fit of their bodies. Almost a bit too natural, like they'd danced together before. Not sure if that was a good thing or not, he kept his mind on remembering the steps of the western dance, enjoying the live band O'Brien's was famous for. The Lonesome Rebels. He hummed along to the catchy tune, trying to keep all thoughts of feeling guilty for enjoying himself at bay. He could sense people watching them with avid interest and he missed a step under the public scrutiny. When the dance ended, his date excused herself to visit the ladies' room. Josh signaled the waitress for another round. His phone buzzed and he was tempted to ignore it. He hadn't been having such a good time in so long, he didn't want it to be interrupted. But duty called and he checked the number, recognizing Rodger Evan's number. The short text message on his screen punched him in the gut.

"Please give Lola my apologies, I have an emergency," he said, jumping up from the table and nearly spilling his mug of beer.

Anna's in trouble. His mind focused only on that terrible reality as he zigzagged through the throng of patrons, mumbling apologies as he bumped others in his way. He nearly plowed down the Police Chief Lloyd Davis and his friend Tom Jackson making their way through the front entranceway.

"Excuse me." He stopped to speak with them, though every cell in his body resented the loss of momentum of getting to her. To make sure she was okay.

"What's happened? You look like something's rocked your world," Tom asked.

"A plane to New York. It vanished from the radar screen a few minutes ago. Rodger Evans texted. I'm headed there now." He'd gotten the intel straight from his friend who was on shift at the Anchor Airport, who knew Anna was on the passenger manifest. It was likely no one else had been notified as yet.

"We'll need to coordinate rescue efforts." Chief Davis was suddenly all business, the glint in his eyes reassuring. "Has anyone from the plane called anyone in the last few minutes?"

In other words, was anyone alive? The impact of thinking Anna could be hurt, maybe dead or dying, sent Josh reeling. He swayed for a moment and Tom used his arm to support Josh.

"Careful there, Detective. Okay, we're heading to the station first. No point in going to the airport just yet. Not until we have more information," Chief Davis.

Josh didn't want to head to the police station. He needed to keep moving, not waiting around for details. Every second mattered. He wanted to fly to be at Anna's side, to see her beloved face telling him she was all right. She had to be. No woman as alive as Anna Hale could possibly be dead, right?

But he had to stand down, no choice but to follow his boss's edict. And yes, it was true he needed to know more before racing in without a plan, though he prided himself on being able to wing just about anything. Anna may have brought out the best in him, a fiery protectiveness, but she also easily upset his natural world often with some of her exploits. But none of this was her doing. She was headed to New York to help her ward, Kelly Smith. Surely fate would not allow such a good woman, a brilliant detective, be taken out of existence before her time? She had too much to offer the world. Such a thing was unthinkable, an abomination on the world. A terrible sense of heavy guilt had him about on his knees for how much he'd been enjoying himself earlier while Anna was out there, hellbent on helping Kelly. Or anyone else that asked for that matter.

His heart thumped uncomfortably and his breathing became more labored as his mind raced with all sorts of scenarios of what could have happened as he followed Chief Davis and Tom Jackson across the parking lot. He reached into his pocket for his emergency inhaler, having suffered asthmatic attacks since childhood, he knew enough to keep it close by, but the plastic device dropped from his tenuous grasp as the world squeezed dark.

THIRTEEN

Anna heard a shout from one of the passengers. Everyone turned to see what the problem was, ignoring the approaching snow machines for the moment. An elderly man had fallen to the ground, clutching at his chest.

"Help! Please help my father!" a younger woman screamed. She bent down to assist him, the worry and anguish on her face made Anna's heart squeeze with sympathy. It was not so long ago she lost her adopted mother Cindy to a similar affliction. Anna began running toward the fallen passenger, with the pilot and crew members close on her heels.

They found the man's skin tone pale, sweat beads on his forehead. His eyes were filled with alarm as he lay prone on the ground, his head nestled in his daughter's lap. The woman kept saying over and over, "You're going to be fine, Dad."

The man's breathing was labored, his pain obvious.

"Does he have a history of heart problems?" the pilot asked.

"Yes. He's on medication for it. He took something for it a few minutes ago, but it didn't help. I think this was all too much for him. Please help him."

The labored breathing worsened. Then abruptly stopped. Immediately, the pilot went into action. He gently asked the daughter to move back a bit before he started CPR on the man, working as efficiently as a machine.

"I know CPR," Anna said to the co-pilot standing nearby. "I can take a turn."

The three of them kept at it for an indeterminable period, but no breath of life returned to the man. Though everyone else knew he was gone, his daughter would not give up hope, pressing them to work ever harder to save her dad.

The tragic scene, fraught with such pain and anguish, sent a complete hush over those present as they fought to save the man's life. Even the snow machines were switched off as they fought valiantly against death.

It was Anna's turn again and she kept up the robotic sequence, trying not to see past this moment. But at the edge of her vision Anna caught a glimpse of Tia now. The sister she'd lost to the Black Rose Killer. A surreal entity who materialized at important moments in time with a message. *Yes, the man is gone.*

Finally, sweat stinging her eyes and Anna having once more turned the CPR actions on the victim back over to the pilot, Anna approached the young girl with sympathy riding high in her eyes. She pulled her close. Hugged her. Someone had to tell her. To continue the charade on a dead man was wrong.

"What's your name?" she asked.

"Keri."

"I think your dad has moved on, Keri. He's probably

not able to come back, even if he wanted to. I think he's with family now on the other side."

"With my mom?" Keri's voice thickened with tears.

"I believe that's very likely," Anna reassured her.

"Stop, okay, you're torturing him now," Keri said before bursting into tears. Anna pulled her back into a hug and let the young girl cry on her shoulder until she was spent.

Another passenger handed Anna a bunch of tissues and she handed them to Keri. "Dry your eyes and blow your nose. You'll feel better."

The young woman accepted the tissues and took a deep breath.

"Thank you."

"I'm Anna, by the way."

"I know. I've seen you on TV. You're a private investigator."

Today she wished she was a miracle worker and could bring back the departed. "I'm sorry for your loss."

The pilot took a moment to close the father's eyes. Then bowed his head. "Our heavenly father, we thank you for this man's life, for his hard work of raising a family and a fine daughter. We pray for his mortal soul as he descends to join you in heaven. Rest in peace. Amen."

"Amen," the crowd echoed the pilot's final word with reverence. Right now, the pilot was their minister in this temporary community build of resilience and need, the man in charge of seeing them safely away from the crash site.

Anna stepped away and worked her way through those standing around to the perimeter of the group, brushing shoulders with those still caught up in the pathos of the last few minutes. She needed a moment alone. If only Tia would come back, just for a little while, share with her all she had learned on the other side. The mystery of death, the veil over the next world, was difficult for all humans. Who or what was out there, waiting? Curiosity and the need to know, to be in control of things, made this final call eat at her. She had to shake it off. Others needed her in this world.

Still, she lingered a moment longer. She took a deep breath and stared at the full moon rising, the blue glow enhancing the white snow and turning the White Mountains surreal. This was her land, her people, her time to make a difference. Don't waste a moment, Anna, too soon this earthly time shall pass. A pack of wolves picked up the "Amen" still lingering from the short service over the dead man and their ancient song echoed in the night, sending chills down her spine. *What awaits me now?* For she knew well enough a certain type of wolf call was a challenge. A call to arms.

FOURTEEN

Josh came around, finding himself on a gurney outside O'Brien's near an ambulance. He sat up, yanking off the oxygen mask. The events of the last few minutes fired up his brain and his determination to get a move on took over. He pulled away from the first responder trying his best to keep him on the stretcher and shambled to his feet.

"Josh, we need to take you in. Have you checked out. You had a bad attack."

Lola was suddenly right there in his face. "Listen to the man, Josh, he knows what he's talking about."

"No time. Anna's missing. Her plane went down. I just need something to relax me. I'm not going to the hospital."

"Okay, we can't make you, but you should have a check-up soon. At least do that."

"Soon as we find her."

Tom moved in to help him, but Josh waved him away. "I'm fine."

Josh then thanked the two medical personnel, both

leaving still shaking their heads, before he strode over to his truck, ignoring Lola's best efforts to stop him by grabbing at his arm. Tom followed him.

"I'll drive," he said, pushing him aside.

"What are you doing here?" Chief Davis frowned at him as he entered the squad room with Tom a few minutes later.

"Doing my job. I've been checked out and I'm fine. What's going on? Any updates?"

Thankfully his boss decided not to press it further. "Okay, listen up. Flight AA1824 has gone down in the White Mountains. Reports are just coming in from the pilot and crew; passengers have been banged up pretty good and there are a few concussions, and unfortunately one fatality, a male passenger. The pilot pulled off a miracle after some bad turbulence and a loss of electrical power, setting it down on an old runway in the valley. A crew is being assembled at the airport for rescue as we speak and a pair of helicopters will be heading to the scene to rescue the thirty-seven passengers and four crew members shortly."

"I want to be on that team, Chief," Josh announced, stepping forward. All he had heard was one dead, male. Not enough to reassure him his Anna was one hundred percent okay, but enough to stop his heart rate from highjacking his body a second time tonight.

Chief Davis balked, shaking his head. "You were lying flat on a gurney less than half an hour ago. I don't think that's a good idea, Detective."

Josh ran a hand through his hair with frustration. "I have to be there. Anna needs me. I'm fully recovered. The paramedics gave me a clean bill of health. It won't happen again." A bit of an exaggeration, but he wasn't taking chances. He had to be on one of those choppers.

"I'll go with him, Chief, keep an eye on him," Detective Browne said, getting up from his desk.

"I will as well," Tom said.

The chief looked undecided for a moment but relieved Josh by saying, "Then you'd better get a move on. But Tom, you aren't eligible to go on an official rescue flight. Nothing I can do about that."

Josh took off at a half run for the parking lot and his cruiser, Tom and Browne following close on his heels.

"I'll drive," Browne said, moving to open the driver's side door.

Josh wanted to object but held his tongue. The guy had stepped up to help him.

"Take my truck," he said to Tom, throwing him the keys. The back seat of the police vehicle was far too confining for Tom to ride along, built on purpose to make prisoners more cooperative.

Josh hurried into the police cruiser.

"Use the siren. I don't want those choppers leaving without us." Josh sat in the passenger seat, his right leg jigging up and down, desperate to get on with it.

In less than five minutes, they pulled into the airport. Josh caught a glimpse of the two huge black beasts being boarded by a couple of people. He jumped out and made a dash for the nearest one. He pulled out his gold detective badge and flashed it at the pilot. "Chief Davis has authorized me and my partners to go along with the rescue of passengers on flight AA1824."

"There's only room for one of you," Micheal McCann warned.

"Fine. I'm the guy."

Browne shook his head while Tom frowned, looking prepared to duke it out with someone for their seat. "Figures. I'll stay behind and take the flack," Browne said.

"Thanks, buddy, I owe you one." Josh nodded at his partner and climbed aboard the chopper. "I'll keep in touch," he reassured Tom.

After buckling in, he nodded at the other man he knew on a casual basis, Ray Samson.

"I heard Anna's on the flight," Ray said with a grim smile. "That's why Micheal let you come aboard."

"Yeah, I know I'm taking up a seat, but I haven't been able to reach her."

"Say no more."

Josh appreciated the pilot's and co-pilot's generousness in allowing him to head out with them. "I owe you guys one."

"Buy me a beer next time we're in the Yellowhead and we'll call it even," Ray said.

"I'll take a whiskey, neat," Micheal added before he donned his headgear in preparation for takeoff.

"I'll buy you all the rounds you can handle," Josh said. "Soon as we get Anna and those passengers home safely."

No one had to the time to reassure him about that being a guaranteed outcome before protocols were enacted by the pilot and the flight tower. In mere seconds they were airborne and flying toward the crash site.

FIFTEEN

Anna strode purposely over to the six men standing by their snow machines, helmets off, their expressions solemn and respectful as they waited to be approached. She recognized one of them. Mr. Menace from the café, the henchman who wouldn't let Emily Stubbs in to see her sister. She forced a smile she didn't feel and gave the man an inquiring look.

"Don't I know you from somewhere? I'm certain I saw you just recently." She gave him a perplexed look before slapping her forehead. "Right. Lucky's café yesterday. You were with another guy, younger." He appeared to be the leader of the small group of males.

"Right." The man studied her face for a moment. "Did you get a place?"

So he was paying attention. "No, unfortunately. By the time I got there it was gone. I'll probably just stay at the hotel for now. Not like I can't afford it or anything else I want." She threw it out there as bait.

"What? Did someone leave you a fortune?" Mr. Menace gave her a sharp look.

"Let's just say I don't have to work anymore. I can follow my dreams for the foreseeable future. Thank you, Aunt Gladys." She made the double-handed prayer sign with a sigh of gratefulness.

"Lucky for you. You new in town?" Thankfully the guy didn't appear to know who she was. A product, no doubt, of living off grid most of the time. She hadn't been mentioned by media for a while now, meaning her cover was less likely to be blown if the guy didn't visit Anchor often. Since she hadn't brought along a disguise, it was a favorable development.

"Yes. I'm on a mission to meet someone." She opened her eyes wider to try to make herself seem more like a zealot and less like a cynical study of human nature. Not that she didn't believe most people are good, but she'd been up against the worst of them too and it tempered her beliefs. "That's my dream." She looked at the vehicles as if she were just seeing them for the first time. "That logo on the hood, it's the same as in my dreams. That's weird, eh?"

"How so?" Mr. Menace crossed his arms over his chest, giving her a rather jaded look for someone in a commune built on faith and zealots.

She took off her glove and pushed up her jacket sleeve. "See, I got this tattoo because it means something to me. It's exactly the same. Wow, what are the chances of that. It has to be a sign, right? Where are you guys from? Are you part of the Circle of Friends?" She gave them all an awed look right out of the playbook.

Mr. Menace gave a nod, while the others gathered round and glanced at the fresh tattoo. Chris Browne had done good work. It was a perfect rendering of the tattoo on the man in the hospital. It was pretty. Too bad it was used to represent a cult.

"It's all meant to be then. I was supposed to be on this plane, headed back to New York and then taken right out of the sky, landing me here. Wow, I don't know what to say."

The pilot came up to the group with a few others, interrupting a play that had gone splendidly in Anna's opinion. She'd improvised, but it was all plausible. Or should be to the cult members who were notorious for looking for signs of the coming apocalypse and other such alarming things.

"Where are you men from?" the pilot asked.

"We're from Ironwood. Just out on a winter camping trip," Mr. Menace said.

"You're a long way from home base."

"It's part of our survival training and a bonding exercise. We'd like to provide any assistance you need. We have warm blankets and a small camp stove."

"Thanks, appreciate it. The blankets would be great for some of the passengers. Not everyone has warm footwear or a proper jacket. I don't know how long until rescue arrives exactly, but we've been assured they're on their way."

The pilot looked exhausted, but focused.

"That's good news," Anna said, giving him a genuine smile. Poor man. He'd done an amazing job of landing the plane, saving everyone onboard. But no doubt, he'd carry the older man's death to his grave. So would Anna. She'd felt him go, leaving the mortal plain for whatever awaited humans.

Everyone worked together, making sure those most in need had a warm blanket. Those without proper boots sat on a snow machine to keep their feet out of the cold snow. Not twenty minutes later, the incoming buzzing sounds of aircraft, then the final whooshing of rotating chopper blades entering airspace, resounded in the moonlit valley. If not for one man dead, it would have been a celebration of being alive. But mindful of the loss, the cheers were subdued when the two S-92 SAR helicopters landed. Anna had always thought the aircraft looked like huge insects, something out of pre-historic times.

The first had barely touched ground when the side door flew open and a man was jumping into the snow and frantically looking around the crowd. Josh and Anna's eyes met at the same exact second and he ran straight toward her, his eyes filled with such high emotion she swallowed hard.

They hugged, long and hard, unable to speak for a moment. Overcome by feelings she couldn't give an exact name to, she took a deep steadying breath, trying to find the right words.

"I'm sorry you had to go through this, Anna," Josh said.

"Not just me. All these people have. Well, it's okay now. You're here."

"I need to help them get everyone out now, but later, we have to meet up. At your place. Okay?"

"Of course. I'll wait for a later ride. I'm dressed warm. Don't worry about me."

The howling of wolves breaking out in the distance didn't exactly punctuate her remarks favorably, but both of them decided to ignore it.

In short order, the two aircraft were filled to capacity with passengers, the extra crew from the plane and the helicopters, and the warmer dressed passengers opting to stay behind. Josh decided to wait until the last trip as well which would be hours away, refusing to leave her.

They stood side by side, watching the helicopters navigate the valley with their precious cargo.

The members of the Circle of Friends eyed the pair from time to time, obviously wondering about the connection. Well, nothing else for it. She'd show up at their compound soon enough and could only hope to be let in. Either that, or she'd have to come up with a Plan B. And there was always a Plan B or C or even D, if necessary, tenacious being her middle name.

SIXTEEN

Anna and Josh buckled themselves into the helicopter seats on the final trip of the night, grateful to be leaving the desolate location. The moon had risen far higher in the sky, making its way across the heavens, a beacon of light that called to her on an elementary level. They held hands, a simple action, but necessary, the connection making her feel grounded. Right with the world.

"You'll soon be home," Josh said.

"Home. Love that word," Anna replied, bestowing a warm smile on Josh. She was alive. The realization hit all over again and she squeezed his hand, wishing they were already there and sharing a celebratory drink together.

"One of the best words in the English language in my opinion."

Josh looked so focused on her, like he had something on his mind. Something of much importance. She got it. When death's hand looms too near a loved one, it changes a person. Makes them either grateful for what they have or helps make a decision for them. Some people moved on from whatever situation they were in, abandoning families even. Others embraced opportunities they might be denying themselves, thinking to save it for the future. Well, sometimes the future hits one smack in the face.

"Yeah, it is."

"Like friends and family. And love."

"You feeling all lovey-dovey tonight?" she teased.

"Maybe."

"What were you doing when you got the call about my plane going down?"

Josh cleared his throat. "I decided to go to O'Brien's."

A certain clenching of her stomach made Anna hyperaware. *Lola*. "You need to get out more, Josh. No harm in that. You work too much."

"So do you."

"Who else is going to do it? It's a calling."

"Yeah, I know. Just don't forget you're human. With normal human needs if you'd only pay attention."

"Let's not go there tonight." She pushed all thoughts of Lola and her annoying invite aside. "Let's just pretend to be two normal people grateful for each other's company after an unexpected ordeal that led to the best outcome possible. I'm home safe and sound. All that matters."

"Works for me."

They sat quietly and held hands for the remainder of the journey. They'd landed and were headed for Anna's place in Josh's half-ton Tom had thoughtfully left after a short debriefing at the airport.

Josh turned into her driveway, a certain look on his face that had her wondering what he was thinking. But she said nothing, just wanting to get inside. She needed to greet Friday and Diva, text everyone to let them know she was fine, and open a damn good bottle of whiskey.

An hour and two stiff drinks later, Josh and Anna were in the living room, facing each other on the sofa. Friday and Diva lay on the floor close by, both fast asleep. The rare domestic bliss felt good after a day with an uncertain outcome. A day where life and death hung in the balance. She felt relaxed, knowing the next steps required in getting close enough to Faith Stubbs to have a heart-to-heart with her. This might be her last night at home for a while, depending on how long it took to get the cult member alone. She needed to make the best of it.

Josh picked up the bottle and topped off their drinks, his actions familiar and comforting. He was her rock, the one person in this world she knew she could truly count on no matter what happened. It was like she'd known him forever. Yes, sometimes she was guilty of taking him for granted. She thought nothing of calling him day or night when she had need. It was wrong. He deserved better than that.

She took another sip of the excellent whiskey and set the glass down on the coffee table. "You know, we often talk about my life, but it's not often you share with me what's in your heart, Josh. What your dreams are for the future?"

Josh gave a crooked smile. Anna took a deep breath. That look, right there, almost a little boy look filled with mischievous overtones, made her melt with affection for him. Her belly warmed by the liquor spread the sensual sensation further downward and she took a deep breath to steady herself. Careful.

Josh looked for a moment as if he was going to make light of the question, then his expression shifted. Perhaps the alcohol had kicked in, because his handsome mug took on a thoughtful thousand-yard gaze.

"I have been giving my advancing years some thought."

"What? You're all of thirty-seven?" She scoffed.

"Thirty-eight next month. Time's slipping away, Anna."

"But what you're doing, what we're doing together, catching the bad guys, *really* matters."

"Hmm. But what about love? Having a human connection beyond victims and cases. Someone to share the highs and the lows with. Or just the everyday minutia that makes up a good life. As simple as 'do we have milk in the fridge?' Or 'who's taking the kids to hockey practice?' So many times, I've wanted to say something—"

He stopped himself, and Anna knew. She didn't want him to say it out loud, make it real. Then they could side-step it later if necessary. She wasn't afraid of serial killers or joining a cult to find a missing person as much as she feared the fallout from admitting what they had been avoiding speaking of for years now. And before she realized what she was going to do, she leaned in and kissed him. Perhaps it was a diversion? But no, in reality it was far more than that, it was decades of denying the intense attraction she'd always felt for her next door neighbor, then adopted brother, and business partner, and finally fellow Wolf Pack Justice member, since the first moment she'd laid eyes on him.

She caught him by surprise. He froze for a couple of seconds. Then he was pulling her in tightly to his broad chest, crushing her breasts against him and kissing her as if his life depended on it. She lost it then, letting everything else drop away. The booze and the urgent need to feel alive after thinking she might die today with a life too soon interrupted all making her feel, no, making her *know*, this was the only moment in time that mattered. She ignored the alarm bells ringing far away in her head with ease as she kissed Josh like there was no tomorrow. No going back. Tonight was theirs. *One night, please, just one night with him before anything changes. One night to remember forever.*

He thrust his tongue into her mouth. Plundered it. He tasted good, the tang of the excellent whiskey melding with his warm breath. He grabbed the back of her hair, the pins from her bun pinging on the floor as the mass of dark hair came flying down, flowing around them. Electric jolts arrowed straight to her core. No man had grabbed her like that. Ever. As if they were the last two people and he wanted her more than life itself. Like she wanted him.

She returned his kiss with greed, hot and searing, surrendering all of herself to this moment. Her arousal dampened her panties. She breathed in the fragrance of sex filtering into the air, the mingling of male and female essence arousing as hell, stirring her senses into a blazing passion of white light. Her blood roared in her ears, an insistent drumbeat mimicking her heartrate.

He ripped his mouth from hers, sucking on her neck, trailing tiny kisses down toward her breasts. She wanted him to go farther. Much farther. He pressed into her, caressing her shoulders, then coming around to fondle her breasts, using his fingers to roll the tender, budded nipples. Her legs gave way. He steadied her, sucking on one nipple then the other through the fabric of her T-shirt and bra. She arched her body to give him full access, her mind screaming, *take me, take me now. Help me forget everything else, if only for one night.*

Fire and ice. Hot passion melted her body into a quicksilver pool of both, swirling one sensation against the other, tugging her into a growing vortex. It near drowned her, pulling her under, unable to see past her want for his man. He held her upright on the sofa, otherwise she'd have fallen over, dissolving into pure lust. Her very bones felt melted, scorched and vibrating with need.

"Tell me what you want," she whispered. His breath scorched her skin where the kisses landed, his beard lightly scratching her sensitive flesh. It drove her wild. He picked her up in arms made golden from the sun. Under her searching fingers, his flesh corded and bulged with solid muscles.

"I want you, Anna. And I won't stop, not until you can't remember who you are." He punctuated each word with a kiss on her flesh, his lips insistent.

"Take me to bed then."

He carried her into the hallway to the nearest guest room, laying her down on the king-sized bed.

He pushed her thighs wide apart, rubbing her through the cloth of her pants. He must have been able to feel her heat, the dampness through the fabric. She circled his waist with her legs. She wanted to be naked under him, have him press that wall of flesh against hers, leave her senseless. *Make me feel alive.*

"Make love to me," she said.

A deep intake of breath rasped.

"I want you. I need you. Inside me." She could not say it any clearer.

He shucked off all the annoying clothing he wore. His fine, strong body emerged from under the layers, chiseled and golden in the moonlight.

"Do you have a condom?" she asked.

"Yes, but it's old." He pulled one from the wallet abandoned in his pants.

"Then what are you waiting for? I'm sure its fine." She quickly shed her own clothing and positioned herself under him. "I want you, Josh."

She drifted back to earth slowly, her body registering aftershocks of pure pleasure.

She reached up and took his face between her trembling hands. "Thank you."

He turned his head to the side, kissing a fingertip as it came close to his mouth. "We're good together," he said with a glint in his eye. "You okay? I didn't break anything?"

"Better than okay. I'm absolutely over the moon. It was perfect." She let her eyes say what her mouth would not—*could not.* She pushed away all other thoughts. Tomorrow she could feel all the regret and guilt she wanted, but not tonight.

He nipped at her fingers playfully. She saw a wisdom beyond his years exposed when their eyes locked for a long moment, but also a vulnerability that took her breath clear away. That a man, a strong soldier and patriot, could feel so deeply...

"Thank God you're all right. I nearly lost it there, when the plane vanished from radar—"

"Shush. I'm fine now," she interrupted, wanting to move on and never look back.

He pulled her closer, murmuring, "That you are, my Anna, that you are."

———

It was still dark when Anna woke up, her head thumping from a tad too much alcohol. She shoved aside regret for giving into her baser instincts and pressed her lips together. How could she have done it? She felt she had used Josh, throwing herself at him to get him to stop talking about the massive one-ton elephant that had been standing in the corner of the room for far too long. She should have left it perched there forever, a constant reminder of what could have been or yet might be was better than this sickening feeling that life as she knew it was done, over with, finished. For now, he would pay the price as much as she would. What was the right thing to do? For once she had no exact plan. No way forward that would guarantee no one got hurt. Fact was, she'd enjoyed every second of last night's tryst. If one could call it that, being only 0500 hours and they'd been so hungry for each other their lovemaking had gone on for practically all the time they were in bed. But to build a life together was risky. She lived a dangerous existence. And she did not want to live any other way. What man would put up with her lifestyle long term, especially once there were children involved? Something would have to give and she wasn't prepared for that. At least not yet. She never said never but hopes for wanting to have her activities in helping others curtailed in any way, slim to none.

Risk assessment: extreme. At least to her heart. There was no bandage big enough in this world to soak up the blood once she came clean about her true intentions moving forward.

She slipped from bed as quietly as she could manage and tiptoed from the room. She needed pain killers, coffee, and a new plan. Not necessarily in that order.

SEVENTEEN

The sight of Anna in the kitchen, hair tied up in a ponytail, frying bacon, and sneaking a piece each to Friday and Diva warmed Josh's heart. Last night had been perfect, obviously for both of them. She looked so beautiful without any makeup this morning, her face relaxed for a change. His heart filled with hope he was smart enough to know might spiral him into real trouble. He moved closer to her, and she noticed him then, their glances locking for a moment. When he saw her press her lips together like she had something she didn't want to say, he pushed his thoughts aside and took her into his arms, kissing her and hoping for more time to state his case. Much as he wanted it to be exactly like this between them moving forward, time spent together every day doing things normal people did, he knew he had to tread carefully. Anna being Anna, meant it would be one step at a time. But hell, it had begun now, no taking it back. And thank God for that. Last night had been amazing. Beyond anything he had imagined and he knew now she was the only woman for him, in every way.

"Careful! Woman working around a hot frying pan here if you hadn't noticed." She pulled away from him and batted him playfully with the metal tongs. But he'd felt a certain stiffness in her body that had not been there a couple of hours ago. Much as he tried to avoid it, dread roiled in his stomach, worried about what she was thinking.

"I can handle a hot frying pan. What would you like me to do?"

"The bread needs toasting."

They got down to the business of breakfast. They'd done it many times before, just not quite like this, with so much riding on it.

"What's the plan for today?" he asked, sitting down across from Anna in the breakfast nook overlooking the spacious backyard. A full moon still hung in the sky, bright and shining over the jack pines that lined the property. Further north was the Strobel funeral home, now closed and shuttered since the Black Rose Killer turned out to be the mortuary owner, Elvis Strobel. The eerie thought did him no kindness this morning and he wished it away. He didn't want to think of death right now, he wanted to be involved in life with Anna.

"I'm going to Ironwood to check on Faith Stubbs. Not sure how long I'll be gone, but it may take a few days. Can you hold down the fort while I'm away?" She avoided his eyes, paying strict attention to finishing her breakfast.

He stopped himself from raising the obvious objections, knowing loggerheads wouldn't help his case any. He congratulated himself for knowing this was the time for wisdom and self-restraint. Maybe he was learning something about women after all, or at least, this particular woman, the one he'd cared about since time began. The first moment he'd laid eyes on the frightened little girl with the skinny legs and hungry stare had cut him to the bone. The things she'd been through so early in life were more than most adults could handle. First, her stepfather murdering her mom, then leaving Anna to burn alive in their house. No wonder she wasn't like other women. Anna was an original, no getting away from that. Problem was, how to assure her he understood all this? Would never ask more of her than she could give if she would only give them a chance?

When he didn't sink his teeth into her comment and rant on about how bad an idea it was, she gave him a puzzled look.

"You okay with it?"

"Sure. You're working a case, right?" he said, lying through his teeth. His jaw ached from the restraint necessary and he might need to see a dentist soon, but he enjoyed the expression she manifested when she arched one eyebrow and a small smile played around her full lips. It got him thinking about how wonderful they tasted and how responsive she was. He quickly shut it down. This wasn't the time to be sidetracked, this was the time to focus as if his life depended on it. Because it did.

"Yeah, I am. And I sense it's going to get complicated and messy before it gets better."

He snorted. "Has it ever been any different. How can I help?"

He could tell the conversation wasn't going the way she expected it to. One small win in the battle to victory.

"So how did it go with Lola last night?" She lobbed

the second grenade of the morning and it wasn't even 0700 hours yet.

He shrugged. "Not much to say really. The group had a couple of drinks and then I got the call from Rodger about your plane vanishing from radar."

"Group? That surprises me. I thought Lola would be smart enough to get you alone. Easier pickings." She smirked, picking up their plates and removing them to the sink for rinsing. He followed her and began to help tidy up the kitchen, taking the plates from her and sliding them into the dishwasher.

"Well, one other couple. Susan and Ray."

"Aw, clever, the engaged couple ploy." This time she was the one to snort and shake her head while rolling her eyes.

"I guess. Do you want me to follow you to Ironwood and set up surveillance audio?" he asked, heading to safer waters.

Anna looked undecided for a moment, rolling it over in her mind. "It's important not to alert them to my real intention for being there, but actually, it's a good idea, if you can keep your distance and remain undetected? I'd appreciate the backup. But what about your job? I could ask Tom to do it?"

"I've got time coming to me. Hell, I've put in enough overtime these past few months to warrant a few weeks off."

"Okay then."

He let out a full breath. Third missile unexploded on the battlefield. He was going for broke this morning. "I need to drop by the pharmacy, but I can be ready to leave in an hour."

"Perfect." She gave him a narrowed glance as she finished up her tasks. "I don't know where you hid the real Josh this morning who'd be screaming bloody murder about my wanting to join a cult, but for now, works for me."

Josh's phone buzzed with an incoming text. He'd laid it on the table and Anna retrieved it for him. She glanced at the screen and frowned.

"Thanks for the dance, PIC. Hugs, Sig. xoxo."

Josh felt his skin heat. He began to sweat. *Fuck. No.* Not after all he'd done to make things possible between them.

She handed him the phone with a brittle smile. "Lola apparently sees things different than you. PIC and Sig?"

"It was silly really. Stands for partner in crime, because of the man I found unconscious on—"

"No need to explain." Her expression changed to ice. "On second thought, I can't ask you to take a week off from your job. You got a case you're working. We need to know more about that guy and why he was found where he was? He's connected to the cult. I'll call Tom instead."

"No! I can do both, until the guy comes around and starts talking, I can't do much anyway. I need to be there. Don't shut me out, Anna." This was so much more than just one case. This was a possible first step in moving forward as a couple.

He saw the hesitation in her eyes and his heart slammed into his ribs. He stood a chance.

"No, it's not a good idea." She hurried from the room before he could answer. Five seconds later, the door slammed on the war room.

"That went well," he said aloud. Both dogs gave him a look of utter sympathy before getting up and trotting away. "Sure, abandon me now." He ran a hand through his hair, wishing he could turn back the clock and not have had a dance with Lola. But then, he'd not have made love to Anna, and no way in hell would he give up that for anything on this earth. It was a night he would never forget, would relive over and over in his mind with hopes of repeating it. *Please, I'm on my knees here, let her come to her senses before it's too late.*

EIGHTEEN

Tom answered on the first ring.

"Got time to head up north to Ironwood today, provide a few days of surveillance for me as I tackle the logistics of getting accepted by the cult as a member?" Much as she wanted to see Kelly, this had to take priority for now. Besides, how long could it take realistically to talk with Faith Stubbs and find out if there was any hope for her wanting to leave? She'd soon get a feel for the place, find out if the man in the hospital had been abused in any way by someone there since he couldn't as yet tell them himself. Then she would know what to do.

"You bet. I can be packed and ready in an hour. Pick you up at your place?"

"Yes, I'm at home."

They hung up, and Anna hurried to pack a few things herself. How much cash should she take? She opened the newly installed wall safe behind the mountain painting and used biometrics to unlock it, a thumb print laid on the discrete door scanner. A possible thief would have to cut off her left thumb to open it. She comforted herself with the thought that most petty criminals wouldn't have the guts to do it. Though if she was missing a thumb, good chance she was already dead.

She piled a small stack of hundred-dollar bills into the duffel bag that held a few changes of clothing and some personal effects, then slipped a thousand dollars into her pocket. Easy enough to make the promise of more later, once she had joined. Satisfied she had enough to bribe the gatekeepers, she closed the bag and tossed it onto the sofa. The doorbell rang and she went to answer it.

Tom stood there, revealed by the monitor, one of many connected throughout her residence. She planned never to get surprised by anyone at her house ever again. One trash can filled with burning fashion dolls was enough in this lifetime.

"Morning," he said, stepping inside and giving her a keen look. "You know, it's not going to be easy for you to adopt the necessary humble expression a cult would most appreciate."

"All too true," she said with a chuckle. "Which is why I'm bringing lots of bribe money."

"Good thinking. But aren't we supposed to *make* money for solving cases, not spend yours?"

"It is what it is. Emily Stubbs is poor and can't afford to pay anything. Another pro bono case."

"I have a lead on a case that might bring in some real cash. A custody fight. Grandparents seeking full custody of their two grandchildren and need to prove their daughter-in-law's an unfit parent. The grandparents are loaded. They don't care what it costs to find the goods on the mother. Apparently, she won't allow them access after their son died in a tragic accident. They blame her for their son's death though no proof of any wrongdoing was found by the detectives who investigated it. But I've been checking out the woman, she does have a checkered past, much as she tries to hide it. A couple of red flags worth looking into."

"This feels important. A custody battle with children involved. Any hint she might pull a runner?"

Tom looked hesitant to say for a split-second. Anna knew right then what the deal was. "You have to get on this thing right away, Tom. The safety of children is too important to put off. I can handle Ironwood alone. Just going in to talk to a member, nothing else. I could be done and have the whole case wrapped up by later today. Either Faith Stubbs wants to leave or she doesn't. Then I can head to New York and see to Kelly's friend. Find out what her deal is."

"No. I don't like the idea of you going in alone without backup."

"I've got my big girl panties on," she said with a cheeky grin, knowing how he didn't care for the expression. "But warn the grandparents if nothing is found, they will have to accept it. We don't make up something that doesn't exist just because they have deep pockets. They're only entitled to the truth. If she's a good mom and had nothing to do with her husband's death, then they will have to go through the courts."

Tom shook his head like he wanted to object more to her going to Ironwood by herself but knew better and wisely kept his mouth clamped shut on the issue.

"Okay. Need any help here?" He looked into the living room where she'd left her one bag. "Traveling light, I see. You're what we men like to call *low maintenance*. Nice."

She snorted. "Except when I'm on a honeypot stakeout." Her own words brought back the image of her standing in frigid cold weather on the steps of a movie producer's country estate north of Anchor in just a slip of a dress, blonde siren wig, and lipstick, freezing her damn ass off. "No, just got to drop Friday and Diva off at the agency with Charlie first."

"I can do that. Save you some time."

"Sure, thanks."

Friday and Diva came scurrying into the room in tandem, like they already knew the deal. Diva was carrying her favorite squeaky toy in her mouth. No way could she separate the pair now, they'd grown so close, even though Charlie had offered to take Diva, the dog she'd rescued from one of the victims of the Jack the Ripper case. The memory was bittersweet and she pushed it aside. Now was not the time for maudlin reminiscing.

Anna bent down and gave them both a hug and a pat. "See you guys later. Be good or be careful."

Tom gave her a certain look, head slanted sideways like he had something serious on his mind. But he didn't share it and leaned in for a hug instead. He patted her back with affection before letting her go. "Be careful yourself, okay? I've grown fond of that face. Don't want to see it altered in any way. Don't become a Moonie or anything like that, promise?" he teased.

"Never. I'm my own woman. Like you said, the hardest part will be adopting a faux expression of being a little lost and needing guidance from Mother."

"Mother?"

"That's what the woman who runs the cult calls herself."

"What's her real name?"

"I ran the photo through face recognition software and discovered it belongs to Mary Jane Wattley a.k.a.

Magic Mary, a former resident of Vegas. Kind of fits, knowing the showmanship necessary to put on a production in Sin City. Talented broad, knows how to conjure up magic. Rather useful ability I should think. She looks like Doctor Molly, my former therapist, only with platinum hair and a far more angelic expression."

"How did she end up in Ironwood of all places?"

"Good question. It's on my list. But more importantly, is she keeping anyone there under duress? Are people free to leave if they decide the Circle of Friends is not for them? How much brainwashing is going on?"

An incoming text pinged and she pulled out her phone to check it. Josh.

> We may lose and we may win, but we will never be here again...

She swallowed hard. Josh had brought out the big guns, his go-to place when he was melancholy, channeling the Eagles. Even so, his astute words hit her in the solar plexus in spite of knowing this and she blinked away a few tears. Of course they would never be in this exact place ever again. People change, they grow. Uncomfortable with the suggestion of what this moment had meant to him, she did the only thing she could. She texted back in a lighter vein using her own song title. Better to suggest living in the moment than worrying about what is yet to be, right?

> Where's the Fun in Forever.

"Everything okay?" Tom asked.

"It's fine. I'll catch up with you when I can. They probably don't allow cell phones, so I'll have to be very careful and hope they don't find the second burner phone I'll be attempting to hide from them."

"Okay, I'm out of here."

Tom opened the door for Friday and Diva, then closed it behind himself.

Anna picked up her bag from the sofa, then took a final look around. An acute sense of loss suddenly hit her as she closed and locked the front door of her home. A realization she might never be here again overcame her and she found walking away difficult. Damn Josh for putting the lyric into her brain.

NINETEEN

"Brother Lazar's been found," Brother Adam announced in the doorway to her dressing room. He stepped closer and his scarred face was reflected beside hers in the large vanity mirror, his eyes intensely focused on hers. Mother stopped mid-application of anointing moisturizing cream to her freshly scrubbed skin. She studied her first lieutenant. Though she knew his looks frightened others, gave even the staunchest supporter pause, Mother did not see the outward battered shell, but into the brother's staunch heart and soul. He was her first believer. The man who had listened to her when she'd first burst forth from the Mojave Desert, after forty days and forty nights wandering alone looking for timeless answers. She'd found them. In a vision of bright light when the Archangel Gabriel had descended before her and held out his hand to her, promising eternal life if she followed him.

That was five years ago. Five years of listening to his voice and council. Now a full year at Ironwood had spread his word and brought fellow believers on board with the Messengers' help. Soon they would have enough brothers and sisters, the perfect complement, two hundred and twenty-two committed souls united together into the Circle of Friends. She caught sight of herself in the mirror, appreciating the perfect visage that shone back at her, the sense of being on the verge of greatness. They were so close to that number now she could taste success. Each person had been carefully vetted. Only those who understood the importance of what they were being offered were picked to join them in their vision quest. Anyone not prepared to put in the effort required had been weeded out, no different than nature eliminating the weak.

"What would you like me to do?" Brother Lazar asked coming closer and slipping to his knees beside her. She lay her hand on his head, feeling the coarse, springy texture of the dark, unruly locks. The heat of the vibrant scalp beneath.

"We will pray on it." He bowed his head while she allowed her mind to free itself of earthly bonds, allowing it to open to the universal soul she knew inhabited all living creatures. A flash of insight came in mere seconds, startling her with its intensity.

"Go to Brother Lazar and tell him all is forgiven. Tell him Mother loves him and only wants what's best for him. But tell him he must think of bigger and better things going forward, what is best for everyone, not be selfish and close himself off. Pulling away from the Circle of Friends will only bring disappointment and pain to his life. Bring him home, Brother Adam. It's a test. I see that now."

"I will do as you ask." Brother Adam stood up. "When shall I say you will be joining us?"

"Soon, tell them Gabriel and I are sharing council and are not to be disturbed."

Mother sighed as he strode from the room. She turned back to her nightly task. She was preparing for yet another evening speech and revelation, applying cosmetics that cost an arm and a leg. Much as she enjoyed the results her prophecies produced before breaking bread together, giving her followers hope in dark times, sometimes it was tedious to go through the motions over and over again. It reminded her too much of Vegas and shilling for the tourists on the strip. A job from another lifetime. Yes, this was far more important work, but did it have to be so damn repetitive? She missed the freedom of a day without so many responsibilities. One day of doing completely nothing was a luxury she had to forgo. She had so many people hanging on her apron strings it was a wonder she could stand upright.

You're being selfish once again. We are all called upon to do our part, nothing more. Give people what they need, what they want, and you will be rewarded. Not now, but when we pass on, our deeds are listed for all to see. Do you want your bargain to fall short of ascending to the heavenly gates? Be unable to spend eternity with your own family? But instead of her beloved Gabriel's voice speaking clear as a bell close to her ear, it was the gruff voice of her dead father. A man she loathed with every fiber of her being. A man who had abused his position of power in the church and his own family. She shrugged the intrusiveness away, rubbing absently at the side of her head. She'd had more than enough practice of avoiding him in the past, though he was coming to her more often, creeping in like the snake in the Garden of Eden, his whispers evil and meant to intimidate.

Why had Brother Lazar left to begin with? His betrayal perplexed her. Was she losing her influence? Her power? Always, it was Mother who eliminated the unchosen, not the other way around. The graveyard for the unwanted was a testament to her strength of purpose, a test each and every time to her resolve. Then she set the conundrum aside. End Times loomed too close to dwell on what would not be allowed to affect the final outcome, not with the last gate poised to open soon as the threshold was crossed. Any day now it would be upon them. Better to spend these last days in preparation, not dwelling on one brother's failure to live up to his commitment. But still it stung her sense of pure righteousness, and she vowed to find out why he had turned traitor to their heavenly cause.

TWENTY

Anna parked her truck out of view of the Circle of Friends compound main gate, a good half mile back from the fence. She'd walk in from there, giving her a better opportunity to reconnoiter the area. Get a sense of things before she presented herself. On the survey map, the group's property encased a full section of land, six hundred and forty acres of poor land nobody in their right mind would choose. Maybe that was the point? Who in their right mind started a cult, or joined one, in the first place. Ironwood had a long history of survival groups living in isolation there; since WWII people had been hiding out in the desolate area, from former Nazis to the current cult bearing the name Circle of Friends. It was the kind of place that bred evil, like Elvis Strobel, the Black Rose Killer.

But with such poor quality land, how were they eking out a living? They had to be dealing in some lucrative enterprise to feed and clothe so many people. Such things don't just fall from the skies, no matter how angelic its founder looked.

She wished she had Friday at her side as she made her way along the sturdy snow-lined fence in her thickly lined boots, carrying her small bag slung over one shoulder. She kept a keen eye out for intruders. Not only would her wolfdog enjoy this assignment, but he'd add some literal teeth to anyone thinking of doing her harm. Her assessment of risk was moderate at the moment, but it could change quickly if the people on guard duty took a dislike to her showing up unannounced. Maybe they weren't like most people who were swayed by the offer of money? Chances were good though it would help her case.

She moved quickly. The air was crisp today with forecast for snow later. She hoped it would hold off long enough to get inside, speak with Faith Stubbs and be on her way.

At the main entrance, she stopped at the gate. She needed to wait for someone to notice she was there. A camera was pointed directly at her, meaning it was just a matter of time.

Not ten minutes later, she had visitors racing toward her on snow machines similar to the ones at the crash site. The same sleek black paint jobs with the iconic dove logo a nice touch. She hoped her own tattoo would be the ticket, along with the bribe money.

She smiled soon as the two men disembarked and strode toward her, their expressions noncommittal. She recognized Mr. Menace but didn't know his companion. She stepped forward, trying to look happy and pleased to see him.

"Hi, I'm Anna, and I'm hoping to join up with all of you. We met at the airplane and I've thought of nothing since then but of coming here. I must have been saved for a reason, right?"

"How did you find us?" Mr. Menace asked, pursing his lips. His scar was obscured by his parka hood, pulled and laced in tight around his face. Both had pulled off their helmets and laid them on the leather seats of their vehicles.

"You're on the internet. I just put a photo of my logo in and you popped right up. And now I'm here."

"And now you're here," Mr. Menace confirmed, his eyes narrowed with suspicion.

"I've brought funds to donate. You know, to help out. Even if I'm not allowed in, I want you to have it. I think what you're doing here—what you stand for—is important. Please, accept the money in the goodwill it was intended." She rummaged around in the bag she carried and pulled out a thick was of one-hundred-dollar bills, holding them out toward the two cult members.

A subtle light went on behind both sets of eyes of the men watching her intently, like an insect under glass. The image made her shudder, and she shook it off. Now was not the time for theatrics.

"You are aware that we know who you are, right? Anna Hale, the woman who solved the Jack the Ripper case, among others. One who has spent her life and her fortune finding justice and not backing down from authority. Rebel for the cause."

She gave him a sugar-sweet smile filled with hope. "So television and the internet are allowed out here? That's good to know. I was a bit worried I might have to give up *everything*."

"Cell phones are turned in before entering and members don't have access to the internet and social media. It distracts from why our brothers and sisters are here. To become closer with the creator."

"But you just said—"

"Mother knows everything. She said Anna Hale would be arriving today, and here you are. And now I need to know why?"

His expression defied her to say anything contrary. She swallowed the BS with difficulty, managing to keep a smile pasted on her lips. She was afraid of coughing up a hairball. "Of course. That makes so-o much sense. Mother would know. Yes, I'm Anna Hale. But the life I've been leading—all the money and fame—none of it has any lasting meaning. My adopted parents, they wanted me to find a cause. We spoke of it before they died. Find something that mattered, they said." That part was true, though she doubted either of them meant joining a damn cult. "And when I found Mother on the website one night, I wanted to come then, but something stopped me. Whispered it wasn't time. But now, being saved along with all those other dear souls, well, I knew it was a sign. That I had to come. I dreamed of Mother—of helping her. Please, I need this. At least let me speak with her. If she decides she wants me to go, I will, much as it hurts." She placed her hand over her heart to emphasize her point. "But I insist you keep the money. It's the least I can do if you won't let me help in any other way, with the labor of my own two hands giving service."

Her words died away while she waited for someone to speak.

"Look!" the younger guy finally said. Anna tagged him Mr. Eager in the moment. He pointed at the sky. "An eagle flying overhead. It's a sign, Brother Adam. Mother needs to know this."

Huh. Brother Adam. Go figure. Who was Mother? Sister Eve? Now was not the time to inquire. Anna glanced upward, enjoying the majestic show of the eagle surveying its territory, its luxurious wings outspread and catching the wind currents that were a given most days in the turbulent Alaskan atmosphere. Perhaps it was a good omen. She could use one. Get this bullshit over and done with and catch a plane to New York and see Kelly. But most of all, get over the bad feeling she had about hurting Josh. Would he forgive her? Jumping into bed with him had been a thoroughly bad idea, wonderful as it had been at the time. Had her own motives been pure? It couldn't be the alcohol alone that had lifted all her inhibitions and restrictions on being intimate with her best friend in all the world. Not when she knew it would change things between them. Forever. If only she could roll her life back twenty-four hours. Get on a different plane. The futility of the idea hit hard, filling her with bittersweet regret. Crap. She had to keep a lid on her emotions, get the job done.

No one seemed to notice her momentary lapse, both men still enthralled by the golden eagle. Or at least one of them was while the other was now back to studying her.

"So what do you say?" she asked brightly. Yes, she realized, the eagle was a sign, but not the one these clowns thought it was. The sign was meant for her alone. A reminder of what Josh had texted earlier about never being here again. How long until there truly was no going back? *Stop it. Keep your mind on the job.* "Can I get a short audience with Mother? I'll wait for days if I have to."

"Why not? Your arrival is propitious, it seems," Mr. Menace a.k.a. Brother Adam said. He turned and walked away, speaking into the radio on his shoulder, similar to law enforcement gear. Ironwood was into modern gear for security guards but kept their members in the dark. Had cults ever been different in the history of the world?

Five minutes later she climbed on the back of a sleek snow machine. She'd already turned over her cell phone, her backpack then claimed by the driver. How much of the money would Mr. Menace give to Mother? She'd bet not all of it unless he was in cahoots with the shyster and wasn't worried knowing he'd be given a generous slice of the proceeds when this gig played out. Mary Jane Wattley would need confidants, people close to her she could trust to keep her secrets. What would all these members think if they discovered their exalted leader was nothing more than a sleight-of-hand con woman operating in Sin City? Her ace in the hole was a video of the woman performing her two-bit act on stage, making a shower of fireflies descend from supposedly thin air, a very effective trick unless you knew how to do it. All such acts were the same. Anna had nothing against a good magician plying their trade, but a cult leader using it to sway her members disgusted her. Not to mention the use of AI to recruit new members grated on her.

As they drew closer to the main buildings that made up Ironwood, Anna noticed a scorched building, most likely a barn judging by the roofline. It appeared recently burned. A few people were engaged in pulling off fire-charred two-by-fours and piling the debris on the flatbed of a trailer. It was hooked to a half-ton, dual-wheeled white Ford truck. The group members looked over as the trio as the two snow machines came into the large open yard situated mid-center of the compound. A couple of people waved at them. Straight ahead was a spacious two-story building with a front veranda while on either side, one pointing east and one west, stood two low-slung, very long dormitory-style buildings that reminded

Anna of the military. Assorted other smaller buildings, some low in stature, some taller also littered the countryside. A large barn was also in evidence and a tall silo. A couple of trucks stood outside the entrance to a large garage. Both had the same logo similar to the snowmobiles painted onto their doors. What businesses were these people engaged in that provided for such numbers the size of the housing suggested? They appeared a hell of a lot more profitable than in past years.

When the machine came to a stop, she scrambled off, needing to create some distance between her and the man driving. Without a doubt, he gave her the creeps, not because of his scarring, hell she had her own, but because of his snake-like vibes.

"Come. Mother will want to see you now."

The younger man strode away leaving Anna no choice but to follow Mr. Menace up the broad staircase to the front door of the two-story dwelling. He knocked, still holding her backpack, then went inside when a green light blinked above the doorway.

He led the way into the vestibule, his expression subdued. Respectful. Mother must bring out the best in everyone. She'd have normally snorted and made a scathing remark at the idea but held her tongue. She needed to check this place out, and getting thrown out now was not the point of being here. People might need her help at Ironwood, maybe more than just Faith Stubbs. Something in the very air of the compound was wrong, off-putting, like a place housing stored memories of a past where horrific events had occurred. Places can absorb energy, good and bad; Anna was certain of it. Who hadn't felt the creep factor of dread from a location where evil events have happened? She'd once encountered a similar sensation when entering a reportedly haunted asylum in West Virginia, turning straight around and abandoning her college friends to their freaky experience. Anna felt life held enough dread of the unknown, why add to it?

Her escort did not stick around but set down the backpack and left her there without another word, closing the door quietly behind himself.

Anna studied the room while she waited, sitting down on one of the ivory and white striped twin sofas that faced a coffee table with a bouquet of silk flowers— red roses—arranged in a cut-crystal vase. A framed, white feather attached to black matting hung in a place of honor over the fireplace. The vaulted ceiling was a nice touch, and the thick draperies over the windows and scrumptious fabrics used in the furnishings gave a sense of another time, a more genteel era. The gilded ornate mirrors were a bit over the top, as was the scent of roses permeating the air far beyond the explanation of one dead bouquet, but hey, Mother had an important first impression to create.

Anna was about to get up and stretch her legs when the sound of an angelic chorus softly filling the room stopped her. Even the lighting changed, became far brighter. Anna blinked repeatedly, letting her eyes adjust to the new intensity.

Then a set of double doors opened up and the scent of roses became stronger. Anna sneezed, ruining the illusion, then blew her nose loudly.

A tall woman, bordering on six feet in height, came forward. She walked very regally through the center of the arched doorway, her outline glowing from the light emitted by her garments as if she was plugged into an electric socket. Hell, maybe she was. Not out of the question for a former Vegas entertainer.

"Anna Hale," she breathed out her name in a voice reminiscing of smoky bars and saxophone players. "You're here. I've been waiting for you." The low timbre of her tone was in contrast to her saintly demeanor, her arms upraised to embrace her as if she were her long-lost family member returned from the dead.

Anna obliged, hugging the woman briefly. But the woman who called herself Mother held on well past the time of social comfort even though Anna had dropped her arms already. She began counting the seconds as she was latched onto like the woman was in fear of her running off, getting to thirty before she was finally released. What was that about?

"Sit. We need to talk. Would you like a glass of wine? Tea or coffee?"

"Just water, thanks."

The woman got two bottled waters from a small fridge built into a side cabinet. She handed one to Anna with a smile. "I'm so pleased to finally meet you. I know of your exploits; I'll state that right up front, and I applaud your efforts to eliminate evil on this earth."

Well, that was an unexpected development. "Yes, I am in the business of helping others find justice. You seem to be all about helping others find a new path forward?" Question was, a path to where, except to being fleeced of money and possession, maybe even identity, as they handed over everything to this woman. Anna had to swallow the instant anger following the reminder to keep from exposing her deep-seated animosity, at least for now. She was on a case and had a job to do. Quicker she got through this interview, quicker she could get about resolving things. She could swallow her own self-righteous bitterness at people being taken advantage of for an hour in aid of the Stubbs family.

"You don't agree with my methods? But we've just met. I assure you I care very deeply for these people who have chosen to swear over their lives to me. I'm here twenty-four-seven seven making sure everyone is cared for, have their needs met. I love every one of my followers equally. Every one of us has a part to play."

"I see. And what is my part?"

"Why, you're the final piece of the puzzle. The answer to my prayers. Number two hundred and twenty-two." The woman's pale irises lit up with a holy light that was more frightening than illuminating. Anna's inner wolf began to growl and patrol the edges of her vision.

"What is the significance of the number?"

"It's the completion of all we stand for here. If you really are on a vision quest to join with us? I need to get to know the real you, Anna, before I can allow you to be with the other members. Do you consent to spending time alone, speaking only to me, for a trial period?"

What the hell! Was she in the twilight zone? Of all the things this woman could have asked, this was the downright weirdest one. *Risk assessment: growing.*

"How long are we talking about?" Anna couldn't abandon her life for days on end. She needed a timeline. It was not as if she thought Faith Stubbs or any of the other members were in immediate danger. But Faith and Emily's mother, being ill, could be, if she were indeed as desperate for a liver transplant as Emily had indicated. She needed help from her daughter, help that may or may not be forthcoming, something not up to Anna. But she had to weigh it against Kelly's request. Her charge needed her. But damn, she might not get this opportunity again either with the perfect chance to find out what was going on at Ironwood. The decision weighed heavily on Anna. Damned if she did and damned if she didn't. Not for the first time she wished she had a clone.

The woman shrugged, her eyes wide open and guileless. "As long as it takes. I must be sure of your intentions, if they are sincere."

"Since you know who I am, you must also realize I can't just stay here without letting others know. I slipped away today to see you. After the recent experience of a near miss of my plane going down, I felt the sudden urge to come here. To seek a different path. To find more meaning in my life."

"Of course you did." The beatified smile gleamed, the perfectly plumped-up lips moist and inviting. The woman certainly knew how to present herself. "I can arrange for you to get your phone back for one final text, letting friends and family know that all is well."

"And I can leave anytime I want?"

"Why would you want to leave?" A perplexing expression as if the woman was the most naïve person on the planet passed over the perfect face with the expertly applied cosmetics. Of course, she'd had lots of practice in Vegas looking her best for her act. "But yes, after your trial period, you're free to leave. All I ask is for you to give me the time to show you the good we do here. And will continue to do. I believe you will find out that we have much in common, driven to better the lives of others. We just come at it from different perspectives, mine is grounded in gospel, while yours in secular, but no less caring. I see the good in your soul, but also the burden you carry. No good deed goes unpunished."

Damn it, the woman was slippery as the proverbial eel, avoiding any mention of when that would be and pretending they had anything in common. They were nothing alike. Anna would never take all someone had to help them. Instead, she was depleting her own funds. But they could hardly hold her here against her will. And no matter what she said in a text, after a few days, someone would get suspicious and come for her. She could see Josh charging in with Tom and Zeke at his back. So there really wasn't any danger to her person. Just to her spirit, having to hide who she really was while tricking the woman into thinking there was hope in having her join her cause. She also needed to know more about the so-called First Call and the significance of two hundred and twenty-two. And make dead certain no one at Ironwood was being abused.

"Okay. I'll give it a couple of days." The wolf pack now howling in the distance wasn't easing her nerves any even if they were just in her mind.

It was then she noticed the blood seeping through the woman's white dress on the right side near her ribs.

"You're bleeding. Are you okay?" Had the woman been recently operated on? Nothing had happened in the room to account for it. The cult leader then held up her palms and blood also dripped from her hands, staining her dress further.

"What the hell is going on?" Anna asked.

"His gift," she said. "My feet as well will bleed now. The time draws near. This is the sign of our Lord returning. The Five Sacred Wounds."

Before she could move away, the woman reached out and anointed Anna's forehead with the sign of the cross drawn in the fresh blood. Or was it real blood? Some kind of cheap parlor trick seemed far more likely. So this was the kind of stunt she pulled to influence her followers. It was wasted on her.

"Where are your towels?" Anna got to her feet,

waiting to be directed to the linen closet. Now that she knew the woman was fine, not recently recovered from anything other than being foolish enough to think a thinking person would fall for such a thing, she could focus on dealing with the mess. "It would be a shame to see it stain the sofa. It must have cost a fair amount."

But the woman didn't take her up on the offer, instead held up her hands even higher, allowing the red substance to flow down her arms and drip over the furniture. The shower of blood would have been horrifying if Anna didn't see straight through the ruse.

"I ask you, Lord, to help me bring this burdened woman into the light. To open up her heart and relieve her of her suffering," the woman said in a pious tone of voice. She closed her eyes and remained silent for a moment.

Anna stood by uneasily, wondering what was coming next. She was worried the woman might have a seizure or something worse. Was she on the verge of a stroke from a brain tumor, perhaps? The theatrics were wasted on Anna, but it didn't seem prudent to say. Now she was more certain than ever she had to make sure the people here were okay. Their leader was proving more than a little unstable.

Suddenly the woman dropped her arms and stared at Anna with wide open eyes. She had the thousand-yard stare down perfectly. Her eyes rolling back in her head or their looking opaque and unfocused could have worked equally well.

"He says he's been waiting for you to come back to him since the fire when you crossed over to the other side. When it wasn't your time to go and be with Him. You were just a teenager, with so much yet to do to help others. A gift you have been blessed with and nearly depleted these past years. Your burden is His burden and it will be lifted when you come to Him a second time. Your two mothers, birth and adopted, and your sister Tia are waiting there as well, happy in the Kingdom of our Lord."

Stunned, Anna stood perfectly still, taking in the woman's words and their meaning. How dare she! She clenched her fists, unsure of how to proceed, knowing there was nothing to gain in confronting her. And damn it, how did she know she'd had a near-death experience when her mom was beat up by her stepfather and left to burn in the fire he'd set meant to take Anna's life as well? She seldom talked about it. What had happened the day the fire nearly took her life and left her scarred. The one that had taken her mother away from her forever. It had to have been a lucky guess. No way could she have known about it. To use her own hope that one day they would meet up again against her sickened Anna. What had this woman done to others to make them stay with her? What secrets had she uncovered and used at their expense? Many religious cults used "confessionals" held in different forms, collected only to be used against the member. But it appeared at Ironwood, the practice of gaining intel had been widened to gathering before the prospect was even embraced in the fold. Downright villainy.

TWENTY-ONE

When Josh got the text back from Anna, stating she was spending a couple of days at Ironwood, he tossed his phone down on the bar table in disgust. Figures. *She'll use any excuse to avoid me now.*

"Bad news?" Browne asked. It was Friday night and a few members of the force were having a drink at O'Brien's, the preferred watering hole of locals and lawmen. Josh had a quick flashback to having a dance with Lola. Could it really have been only twenty-four hours ago? Since then, Anna's plane had gone down, they'd spent the perfect night together, something he'd dreamed of for years, and his life had moved on with the new hope they would move forward together, but apparently Anna wasn't even considering it. The realization that they might never be together as a couple ate at his core. He had to slam a lid on this thing or he'd end up doing something stupid. Like get drunk and into more trouble.

"It's fine."

"A woman?"

"Yeah, how did you know?"

Browne snorted. "Isn't it always a woman? Talking about women, there's that hot one now that's been sniffing around you, buddy."

Josh didn't need to look around to see who his partner meant. Lola. He sighed. Last thing he needed now was Lola complicating his life. He immediately felt bad thinking it. Lola was only a gal out looking for love, a partner in life, same as he was. Problem was, he knew who he wanted and she was not having any of it, by the look of things. He knew himself to be a man who would stay loyal forever if his relationship partner would commit to only him. Like his father, he believed there was only one woman for one man. And it was binding. But his dad had never had to face a woman who wouldn't admit to having a life outside of her own interests. His mom had loved his father unconditionally, following him all the way to Anchor from Kentucky when it was best for the family. Anna seemed to find it easy to give up on dreams of having her own family one day. Or did she even have the dream? Problem was, he was more and more certain he wanted a family. Whenever he spent time over at the Browne household, who had recently received the precious gift of their first grandchild from their oldest daughter, he was hard-pressed not to set a timeline. Maybe it was him? Maybe Anna might feel differently if the right man came along? Shit, all this second-guessing was wearing on him. It didn't help that she had barricaded herself up at Iron-wood. She wouldn't be available, even to text, for a couple of days. What was he supposed to make of it?

"Well, howdy, Josh," Lola said close to his ear, her warm breath grazing his cheek. She'd bent down to say it over the loud volume of the bar patrons, giving him an unrestricted view of her ample assets in her low-necked form-fitting top.

"Lola," he said, keeping his tone neutral. "How are you?"

"I was wondering where you had run off to last night. But then I heard your sister's plane had gone down." Lola stood close to his side. Last thing he wanted was to invite her to sit down. Instead, Browne did it for him.

Lola slipped into a suddenly vacant seat beside him and turned those huge doe-like eyes on him. "Is she okay?"

"You'll have to ask her that. She's out on a case at the moment." Shit, he shouldn't have said that. Now it sounded like there was a rift between them. Even though it was the truth, he didn't like others to know his personal business.

"She must be fine if she's working so soon after being in a plane crash. I admire her gutsiness. Not sure I could manage it. Probably take a few days off at least. Anything new about our John Doe?"

"Yes, a couple of hours ago, he was identified. John Mosely. We found out his family is looking for him. He up and vanished from New Jersey about six weeks ago and landed in Alaska of all places. His parents are headed up to see him on the next plane. I wish he would wake the hell up and tell us what happened already, but the short periods he's conscious, he's not always lucid. But it's early days and the doctor's optimistic he will regain some memory in time, if not all of it."

"Ya gotta wonder what happened to him," Lola said with a small shake of her head. Her fair hair caught the light as it swayed on her shoulders. She had grown into a good woman, deserving of a man who would love her for herself. She had a right to know that he could never be that man. His torch was lit for Anna and would always be, no matter how much it hurt to admit that she might never feel the same.

"Fingers crossed that his memory is improved by the arrival of his family."

"It can only help to have loved ones around. We all need someone we can rely on in the hard times. Easy enough to share the good ones. But I think too many couples get together thinking it's love that will get them through the rough ones. Takes far more than that, though love and friendship is important. It takes guts and commitment, a choice really, to go the distance with the other person. If two people make that decision together, nothing can stand in their way."

"Wow, Lola, that's a speech I would love to see you give at all wedding receptions. Cuts straight through the bullshit with laser focus," Browne said, raising his glass in a toast to her. He nodded at Josh who would have given his left nut to have Anna say the words to him. "Look out for this one, buddy."

"Well on that note, I'm going to leave you to it. I just came in for a drink. I have company coming from Fairbanks tomorrow and I need to prepare for them." Lola got to her feet. She leaned over and kissed Josh's cheek. "Call me sometime. We didn't get a chance to finish our first date."

Browne watched Lola walk away, his expression making it clear he enjoyed the view. "You need your head examined if you can't see where that could lead. She's got a decent head on those fine shoulders."

"Yeah, she's come a long way since high school. Hard to believe now she was into Goth to the point she dyed her hair black and wore chalk white makeup. Hell, she looked like a vampire just crawled from the crypt with her other friends doing the same. Crazy damn fad." The image made him shudder. Remembering his own time in a coffin during the Black Rose Killer case didn't help his mood any. The terrible claustrophobia had been crippling, his near-to-death experience still haunting his dreams. But Anna had rescued him. Gone the distance to save him. Could he count on her now? Would she bend her rules enough to allow him to be a bigger part of her life? Doubt crept in, making him wonder if he would have to give up on his dreams of a wife and family to stay loyal to Anna. Could there not be some kind of compromise? But if so, what the hell would it look like?

"Would you like another drink?" the waitress asked, gaining his attention.

"Yeah, and make it a double."

TWENTY-TWO

Sister Beatrix glanced at the newcomer as she unpacked her belongings into the small cupboard built-in between their bunks, noting the rosy cheeks and well-groomed hair. The polished look often meant someone who came from money. Her new sister was pretty, too pretty. She made her feel like an unmade bed, all disheveled and rough around the edges. She'd been assigned earlier today to help Sister Joan get familiar with the Circle of Friends, teach her the daily schedule of what needed doing to keep the place running smoothly. She was happy to help Mother with assisting the new member, hoping to impress her with her dedication. She'd have Sister Joan whipped into shape in no time. But with her First Call looming on the horizon, this all just might be a waste of time.

"Every day, you need to make your bed and put your things away. Mother likes things nice and orderly," she said. She was dead certain this woman had never had to lift a finger in her life to do a thing for herself she couldn't hire others to do for her. She had hot house flower stamped all over her.

Sister Joan stood back up from stacking her personal grooming supplies on a shelf. "Not much room. Where do we hang our clothes?"

"We keep them in the communal dressing room on hangers. You put your name in the slot above your clothes. I'll show you next. You'll need to sew your name in them as well."

"Just like summer camp," Sister Joan said with a smile. "I already did that."

Sister Beatrix raised her eyebrows, surprised. "Really? Yourself?"

"Not like I haven't done it before. I loved going to summer camp, getting away from living at home." The young woman made a face.

"You have three days before answering First Call. Are you ready?"

"Of course. I can't wait to move on, be washed of all my sins. I just wish my sister would try it. She probably needs to do it more than me. What a pill. Mean to the core."

Sister Joan's placid expression, her skin smooth and unblemished in any way, rubbed her the wrong way. And talking so poorly of her family. Well, truthfully, they did have something in common there. Sister Beatrix's own family left *everything* to be desired. If she never saw any of them again, it would be too soon.

Intrigued in spite of her misgivings about needing to compete with someone so attractive for Mother's attention, she asked, "What did your sister do to you?"

"What didn't she try to pull would be more like it. She hated me since the day I was born."

"Why?"

Sister Joan's shoulders drooped, though she tried to keep the smile pasted to her face. "Not that it matters now, but she blamed me for our mom's death."

"Really? Why?"

"She died when I was born."

"That sucks." A wave of unwelcomed sympathy swept over her.

She shrugged, trying bravely to show she was okay, even if she did speak in platitudes. "It is what it is. So, how do we make our living here?"

"That's what I'll show you next." She didn't say that the suitcases full of money she'd brought to the group would be of a greater asset than any of her new sister's tasks going forward, though as a group, by consolidating their efforts, they had achieved a lot at Ironwood. Had learned how to market and distribute a product that brought a decent sustaining income to the circle.

She led the way, stepping outside the dormitory to access the barn. A cold, bitter wind was blowing in from the north, filled with the heavy promise of snow. She didn't mind snowstorms, the sense of being cut off from the rest of the world. She found solace in the quiet times such events brought to their enclave. No outside work could be done, though in reality more was done inside than out. Something Sister Joan was about to find out. Normally, she wouldn't be allowed into the location of their greatest money-raising venture, not until she had risen from First Call. But Mother had changed things around, not spending the first few days with the prospect alone for some reason and it wasn't her place to question it. She must trust the new plan. Mother knew all.

Inside the barn, Sister Beatrix pushed back a throw rug and yanked up the trapdoor. Underneath was a staircase leading down under the building. Sounds of conversation and echoes of people moving things around greeted her ears.

"We work underground to save on heat," she explained.

"That makes sense. What are we making?" Her new sister seemed eager to learn.

"Herbal medicines. We use hydroponic methods to grow our own food and we even have a medical lab. You'll see. We're nearly self-sustaining now. Most of our electricity comes from solar-powered grids. And we burn wood. We still need gasoline for the snowmobiles and vehicles, but some are hybrid."

She clamored down the steep staircase that had been outfitted with hand railings, then waited for Sister Joan to join her at the bottom. The new member looked around in wonderment. "Wow, this is some enterprise."

"We pack the pills into those white doves over there for shipping and distribution. Our products are very popular." She pointed out the stack of crates holding hundreds of white doves. The rest of the space was taken up by long tables where worker bees filled up small plastic baggies from trays of pills to be inserted into the plastic birds.

"Are the pills vitamins?" Sister Joan asked.

"Yes. Specially made to enhance the health and well-being of anyone who purchases them. It's a special blend created by one of our members that has a degree in chemistry. He works in a separate area with a couple of assistants and oversees the lab. It's great. I take one every morning and I've never felt better." In reality, she wished she could get her hands on more. It took the edge off her exhaustion but Mother said they were not to be greedy, that once their daily work was done, there was no need for it. She continued her spiel, pleased her audience showed such keen interest. Maybe her new sister wasn't the pain in the ass she expected. "We ship any extra out of the country to bring in some income. Mother says we don't want to sell around Anchor or even in Alaska, because that would draw unwanted attention and we'd be swamped by people breaking down our fences for all the wrong reasons, wanting to get in on the business end and not for the ideology that sustains us. Most of our income comes in from across the border we share with Canada in the province of British Columbia."

"How can I help?"

"You can insert the vitamins in the doves. It's easy. Or you can help in the garden. The lab requires special skills and no one's allowed in without security precautions. Suiting up and the like. Makes them look rather alien."

"I think I'll start here. Why does everyone wear gloves and masks and hair nets?"

"To keep the pills pristine. No one wants hair or germs in their stuff, right?" Just as she got Sister Joan settled at her new workspace, a loud sound like thunder erupted from somewhere nearby. The cement floor trembled slightly beneath her feet.

"What was that?" Sister Joan's light-blue eyes widened with concern as she clutched at her arm.

"Not sure. Alaska's known for earthquakes. I'd better check on it. Wait here."

Her heart thumping madly, she ran down the alleyway between the tables laden with supplies. Just as she was about to open a door that led into a back room, another person came racing out of the room, knocking into her. She stumbled and reached for something to hang on to, flailing at the air.

"Sorry, sister." Brother Abel grabbed Beatrix at the

last second to keep her from falling onto the cement. "You okay?"

"I'm fine. We heard a loud bang. Everything okay?"

"I'm headed to check on it. Wait here." He dashed past her, headed toward the stairs. The gasoline fire of just a few days ago was still front and center in her mind. Had another similar disaster struck? Tensions had been growing among the circle, whispers that reached her ears on occasion that all was not smooth sailing. She'd been ignoring the rumors, figuring there was always a bad apple or two in every group. But whether it was bad luck or sabotage creating the disasters, either way it gave her pause.

The intercom suddenly sparked to life. "Mother asks that all her sisters and brothers join her in prayer in the dining area now for an important revelation. Please drop anything you are doing and join her."

TWENTY-THREE

Anna heard the loud announcement of everyone to head for the dining room. She was sitting on the single bed in the small room assigned to her. The cult leader had shown her to the cell-like room, then left her alone with the explanation she needed to use the time to pray and meditate. Right. This was the ideal opportunity to find out what was going on at Ironwood and she wasn't intending to waste it. Soon as she heard the front door close, she waited an extra couple of minutes to make certain the house was empty before quietly getting down to work. She removed the bugs she intended to plant in the main room from the money belt she'd strapped around her waist under her clothing, then left the room. She quickly concealed one on the light fixture shining down on the framed white feather picture box and one on the opposite side of the room, in a lamp by the sofa. *There, this section of the house is covered.* Time to check out the other rooms. She did an efficient recon of the ten-room house finding only one door locked and inaccessible, planting electronic surveillance equipment in most of the rooms before circling back to the front area.

She zipped up her parka, figuring the dining hall had to be the large complex situated behind the main house. Neither of the two dormitories would work. And no other building was large enough for over two hundred people to sit down in comfort.

She checked through the peephole to make certain no one stood on guard outside the house, discovered the way was clear, then ventured outside. As expected, the grounds were deserted. She caught a glimpse of the door closing on the suspected dining hall when she rounded the corner. Perfect, everyone was already assembled. She hurried across the short distance, aware of exposure, but calculated it was more than worth the risk to hear first-hand what bullshit the woman preached to her converts. She needed to gather any intel she could. It was risky of course, if she was spotted. No doubt she'd be thrown out on her ear, but she couldn't just twiddle her thumbs waiting for something to happen. Five minutes alone with Faith Stubbs was all she asked.

She slipped inside the dining hall, pleased to see she was inside a vestibule-like space that doubled as a cloak room, adjacent to the main room. She peered around the corner to check on logistics and decided to hang out where she was. Everyone was assembled inside, situated along long tables with steaming bowls of food at regular intervals. Even bottles of red wine. She could hear well enough with the door open to the main hall and it avoided being spotted by anyone. She chose a spot near the window and sat down on the floor; half hidden by the hanging outerwear. She didn't have long to wait. The only distraction was the scent of savory food that permeated the air, making her aware she hadn't eaten in hours. Was she meant to fast for three days? If so, she'd be diving into the handful of protein bars she'd also planted in her waist pouch.

"Evening to all my chosen children. I am pleased to break bread with all of you on this special day. For this is the moment of highest calling. No longer are we waiting in limbo for our numbers to be fully realized. For tonight we have achieved our greatest dreams of uniting all those who feel as we do. Our last two chosen have arrived. Sister Joan and Sister Anna. *No fear. We are the chosen.*"

"*No fear. We are the chosen.*"

The reciting of the exact same rote words spoken by their creepy leader sent a spine-tingling chill through Anna. Was she meant to be Sister Anna?

"I ask that you raise your glasses in a toast. Heavenly Host, we thank you for this fellowship, for the love and the blessings of living only to help others. We pray for peace and understanding in this hard world as we work to provide an example of living for more than our own selfish needs, for being generous and seeing the good in others. For praying for their healing and their hearts to open to aid others in becoming their best selves as we ourselves strive for daily help to gain perfection and become the epitome of kindness and understanding. To go forth in this world as directed by Him with love and mercy."

Well, the message didn't suck. The unwanted thought struck that she sometimes only lived for one need, to provide justice to others, not to work on becoming a better person or having an open heart. Damn it, this woman was good at her job. She even had her questioning her lack of generosity toward those just wanting to spend more time with her away from her mission.

Josh rose in her mind and she swallowed. Fuck, this was *not* the time to second guess herself.

Had the woman cleaned all the fake blood off herself? Anna couldn't see her from her vantage point, only the lineup of outdoor clothing hanging above her, mostly of the camouflage type popular to the north. Personally, when you're out hunting, maybe favor a bright yellow and black safety jacket to draw attention to yourself to avoid being shot. Accidental death from hunting was not uncommon.

"In three days, the final two will be tested by First Call. If they are chosen, we will be ready."

There was that term again, First Call. What did it mean?

A loud bell sounded.

"We have visitors. Please enjoy your meal and give thanks to those sitting next to you for their service. I will leave you now to your repast. Enjoy and celebrate this moment. All of you will be issued an extra vitamin tonight in honor of this occasion. *No fear. We are the chosen.*"

"*No fear. We are the chosen.*"

Anna pressed herself back tighter to the wall. Any minute the crafty leader would be coming past the cloakroom. And exactly what kind of vitamins was the kook talking about?

When the door closed behind the cult leader, Anna arose from her hiding place and made her way to the door to the dining hall. She knew what Faith looked like from a photo her sister had shared, and she glanced up and down the long tables, searching for the familiar face.

Was that her? If so, the woman had certainly lost weight, her cheeks sunken as she picked at her food like it might poison her. No one else looked a possible candidate and Anna slipped from her hiding place and strode up to the woman as if she belonged there. She crouched down beside the person's chair, gaining her attention. She had to make this quick, others were alerted to her presence now.

"Are you Faith Stubbs?" she asked with a smile.

"What? Who are you?"

"I'm Anna Hale and your sister Emily asked me to speak with you to see how you are doing?"

"I'm Sister Beatrix. I don't know any Faith or Emily."

The woman was a bad liar. She averted her eyes, the color rising in her cheeks. But Anna was pressed to get the information across required and she went ahead and recited the facts. "Your sister says your mom is very ill, dying, and needs your help. If you want to see her, I will get you out of here. Do you want to leave?"

"No. I belong here. Why would I ever leave Mother?"

"What are you doing here?" another voice intruded on the conversation. Anna glanced up at Mr. Menace. She held back a groan and got to her feet. Well, at least she'd touched base with Faith. But Emily would not be happy with the results. And neither was she. Something felt off at Ironwood, something drawing her in to solve an even bigger mystery. Her curiosity demanded answers. And her wolf instincts vibrated with a sensation that this place held some deep, dark secrets she had to expose to give the members a chance to decide for themselves if this was really a place they wanted to be.

"Just speaking with an old friend. Sister Beatrix." She smiled sweetly at the annoying asshole in efforts to disarm him.

"You were meant to stay put. Come with me."

Anna had no choice but to follow him back through the hall and out into the cold. She'd not even been offered a meal for her trouble. Her stomach growled to settle the point.

"I didn't know it was a crime to speak to a member," Anna said, striding alongside the guy.

"You were specifically told not to interact with the other members until it was time. You must prove out first." His tone was hard-edged and hardly charitable. He looked far more dangerous away from the others, radiating a certain level of seething anger, like that was going to stop her.

"I thought this was a group that prided itself on love and understanding? Of giving of themselves over to doing good deeds to better their chances of someday getting into heaven. Was I wrong? Is it all fake?"

He was silenced by her accusations, a noticeable tic developing under his left eye. She clung onto his arm as if they were old pals.

"And I'm hungry. Don't you think feeding me might be a good idea?"

"Fasting's good for the soul."

"Not very charitable if it's not voluntary. And exactly what is First Call? Not fond of dancing in the dark, if you know what I mean. Especially not when I'm hungry. Maybe we could take a side trip to the kitchen and rustle me up some food? Give us time to get to know one another better, Brother Adam. I don't bite, well, except maybe if I'm driven to it. But I think we'd find we have a lot in common, the two of us. You provide security to protect this place and all those in it, while I'm on a similar mission to make sure others stay safe and are provided with proper justice in the outside world. What do you say? I promise to go back to my room right after I eat." She figured her one chance of avoiding being thrown out on her ass was to appeal to the leader's right-hand guy. Sure, it grated on her, but it was a last desperate ploy to stay put for a couple of days. She was more than certain Mary Jane Wattley would send her packing.

He remained silent. They were almost back at the front door to the main residence when he stopped walking and turned to her, a new light in his dark eyes. One that showed interest in her as more than a possible sister. She comforted herself in how she was good at handling herself around men. Not like she hadn't had enough practice. She held her breath, hoping for a chink in his armor.

"Okay. Let's go around back. I have a stash of food in my room and some fine Kentucky bourbon. We can get to know each other better, Anna Hale. Mother's busy tonight and we'll have the place to ourselves for a few hours."

TWENTY-FOUR

Sister Beatrix was stunned by Anna's revelation that her sister was looking for her and their mother was on her deathbed. No, not her sister, but someone she'd grown up with, who she felt less related to with every passing day. She licked her lips nervously, eyeing those around her. She didn't like to be the object of scrutiny, to have everyone talking about her. She'd come here to find a home, a community with like-minded people. Do something more important that what awaited her on the outside. Mother understood her while her birth mother would never raise a hand to help her unless it was a ruse in some way aiding herself. She and Sister Joan had something in common, a birth family only wanting to use them, destroy their self-worth for their own selfish purposes.

"Are you okay?" Sister Joan asked.

She'd remained quiet during the incident, though like Beatrix, she had barely touched her food. She lay a hand on her arm to reassure her now, a kind smile lighting her face. Though they had met only today, she felt some kind of bond with the young woman already. Maybe they could be friends? She'd never had a friend growing up she could count on. They'd moved around too much, dodging debt collectors, always leaving new possible friends behind in the rearview mirror. She'd hated all the "fresh starts" because she knew it was her parents' fault for being drug addicted. Fucking just say no already! If her mother and father had really loved her, any of their children, they would have given it up, as painful as it was. She believed in her heart all her problems came down to other people's bad choices. She had yet to offer them forgiveness, like Mother modeled. She knew her stance was unacceptable. Maybe she was the problem that every time they got close to the exact number of members needed to ascend to a higher state of being, they lost somebody? If she forgave her upbringing, maybe it would make her new sister safe? It was a radical new thought for her and something she would need to ponder.

"Yes, thank you." She was a long way from okay, but admitting it felt weak, something she didn't want to appear in front of the fellowship.

"You're a heck of a lot stronger than me," Sister Joan said. "I'd be bawling my eyes out or hitting something. I get emotional when it comes to family and all the dirt that brings up. You are amazing, Sister Beatrix."

A sudden glow at the unexpected compliment filled her with brimming emotion. She had no idea how to deal with it or express in words what it meant to her to be given such an awesome gift.

"You should eat. You'll need to keep up your strength for First Call," she advised.

"Bit nervous about it, truthfully. Maybe we can talk later? You can tell me how it went for you."

"Of course. I'd like that."

Beatrix watched Joan eat a few more bites and was pleased she was the reason for it. How was she to explain the upcoming experience of being baptized into the Circle of Friends? It was scary, being held under water until you left your former life behind, rising to become a chosen one. Like she'd stepped through the Janus Gates to emerge a new person, entering one side as a sinner and coming out the other gate filled with unending love to helping save Mother Earth. Yes, it was wearying at times, this new life. The things they were called upon to do sometimes radical. Shocking. But whenever she felt lost or uneasy, she remembered the bad times growing up, knowing her exhaustion would pass and under-standing of the why of things would become clear as the things Mother prophesized came to pass. The cost of keeping her soul pure was believing before knowing. Proof always came later with Mother.

At the end of the meal, everyone bowed their heads and gave thanks, one of the many rituals that pleased her. Even stopping on the hour, every hour of their waking day to give a short prayer of thanks wasn't as difficult a task for her than at first. Life was precious. Time short. *Please let my new friend be okay*, she prayed, her hands clasped together tightly, her wish tangled up with newly unleashed emotions surging through her.

"We take our plate and cutlery to the bin over there," Beatrix said. She picked up her dishes and carried them to the location along with others in the vicinity. Everyone patiently waited their turn in line. She nodded at a couple of people, but for the most part everyone ignored her as they did every night.

A few curious stares though for her new sister and a couple of the brothers gave her lovely body a full one-eighty with lecherous, heavily lidded eyes. One guy in particular, Brother Mathew, made her stomach twist in knots. She wanted to scream, don't be looking at her like that. But she found herself unable to speak, her throat dry and painful. If he touches her...

There had been rumors about him and his bullying, his putting pressure on women to put out for him. She didn't want to believe them. Surely they should be held in check by their love of Mother? Men. She hated them all. Memories of unwanted advances, smoothed over by her druggie and so-called mom who took the money they offered, sickened her. Maybe it was one of the reasons she took no care of her own appearance, not wanting to draw any unwanted male attention her way. The thought was radical for her. Since her new sister had shown up, she'd been in a far different place. She needed to rein it in, save her counsel and energy for Sister Joan. She herself was unimportant in the scheme of things.

"Welcome, sister." A smarmy, male voice woke her from her thoughts to discover the man she normally avoided as she did all the male members in the Circle of Friends standing in front of her and Joan, blocking them from leaving. He held out his hand and she wanted to pull her new friend away, keep her close and hide her from his sight.

"If there's anything you need, anything at all, day or night, I'm always here. Ain't going anywhere. Mother sees and knows all," he said, grinning at his own lame words which he obviously didn't believe or he'd stop this right now. He was like a priest wanting a choir boy and not letting God stop him from his evil intentions. To her, that meant the man of God didn't believe in a higher deity any more than this man who didn't deserve to be called a brother did. For how could you believe and do such harm? You couldn't.

"Nice to meet you."

He leaned forward and whispered something in Joan's ear that made her blush and cast her eyes downward, making her even prettier with the heightened color. Beatrix's hands fisted at her side. Now he'd upset her new sister. What foul thing was he up to?

"We have to go," she said. She pushed her way past the monster, making a path for Joan to follow.

"You aren't the boss of her, *sister*," he said, his lips curling up with disgust. At that second, something passed between him and another brother close by. Then a flash of movement and she found herself flailing in the air, her feet knocked out from under her. She slammed onto the wooden floor; the wind half-knocked out of her. *Who tripped me?* She shook her head, refusing a hand up. She stumbled to her feet and clung onto Sister Joan who hovered at her side.

"You stay away from me and my sister if you know what's good for you," Sister Joan said, pointing at Brother Mathew, her finger nearly stabbing his broad chest. "Or I will tell Mother. I haven't undergone First Call which means I will be confessing personally to her very soon. I'd hate to have to report this to her, but I will for the good of all."

They pushed their way through the throng of astonished onlookers. Beatrix had never been prouder. She glanced back at the brother who had been set in his place, but instead of being humbled as was right and proper according to their teachings, he looked angry, his eyes bulging in his reddened face. This was not over. Her throat tightened with unshed emotions. She wished she'd been the one to say what Sister Joan had said with such bravery. She needed to step up, not be a victim of anyone. She realized even here, at Ironwood, where safety and sanctuary had been promised by Mother, it wasn't a guarantee when the temptation of lust and sin reared its ugliness.

Sister Beatrix vowed. *If he touches her, he will pay.* How she would accomplish it, she had no clue. But she believed in a reason for all things, meaning she'd know when she was called upon what to do. After all, she'd managed to escape once before.

TWENTY-FIVE

Screams woke him up. Loud screams. They pierced the air making it appear to vibrate all around him, making it impossible to see anything in the deep, dark mist shrouding his existence. The terrifying shouts were filled with such pain and anguish it sounded like a mortal soul had shattered into dust. Who was screaming? *Stop it! Stop it!* He clutched at the blankets, holding on for dear life, trying to get the terrifying sounds to go away. "No!" he shouted.

Then he realized the screams had come from him as he came further awake, the nightmare slowly losing its grip on him. Another night terror. This one worse than the last. He'd relived his own death again. The darkness and evil lurking on the other side awaited him with a finality that doomed him to never-ending pain. There would be no redemption for him. No coming back from what he had done.

Was it his fault he'd been born this way? He loved children too much, maybe that was the problem. Did that make him a bad man? One past redemption? He knew it to be true now, ever since he'd consented to Last Call. There would be no forgiveness for him. No washing away of his sins. They had all lied to him. Said it could be done. That God forgave all.

His sin had been judged to be too dark, too evil for him to escape final judgment. Life was now impossible, knowing what awaited him.

A nurse came rushing into the room, her expression equal parts exasperated and concerned. His night terrors were happening more frequently. At least once every hour he was awakened by screaming, his own. There would never be any relief for him. He would end it all if only he wasn't going straight to hell to live among them. The damned.

"Are you in any pain?" the nurse he knew as Jackie asked, her forehead creased into a frown.

He could only stare at her with disbelief. How could she not see it? His evil was leaching out of him, an oily black tar substance sticking to everything he touched or looked at. Even now some of it dripped from her chin, making her appear ghoulish. He blinked the image away. It's not real, he tried to comfort himself. But the idea persisted. Was she one of them? A collaborator with Satan's army?

All he knew for certain was he could never die. Not with what waited him on the other side. But he was living in a century when it had yet to happen. Immortality. If only he'd been born in the future. Maybe if he hung on long enough, a breakthrough would happen? A faint hope at best, but he needed something to soothe him, to keep him from going mad.

"I'll give you something to sleep," she said.

"No!" The last thing he wanted was to relive the nightmare again. The black maws of death, the sharp pinchers tearing at his skin, the fierce fire singing away all his hair. No, better to be awake, on guard. "I don't want to dream it again. It's too horrible for words."

Her expression turned more sympathetic as she straightened his covers. "Maybe you need to tell your therapist about it? They can help. Show you ways to cope better."

They both knew he wasn't coping at all right now. He was a living nightmare, a man with no soul. Was this how someone turned into a zombie? Fear so terrible they would do most anything, even cannibalize others to avoid living life?

TWENTY-SIX

"Where's Mother gone tonight?" Anna asked, managing the moniker for the group's leader without choking on it. She was walking around the suite and picking up the odd thing to check out more carefully. When she'd planted a bug here earlier, she hadn't realized who the suite belonged to. A guy who was into hunting and fishing and winter camping judging by all the photos of candid outdoor shots. He also had a lot of trophies for winning sharpshooter events. Not exactly the kind of person she'd expect to join a cult.

"None of my business," he said noncommittally. He was busy pouring them a couple shots of Kentucky bourbon in flat-bottomed glasses.

"Did you know her before?"

"Before what?"

"Before she became your leader?"

"Hmm. You ask a lot of questions."

"Lingering effects of a dedicated sleuth searching high and low for the truth."

"I thought you were giving all that up to secure a

153

place here among the chosen? If you're not, might as well hit the road, Anna Hale. You'll never be happy here or fit in if you're into asking too many questions. The ideology of the Circle of Friends is to be accepted by the teachings of our dedicated Mother and saint. A woman who has the voice of an archangel messenger whispering in her ear."

This guy no more believed his pretty words than he believed in Big Foot. Question was, how close was he to the leader and did he tell her everything? The very fact he had invited her to his room without her knowledge, meant he wasn't totally on the up and up, giving her some hope.

"I do accept the idea. I just want to get up to speed on this archangel messenger and how all of this came about," she prompted him. "I find it fascinating."

He shrugged, looking somewhat placated. "It happened in the desert. She was lost, alone, starving, and not even having any access to water, close to death when he came to her. The Archangel Gabriel promised eternal life if she embraced his teachings. He's been with her ever since. She even has one of his beautiful white feathers framed."

Yeah, right. More like a white swan feather. She took a sip of the liquor, pondering how to phrase her next question. "You're her head of security. What would she think of you and I being alone like this?"

"You came to me for help while she's away. I assisted you with your questions. Nothing to tell. We've already met anyway. But you're not to be wandering around the compound, bothering others. That's unacceptable and will get you expelled. But I won't tell if you won't. However, a little quid pro quo might be in order."

Eww. Was this how he got his little fun on the side?

"I don't prostitute myself for anyone."

"Who said anything about prostitution? Look, I just wanted to get to know you better. I took the Latin phrase to mean sharing a bit about ourselves. Maybe you should leave?"

"Sorry." The single word pained her. He'd obviously meant more sharing than just conversing but was backtracking now. Not a bad idea. "I may have read this situation incorrectly. Please, let's share a friendly drink. An excellent bourbon, by the way. Tell me, how long have you been here in Alaska?" She settled back in her chair, trying to look contrite.

"As long as she has."

"Where did you two meet?"

"Are you here to join up with us or are you here to cause problems?"

"I'm here to understand. To find my true path forward." Nothing fake about it in reality. She felt she was at some kind of crossroads. The very fact she'd stepped over the line with Josh suggested something more was going on in her life than she was seeing or admitting to.

"Well, only He can help with that. Consider praying on it. Use the next few days wisely to look deep into your heart."

Did he somehow know about the bug she'd planted? He was hedging his bets with the best of them now.

"I'm more interested in you, Brother Adam. You are the more fascinating one here. What's your story?" She knew the outline of his life, of course, having researched it before coming here. How he'd been brought up by a single mother, got in trouble with a gang at an early age before turning his life around. But how much of his belief was real and how much a con job?

"Not much to tell. A troubled childhood that led to my seeing the light with Mother's help."

"But she gets all the accolades while you hide in the shadows." She drank a bit more of the excellent liquor, giving him an inquiring look. "Wouldn't you like to be seen as more? The man at the right-hand side of the throne with all the answers?"

"I do just fine."

"But what is the endgame? This all seems like preparation for something?"

"Not revealed as yet. Besides, what's the rush. The status quo is working fine." He drank deeply of the bourbon, his expression confident.

"Don't you ever worry about outsiders not understanding the good you do here? Think of history. Past events are the best indicators of what can happen in the future. Take Waco for instance. What if the authorities descend on this place? How far is the head of security willing to go to defend it?" That was her worry in a nutshell.

"Waco could *never* happen here. We aren't a damn cult, just like-thinking people who have come together for the common good. We have shared values of living right and valuing life. There's no reason for the law to come to this place. If you go back home, and I take it you will, then take this message with you. We choose to live as a community dedicated to leaving zero footprint on nature. We take climate change seriously and we live to love one another equally."

"So you're saying that if an armed group arrived here, you'd stand down. Not fight if they told everyone they had to leave immediately?"

"That's not the same thing. No one takes away our freedom to live in this way. The right way for us. We own this land, everyone is here voluntarily, and we do no harm. They would be very bad people to suggest otherwise, not us."

A very unsatisfying answer.

"Okay, then tell me what this First Call is all about? Is it a test of some sorts?"

"Nothing more than being baptized. That's hardly a crime."

"If that's all there is to it, why didn't you say so earlier? All this mystery about it makes no sense."

"It's a sacred ritual, not to be bandied about. You're either with us or you're not. Why should we share and maybe cheapen the experience by saying, do this, do that, you're in. No, each must be called for a higher purpose for it to matter to Him." He looked toward heaven to punctuate his remarks.

"Okay. And this call, how does it usually manifest itself?"

"No one can help you there. But it's often a dream, a vision, a sense of the rightness of joining with Mother. Let your heart and mind open. You may be surprised at what pours in."

This guy was good, she'd give him that.

"This has all been very illuminating." She set her glass down, nearly empty now. Where was the promised food? "Tell me how you knew you were being called?"

He shrugged and got up. Walked over and topped up her glass without asking. "A dream. One of the more common experiences for others is embracing joining the Circle of Friends."

"Tell me about it."

"No. It's personal. I don't want to influence your mind one way or the other."

Like hell you don't. Phttt, the amount of bullshit flying

around this room. "Of course, forgive me for asking. But I am famished. What are the chances getting some food? Anything, crackers and cheese or a jar of peanut butter would do."

"I checked, but it seems I'm all out of anything to eat. And the kitchen's closed now. You'll have to wait."

Passive aggressive asshat.

"I should be going." She got to her feet but found herself swaying back and forth, the room spinning dizzily. *Just freakin' great.* Normally she held her liquor better than this. The bourbon was stronger than she realized or maybe it was drinking on an empty stomach?

"Whoa. You'd better lie down."

TWENTY-SEVEN

"John Mosely's awake and asking for you, Detective Pace," a nurse popped her head in around the corner of the emergency cubical. He was there on other business, checking on his partner who'd been brought in with chest pains a short while ago. Detective Browne was hooked up to monitors and was looking off his game with an oxygen tube up his nose, but still pissed at his wife for making him come in after chewing two baby aspirin. She'd gone off a few minutes ago for a needed break and asked Josh to watch over her husband.

"John Mosely? That's a surprise."

"Go and see what he wants, Josh. I'm fine. No need to fuss. Evelyn's always overprotective. That woman's not happy unless she's got a crisis on her hands and someone to fuss over," Browne grumbled. "Just a case of bad indigestion."

"Heart attacks, even mild ones, are not bad indigestion. You need to take it easy, pal."

"Anyway, go and see what the guy wants? It could

prove important. I got nurses to call on if I need anything."

"Okay. But you have to promise to take the flak from Evelyn."

"Done. Used to it anyway."

Josh chuckled and left the room. John Mosely's room was not far, and he stepped inside to see the patient surrounded by an older couple and a young woman.

"I'm Detective Josh Pace. John was asking to speak with me?"

"Detective. Thank you for coming." The older man stepped forward and offered his hand. A stiff man, he didn't smile, but said spoke his words in a measured tone. "And for being there for my boy. I'm Andrew Mosely, and this is my wife, Martha, and my daughter, Jennifer." His wife Martha barely nodded at him, her eyes downcast but the daughter Jennifer gave him a wide smile of greeting.

"Nice to meet you." After shaking hands, Josh moved closer to the bed to see John propped up on some pillows, looking more alert than in days though his eyes were dark and troubled. He'd heard about the never-ending night terrors the man was having and felt immense sympathy for his plight. What had happened that had caused him such pain?

"Hey, John, how you doing?"

"Better since my family got here," he said in a raspy whisper. "You're the man who saved my life. Thank you."

"You did that all on your own. I just got you to the hospital. How are you feeling?"

"Better. Still weak…dizzy, but alive."

"Do you remember what happened to you that led to your being in the middle of the road?"

"It's a puzzle. I see pieces but they don't make any

sense. It could all be a nightmare...not real memories. I just don't know. I have a lump on my head so some of it must have happened."

"Tell me the pieces and we'll go from there."

"A terrible explosion, the stench of gasoline and a burning fire. I see a lot of impressions of holes dug in the ground all lined up in a row. I don't know where I saw them. But there must be ten or more. Also, I keep hearing the words, *beware the messenger*, but they don't mean anything to me."

"Where were you before you came to be on the road where I found you?"

"I don't know. I remember getting hit over the head or falling down and being worried about something. I couldn't see much because it was dark. Then I woke up some time later and it was morning and I began walking for miles and miles."

"Any idea of the timeline? How many days you walked?"

They both looked up as Lola came into the room. She spoke quietly with the family and then joined Josh by the bedside.

"How are you, John? Just checking in again. So happy to see you're doing better."

John gave Lola a weak smile, obviously pleased by her attentions. But it didn't chase away the darkness the man appeared desperate to hide. He looked even thinner than when Josh had found him on the road. "Thanks, I'm better, Lola. Just trying to remember what happened."

Josh was more interested in finishing the interview than more social interactions with the woman who kept showing up it seemed where ever he was. He knew he was being unfair, but he was in an awkward place at the moment and wasn't certain of the path ahead. He did know he needed space to figure things out. "This explosion and fire, John. We can send in an aerial spotter team to check the area. If you know how many days you were walking, it would give us an idea of the distance we should check?"

"I think at least three days. I remember the cold nights and the relief at being alive in the morning. I do remember one night I slept in a line shack and it had firewood, though no food. The doctor said it would be like this. More and more of it would come to the surface," John said.

"Okay. We'll see if evidence of the fire is visible from above. If you remember anything else, please call me."

"Josh, I need to speak with you before you go," Lola said, laying a hand on his arm. She looked good but then she always did. No paramedic filled out their uniform better than she did.

"Okay," he said. "I'll be in the waiting room. But I can't stay long."

He gave the family a few last words and left them alone with their son. Lola followed him into the hallway. "Have I done something to offend you, Josh?" she asked, working hard to keep up with his wide strides.

"What? No, I'm just busy working a case."

"I have a friend from high school that joined with the Circle of Friends a couple of years back. He said he spotted Anna there last night. She was talking with one of the female members."

Josh stopped in his tracks. "Which friend? One of your Goth crew?"

"None of us are Goth anymore. We outgrew it. Just like jocks and sorority girls need to."

"Give me a name."

"David Merino. He was always looking for something, wanted to become part of something with more meaning than what society offers. Not a bad guy, but kind of lost. Better he joins Circle of Friends at Iron-wood than a gang selling drugs, right?"

"You guys still keep in touch? I thought that all contact between members and regular society was frowned on."

"It is. But David had—has—a thing for me and some-times he reaches out when he leaves the compound to get supplies in town. He wants me to join up too, spouting all the good the group does. One of their missions is to achieve zero carbon footprint which is a darn good thing, right? But why is Anna there? She's not exactly the type who would join a group like that."

He couldn't see any reason not to tell her. Lola was on the outside and not involved with the movement other than a connection to an old friend. "She's on a case. Undercover. One of the members—her mother's sick and needs a new liver. Anna went there to tell her about it. If I knew about this earlier, I could have had you reach out to David Merino to have him ask the question. This could have saved everyone some time." Not that it was a bad thing Anna and he were apart for a few days. Hell, they both needed time to think.

"So, you're saying her being there is under false circumstances? She's just pretending she wants to join up? Kind of a sting operation if you ask me."

Lola's snarky tone took Josh by surprise. "She doesn't mean harm to anyone there and if they aren't doing anything wrong, there's nothing to worry about."

"I didn't mean anything bad by it. But other people might see her actions as less than above board. Like she's using them." Lola frowned, looking a bit confused by his intel.

"How else to help the mother? Just let her die because no one can get in to see the daughter and ask her to be there for her own mom? The sister had already tried to see her but was turned away at the gate."

"In my experience, those in the group are running from families that don't care about them. People who have been abused in the past and are suffering from a lack of meaning or good self-image in their minds. Most families have been abandoned for good reason or at least in the mind of the member who left them."

It was a viewpoint he hadn't considered. What if John Mosely had been there at Ironwood? He was found a good distance away, but he had three days to get as far as he did. Though he seemed to care about his family which didn't back up Lola's theory. Unless he had forgotten about what his home life had been like? He had to admit John's parents didn't come across as being overly happy about their son being alive.

"Okay. Let's leave this alone for now. All I ask is you keep Anna's reasons for being there under your hat. I don't want a whiff of this leaking out and making her job harder."

"Of course. You didn't need to say it. Just because I see both sides of things, doesn't mean I don't want to help. I want to get at the truth as much as anybody. No one has a monopoly on it. Right? Not even Anna."

And with that, Lola strode away, not even looking back to see if he was watching her. He knew he'd offended her and that he was being unfair. This was what happened when he and Anna were at odds. It colored everything else, making his life harder. Sure, they always came out of these periods, usually stronger and tighter for it. But what about this time? A certain unease in his stomach gave him the sensation that this time was different. Would Anna always run from commitment beyond her mission to find justice for others? If so, any chance at a relationship was doomed before it began. An overwhelming sense of longing filled his body and soul. Was this how the members of Circle of Friends felt when they wanted to join up? Like they were lost and drifting through life that needed more meaning. Yes, he had a great job, friends, and his sister Zoe on his side. He too wanted justice for others, just not at the cost of never having his own family. Damn it, he wanted to punch something, get rid of some of this frustration with feeling helpless. Past time to visit the gym and bust a few moves on the punching bag.

TWENTY-EIGHT

Anna came awake slowly, her mind an annoying fog. What the hell? Her mouth was sour, and her head throbbed making the case for too much to drink on an empty stomach. She sat up gingerly, holding onto her skull like it was about to fall off her shoulders. She pried one eye open and looked around. She was back in the tiny room she'd been given by Mary Jane Wattley. What time was it? There was no clock in the room. She struggled to her feet and shambled over to the window to raise the blind, only to discover the glass was replaced with the image of a white dove flying against a blue sky painted over it. No way anyone could see in or out though it allowed some hazy light in. Didn't help gauge the time though.

There was a tiny bathroom and she made quick use of it, gulping down a couple of glasses of water. Someone had put her back in her room last night. And that could only be Adam. She had not been molested to her knowledge and was still fully dressed, minus her shoes. She rummaged through the bathroom but could find no pain relievers. Her stomach rumbled and she remembered the protein bars in her concealed belt around her waist. It was then she realized it was gone. Damn it. She searched the room but came up empty. Other than a couple of changes of clothing, there was nothing else in the room. The worst part, her burner phone was gone.

She decided to shower first, then hunt down some food and an explanation. And find out the time. It was discombobulating not to know and she hated the sensation of not being in charge.

The shower helped, throttling her headache back to Defcon one. Dressed in clean clothing, jeans, and a long-sleeved T-shirt, she tidied her bed and tucked her dirty clothes away before approaching the door. Time to speak with the head honcho and get a better reading on things.

But when she turned the knob, it didn't give way in her hand but held firm. She twisted harder and knocked her shoulder against it, to check if maybe it had gotten stuck, to no avail. It was locked from the outside.

She pounded on the door, shouting for someone to come and open the damn door already. When nothing happened, she kicked at it with her boots and screamed even louder. The door withstood her best efforts to break it down, but she didn't give up. Noise would bring someone eventually. It wasn't helping her headache any, but it was satisfying to let out her frustrations on something physical. If she was at home, she'd put in a full hour boxing session on the punching bag to relieve her stress. These past couple of days had been daunting, from the plane crash to not being there for Kelly, to the mistake of going to bed with Josh, which meant she had lots to be pissed at.

When the door abruptly opened, she nearly hit her rescuer in her angry state, striking out at an unseen enemy prowling the edges of her mind. She had fallen into the deep end and it felt good to let it all out. Something in the dark energy of this place was preying on her and lashing out was the only way to get it out of her system. Purify her mind and body.

"Careful!" Mother shouted, ducking her flying fists. "What are you doing? I was only making sure you weren't prowling around and getting yourself into trouble, not to mention upsetting other members. And you overreact like this? Shows I was right to make certain you upheld your promise to stay in this room and pray."

"You had no right to lock me in!"

"Seems by the way you are acting now it was more than prudent. When you've calmed yourself, we'll talk." Mother abruptly turned and headed down the hallway.

Anna followed, breathing heavily, ready to challenge the woman.

"I need coffee. Food. I assume they won't be withheld due to some misguided thought processes on your part?" The words were more biting than intended, but Anna could never suffer fools gladly.

"A simple repast is in order. We don't allow stimulants of any kind, no coffee or tea. But we have herbal choices or fresh cow's milk."

"How about alcohol?"

"Our Lord and Savior allowed wine. I have no problem with it in moderation."

Anna was sweating profusely and could use a second shower, but she followed the woman into a large room functioning as a country kitchen. Its homespun appeal was lost on her, and she strode over to the stove to see what was on offer. One single pot of porridge sat on the stovetop, steam rising as she lifted the lid.

"Is this it?"

"You expect steak and eggs and all the extras? We eat simply here. And live more humbly, grateful for the gift of life. Something I sense lacking from your daily existence, Anna."

Every word the woman spoke could be construed as well-meaning, but it grated at every nerve in her body. The woman was neither humble nor simple in her needs. No one looked like Mary Jane Wattley who didn't have an arsenal of expensive beauty treatments at their disposal.

"I'm fine with it." Anna grabbed a bowl from the stack on the counter and was about to scoop up a large serving when the woman interrupted her.

"I will serve you as you are our guest. Please, be seated at the table." Mother took the bowl and spoon from her and waited for her to sit down.

"Fine." She retreated to the table.

The offering was about a third of what she was hoping for but better than nothing. The leader's portion was even smaller and Anna figured she'd eaten earlier and this was just for show. Otherwise, the woman would be skin and bone like Sister Beatrix. Instead, she appeared well-nourished and healthy.

"Thank you, Lord, for this day and for the food to sustain our lives. We hope to be of service to you and to follow the work of the faithful. Amen." The woman glowed with good intentions. What evil was hiding beneath that placid exterior? Anna could sense it like a wolf scents out a predator.

"Thank you for this opportunity to be here within the Circle of Friends and to break bread with them. To find out how they live to ease the suffering of others and to leave as little footprint on this earth as is humanly possible. Amen."

The woman pretended Anna's additions to her prayers were wanted, and she said *Amen* again with great aplomb.

When she was done eating which wasn't much of a feat considering its scantiness, she took her bowl to the sink and rinsed it. It had taken all of two minutes to consume the bland repast.

"What now?" Anna asked, eyeing the tiny, weeny spoonful her host was consuming.

"We pray."

"Where?"

"God is everywhere, Anna." The woman upraised her arms like she had a huge audience. "In the very air we breathe. It is what keeps us humble and grateful to be alive."

"Of course." The way the woman thought she had a direct line to being the most enlightened being on the planet might grate, but it was also an ends to a means.

"I have somewhere I need to be. You will pray in your room on your own this day."

"I see. What if I'm ready to join now? That last night I had a dream that it was the right and proper thing to do, being baptized?"

Mary Jane Wattley gave her a skeptical glance. "Okay, you can share the dream with me later. First, you must pray."

"No locking me in. That's off the table."

"Then I need your promise you won't disturb the others. You broke your word yesterday. The Lord sees all, Anna."

Anna bit her tongue. Actually, she was shocked she

hadn't been asked to leave. The woman had a use for her then. What was it? The angle eluded her. Wouldn't it just be better to kick her out, right now, for breaking the rules? Someone else would come along and be their number two hundred and twenty-two. It didn't seem like a good enough reason to hold onto a member like her who had no trouble flaunting rules. In Alaska, most everyone knew that Anna Hale was a woman who walked her own way, a pathfinder. One of the many characteristics she knew she shared with the wolf, her spirit guide, along with intelligence, loyalty, and protectiveness.

"Why did you speak with Sister Beatrix and upset her? Is she the real reason you are here?"

"No, that's just happenstance. After I made my decision to come here, her sister, Emily Stubbs, asked me to check on her. Since I was coming anyway—"

The woman's razor-sharp eyes were focused on hers, and Anna made sure to believe what she was saying, staring right back at her. To beat a lie detector, know your words to be true. Many have done it and confused law enforcement. Anna didn't like being seen as similar to a criminal in that regard, but if it needed to be done for a good cause, she was prepared to accept it. Sometimes it was a razor's edge between the good guys and the bad. But it didn't mean she didn't know exactly which side of the thin line she held fast to.

"Coincidence, I think not. But at least now you will be able to calm yourself knowing she is well and here because she wants to be. I have taken a special interest in Sister Beatrix. Her home life growing up was abominable. Made to prostitute herself to pay for her mother's drugs. It eats at her still, causing her to not look after herself as well as she should. But we are making progress, albeit slowly. Hard work is the best medicine, it helps one sleep at night."

The news was unwelcomed even though it rang true, worse than she had been told by the sister and all the more so because it made her feel wrong-footed. She would no more ask the woman to go back to such a deplorable, vile situation than she would cut off her own right hand. She'd worked hard for years now to help women out of bad situations, not deliver them back into them. Did her sister Emily know about it? Was that what she'd been hiding when they spoke? If she did know, Anna would be having a word with her as well as her wrong-minded mother.

"That's new information to me. The decision to leave or stay was always up to Faith though. And I would *never* pressure a person to deliver themselves back into a situation that is harmful to their wellbeing. I won't be contacting her again. If she wants to talk to me, that's different, of course." Strange to hear herself saying the cult was better for Faith than living with her family. In reality, both situations were bad, though this one was not as harmful to her as living with a family that prostituted her. At least it appeared so on the surface. There was so much Anna wanted to know to make sure the young girl had jumped into the proverbial fire from the frying pan by staying at Ironwood.

"Then we are on the same page. Now, if you'll excuse me, I have duties to attend."

"Any problem with me being outside my room if I keep within the house?" Anna hated to ask for permission, but it was necessary.

"No, but if you venture outside again, you will be escorted off the property. Are we clear?"

Anna nodded.

"And if you are really serious about joining us, I will hear your dream tonight after you have spent the day in prayer."

Anna watched the woman sail forth from the room; her outward reflection so perfect she could be the model for a Renaissance sculptor. At least her coloring was right to be carved in marble.

She filled her bowl with the last of the porridge, reminding herself she needed to keep herself nourished. Her dismay at learning about Faith Stubb's former situation nagged at her as she had her fill of the oats. What kind of monster does that to her child? The luck of the draw, like which family one is born into or when illness strikes good people early in life, had always bothered Anna, something she could see no rhyme or reason for. But philosophy was for a different day, not now when she was already feeling off.

After doing up the dishes, she went back to her bedroom and had another shower to wash away the sweat. At least now she had the run of the place. She was on the verge of leaving here, nothing seemed more amiss than like-minded people being corralled by an ideology some would disagree with. Didn't mean they were at harm. Those looking for meaning in their lives who joined a gang of criminals were more at risk for dying young.

She pulled out the minuscule surveillance device she'd hidden beneath the dresser yesterday, wanting to listen in to check if any conversations were happening now. Good thing she had removed it from the belt that held the bugs she'd planted, otherwise all her efforts would have been in vain. It was a last-ditch attempt to find out any intel that could support her theory that something negative was going down at Ironwood.

But when she attached the audio feed to her ear, all she got was silence. She listened in until she got bored, then tucked it back in its hidey hole. Now what? Isolation and prayer were not Anna's thing. She needed to move, to be doing things that mattered. To make some kind of difference. And the last thing she wanted was to dwell on the Josh situation. Of course, just the thinking of it brought all the churning feelings back full force. What the hell was she going to do about it?

TWENTY-NINE

With one swift movement, the messenger pulled the black hoodie up and over their head. Time to deliver the words. They strode with purpose toward a side entrance, avoiding the flashing lights and keeping their face turned away. Cameras were the least of the messenger's concern but why tempt fate? The silicone prosthetics they'd applied and black-rimmed glasses should be sufficient to disguise themself. Unlikely even their own mother would recognize them now.

They made their way to the side staircase, avoiding the elevators, and climbed to the second floor where the person they needed to deliver their message to was recovering. They stood and listened at the doorway to the room to check if he was alone. They held a small bouquet of wildflowers in their hand just in case the patient had visitors. But he proved to be alone, and they walked swiftly into the room, pleased to find him awake and staring at them. An excellent chance to talk, to see where his loyalties lay.

"Brother Lazar," they said the words quietly and stepped up to his bedside.

His eyes widened at their appearance, his eyes questioning who they were. He looked bad. Physically and spiritually haunted. It did not surprise them. He was lost now, a soul wandering in the darkness chased by demons. The path he'd chosen.

"I've come on behalf of the archangel to find out why you abandoned us?"

The man's hand crept toward his call button. They quickly grabbed it before he could, then held it out of reach. "Why have you forsaken us?" they asked.

"I don't know what you mean? Who are you? You should leave. My parents and sister are coming back any minute." His eyes looked frantic, like he was ready to do most anything to stop whatever was happening. What did he fear most?

"You know that's not true. They are having a meal together, giving us the opportunity to speak."

"You only want to talk? What about?"

"Why you left us? I've already said as much." They were getting impatient. Soon his parents would be back and it would be too late to save him.

"I had to leave. I no longer felt the calling. What they're doing there—it isn't right." The darkness in his eyes said it had been much more than that, he had fallen into the clutches of the devil.

"You should have come to us. We would have helped you to overcome your doubts and fears. Chased away the darkness and brought you into the light."

"Please, just leave me alone. I won't tell anyone if you go now." He suspected now who they were by the change of expression. The fact that he looked even more afraid surprised them. Did he not know they were only looking out to his best interests? Someone had to save his mortal soul.

"What is there to tell? We were all trying to help you. Save you. What is it you think you know? What has caused you to abandon the teachings? To turn your back on all of us and the good we do." The brother had risen from First Call in a bad way. Perhaps he was a lost sheep, doomed by his life's choices and unable to become part of God's plan? A wandering soul with no place to go, unable to move on was to become a ghost, never blessed in the design of things. The true walking dead.

He pulled back the covers, looking like he was ready to bolt, giving them no choice. "I thought you cared about us. That you were dedicating your life to a bigger cause. I'm disappointed in you, brother. More than we can say."

"I'm sorry, okay, but I no longer believe in what you do. You all brought on this evil. Left me doomed to eternal damnation. Let me go, I'll never tell. Go away." He clutched at his face as if in pain, his eyes closed firmly shut.

"I'm sorry to hear that."

They moved quickly, retrieving the hypodermic from the bouquet of flowers and throwing the fragrant foliage to the floor. In a flash, they were on him, pushing the needle deep into his neck. His eyes bulged with fear then and he let out a strangled cry before they clamped down hard on his mouth with both hands. When he went slack a minute later, his life ending, they let go.

They had to move fast now. They thrust the used hypodermic back into their pocket. They exited the room, unseen, leaving something behind: a single white feather drifted from under their coat and landed on the tiled floor, too busy thinking of their next moves to notice. For they had been called upon to do what others could not imagine. It could have been avoided if only their brother had come back to the flock. Embraced the teachings and realized everything they did was for a higher purpose. It would have given him time to enjoy Final Days. But no, Satan, the archenemy of God and all angels and archangels, had intervened and called him away in a weak moment. Left them no choice. A friend had whispered as much in their ear, keeping them abreast of things.

When they reached street level, they walked away and toward their vehicle, keeping a steady pace and alert for any problems. Once inside the van, they took a few deep breaths, reassuring themselves of the rightness of what they had done. What they had been called upon to do. This was nothing more than one more test, one step closer to knowing all.

They pulled into traffic, their mind going back over a recorded conversation. Sister Joan was next. If she were truly drawn to their cause, Mother would act appropriately. Well, soon it would be decided either way, when she was either chosen or sent her on to her just rewards.

THIRTY

"You promised to explain First Call," Sister Joan said, sitting down beside Beatrix on the stone bench near the woodpile. They had both escaped to the outdoors and away from prying eyes. She breathed in the fresh Artic breeze, wishing she could go back in time and change the past. If only she hadn't lived the life she had, she could garner more respect for herself. But her mother had put a stop to it, making her do those awful things. Sister Joan would never understand how bad it was, what she had gone through. She was tainted, far more than her new friend. Her mother dying when she was born was not her fault. How could her own sister say such a thing?

"It's an important milestone. When you come out of the water, all your sins are washed away." But were they really? She was still haunted by the past rearing its ugly head, more and more lately even as she worked to overcome it. She'd tried to live clean, do all the good she could, but still her skin felt dirty, her soul tarnished. Did First Call work for everyone? Brother

Lazar had not been the same after he rose, his glances her way dark and filled with anguish. Maybe she too was a failure? Her sins too dark to ever be totally obliviated.

"But what actually happens to make you become one of the chosen? Like, does Mother do anything? Is there like a test or something?"

"The test is rising from the water, letting your sins go yourself, with God's help, of course." She didn't say that being held under the water for an indeterminable time was an important part of it. It would frighten her only friend in this world away before they had a better chance to know each other.

"That's it? Sounds too easy to be true. Did you feel it? Your sins being swept away?"

"I did at the time."

Sister Joan's forehead creased with worry. "But now they're back?"

"I guess my problems were a bit harder to fix than most. Yours, however—your mother dying at your birth —are not your fault. You'll be fine." *If the messenger lets her live*. The thought scared her and she bit her lip to keep her thoughts hidden inside.

"But it's not fair that you should be troubled either. No one is to blame for whatever family they are born into."

"Maybe I do need to see my mom and sister, make peace with her to gain salvation before she dies?"

"What? A woman who abandoned you? Made you feel insecure and helpless?"

"I don't know what the right thing to do is anymore. I wish I could go back and feel the healing again."

"Maybe we could be baptized together? Perhaps that would help?"

A radical thought but one she quickly abandoned. "But then Mother would know I'm having doubts."

"But you are."

"Please, don't tell anyone. I don't fit in very good as it is." The Lord knew how much she had tried, but no matter what she did or said, she often felt on the outside looking in. A fringe player.

"I thought this place was all about community? Supporting each other as we worked toward a higher cause."

"Most of the sisters and brothers are nice. Just the odd one I guess are still trying to find their way."

"You're way too good for them."

Never has she had such a staunch supporter. It filled her with such a strange feeling she was unsure even what to say back.

"I know what will make you feel better about yourself. How about we give your hair a nice conditioning and I'll trim the dry ends for you?"

"You'd do that for me?"

"Sure. I brought lots of the good stuff. Just because I believe in a higher purpose doesn't mean I don't think it's not important to also look after ourselves. We only get one body, better treat it right. And speaking of that, you need to eat more."

She grinned. "You sound like someone's mom."

"Thank goodness I don't look like one."

"You want children one day?"

Sister Joan shook her head. "I don't think it's in the cards for me."

"Me neither. Doesn't seem right to bring children into the world. Mother constantly reminds us of the evildoers and how she's doing everything she can to protect us. It gets worse every day out there, she says. So much crime. I'd be afraid to step out my front door now if I wasn't here. Maybe it's why there are no children are here at the present time? Everyone feels the same about the issue."

"It is bad. But I don't think it's hopeless. We just need people to see a better way forward. I was hoping coming here might help me see it. To learn what I can do to help. I guess I'm hoping for an epiphany. Did you see anything when you were baptized?"

Sister Beatrix dug down deep, trying to find the exact words to describe her own First Call. "I remember feeling lighter. So filled with a wonderful sense of purpose I was certain my feet weren't even touching the ground. And relieved to be alive, of course, called upon to be one of the chosen."

"Why were you surprised to be alive? Wasn't that a given?"

She'd said too much. She could have kicked herself. Why was she always messing up? "Yeah, I guess. Let's go in. It won't be long until lights out. That's if you still want to help with my hair?"

"Of course." Her new friend linked her arm with hers as they made their way back to the women's dormitory. *Please, let Sister Joan live and become one of the chosen. I'll do anything to make that happen. Anything. Just tell me what to do.*

THIRTY-ONE

Anna stood unmoving under the overhang of the veranda. The wooden addition stretched across the frontage of the main house, offering protection against the elements and away from prying eyes if one stayed close to the front entrance. She needed fresh air, a new perspective, and answers for why this place gave her the creeps. It was the kind of place even her Tia, her sister murdered by the Black Rose Killer, Elvis Strobel, most likely wouldn't appear in corporeal form to give her any hints or clues, which was really saying something. Tia's ghost had helped solve her own murder, hovering over her own grave. Then appearing whenever things were of the utmost importance. Or going to go bad in a hurry. But not a hint of her here at Ironwood. Not for the first time she wished she knew a sure-fire way to call upon her.

She kept her eyes locked on the landscape, continually sweeping the area of the compound. Not much was going on, most people worked inside in the winter and only a few appeared assigned to cutting logs to length to use in their fire-burning furnaces.

She watched a new figure coming out of the barn dressed in a warm parka, a woman, moving determinedly in Anna's direction. Intrigued, she stood her ground, waiting for her to come up onto the porch. As she got closer, Anna studied her face. She looked familiar. Even with the knit cap covering most of her hair except for a few red curls, her features were definitely known to Anna. *Yes*, it was Tabitha Owens, Kelly's friend from New York. Shocked but thrilled to have the opportunity to speak with the young girl fired her up. Anna believed most things happened for a reason and here was a coincidence that could not be ignored. Of course, how many new cults had begun this year anyway? Circle of Friends did have the best website and app for a cult she'd seen in years. And now Anna had just walked into the path of the very person Kelly was so worried about. Finally, something good was happening in this forlorn place. She stepped forward to greet her, ignoring the edit by their leader not to speak with any of the members.

"Tabitha Owens, right?"

"I was. I'm Sister Sarah now. How did you know?" The girl appeared distracted, like she had another purpose in mind than being sidetracked.

"I'm Kelly Smith's friend, Anna Hale from Anchor, Alaska. The one who arranged for those photos to be taken down. You two go to design school together in New York City."

"Aw, right, I have heard of you. Kelly was so happy about all your help with her schooling. And thanks for taking care of, well, you know." Tabitha blushed. "I quit a few days ago though and she was kind of upset about it. She didn't want me to leave. Have you joined us here as well?" She was trying to gauge how friendly she should be to Anna. Was she an insider or the *other*. Anna worked to keep the judgment off her face. Had it ever been any different since the beginning of time? Every group that ever lived seemed to think they were the only ones who had it right. Though admittedly cults took it one step too far, so often ending in tragedy.

"I'm praying with Mother about it." Closest she could come to admitting the truth.

"You should. It's wonderful what they do here. They are really building something important. Making a difference by living off the land in a sustainable way."

"Yes, they are building something here. Can I help you with anything? You seemed in a big hurry coming across the yard just now."

"I need to speak with Brother Adam. Is he around, do you know?"

"No, but maybe I can help. I know a great deal about security. Kind of my job. I don't know if Kelly mentioned it, but I help solve cases of missing people." She decided saying she was a private investigator might rub Tabitha the wrong way.

"Right." The young girl's face cleared. "I found something when I was cleaning up the water in the shower area. There was a leak and it soaked all the tile in the ceiling. It happened the day we had that big boom, you know, like an earthquake or something."

Anna nodded, intrigued. "Yes, I felt it too. What did you find?"

"Anyway, a black book fell on the floor, a journal, and it's locked shut. I'm not sure what to do with it. No one seems to know who it belongs to and I thought it best to hand it in to security. I didn't read it so I don't know who it belongs to."

"You did the right thing. It's private and I would imagine Brother Adam will give it to Mother."

"Maybe I could hand it to her personally." Tabitha a.k.a. Sister Sarah's eyes lit up with a bit too much zeal for Anna's comfort. That was more than likely the reason she was here with the journal, hoping for an audience with her idol. *Beware of false idols and prophets.*

"That's not possible. She's away right now, working to help others. I'll hand it over to Brother Adam. He'll know what to do with it." Anna held out her hand, wanting nothing more than to yank it off the girl and head inside to begin reading. She couldn't believe her luck. Not only knowing Tabitha was safe to answer Kelly's worries, but also to maybe get a clue about how another member felt about Ironwood. Every once in a while, in a person's life, forces of energy converge. Sometimes it was a good thing, sometimes not. Only time would tell how this moment would play out, but Anna's bet was on the forces of good having a hand in it.

"There was a lot of water damage to it. Not sure if much of it will be legible."

"I'm sure they will want to try to dry it soon as possible." Anna waited with her hand outstretched.

The young girl gave a small sigh. She reached in her parka and drew out a small, five by seven-inch black book. "Here," she said, none too happily.

Anna quickly took the offering and slipped it inside her jacket. "Do you miss going to school?" She had to wonder what would make her give up on her dreams of going to a prestigious New York design academy so young.

"No, I'm right where I'm supposed to be. No point in making all those pretty, useless clothes when there are far more important things going on. This is a special time. We're going to make a real difference here. Just you wait and see. If you don't join with us right now, it will be too late to save yourself. Someone else will take your place and you'll miss out on being one of the chosen. There can only ever be two hundred and twenty-two of us. Ever."

The feverish conviction in the young woman's eyes was chilling. If it was such a good thing, wouldn't they let in as many as felt called to be here? Sounded more like some kind of exclusive club than anything. What did an arbitrary number have to do with anything other than control? Cults were notorious for the leader's need of dominance of its members. Make them all wear the same clothes or haircuts, chant the same words, marry only those approved, no pre-marital sex, sex with only the leader or too much sex. Children or no children. Drugs or lack of sleep at the will of the leader. A host of terrible ideas that sought to do only one thing: control their members every move. But you give up that kind of control for being handed back so-called-enlightenment, then be prepared for your life going off the rails if the leader was a madman or woman. Absolute power *does* corrupt absolutely, leaving only one dark question in Anna's mind. Was this so-called Mother so deluded she could lead this group straight into danger?

THIRTY-TWO

"I can't stay long," Pierce said, rolling onto his back and pulling up the bedcovers. "She's expected back tonight."

Lola sat up abruptly, swinging her feet off the bed. She grabbed a cigarette off the night table and lit it, dragging the nicotine deep into her lungs. "How much longer am I expected to put up with this, *Brother Adam*? Between the crap job with all those damn whiners and needing help with the bill collectors always banging on my door because of my dad, my life is one boring, fucking grind." She missed the wild expectations of high school with the long talks of dropping out and living life on their own terms. She'd devoured the story of Bonnie and Clyde. Sure, it happened a long time ago and she only got to see an old movie with her grandmother on Turner Broadcasting the first time she was introduced to outlaws, but the way those beautiful movie stars had shown it, the adventure. The way they called their own shots. It still fired her blood. It had ended bloody for them, but it wasn't going to for Lola and Pierce. No, they had the perfect plan. They'd be rich and living on the beach, away from the frigid cold of Alaska. She hated her life there and it was getting harder to cover it up. Even cock teasing men to show her power was getting beyond old. And then Josh Pace not taking her up on it had grated more than she cared to admit. He and that damned Anna Hale would pay for the slight.

"Not long now. We have the full complement of sheep with the arrival of a couple of rich ones. The coffers are full. Which means very soon we can make our move. You need to be smart. It will happen quickly. Keep a bag packed. And don't call me on my personal cell. Use the burners. You gotta stay smart, Lola love."

"Then you need to answer my texts. I'm sick of being out of the loop." She snubbed out her cigarette and took a sip of water.

"Now come back to bed and I'll make you forget all about it," he said, a smoldering half-smile making her heart beat more rapidly. He was the quintessential bad boy. The man your mother warned you about. But bad boys were her thing. Made her body hum with lust. The need to conquer them, make them bend to her will, and ride the whirlwind together outstripped any other thoughts on the matter. Nothing turned her on like living life on the knife's edge. How else was there to feel alive? She'd been raised by gamblers and druggies. Hell, she was still paying for their mess. Well, that was over. Anchor would soon be a distant memory in the rearview mirror. She'd leave the annoying Anna Hale and the lame detective to clean up the worst mess they could ever imagine. And won't they be surprised when they realize she'd made them into a pair of losers.

Her phone buzzed with an incoming text. She checked the message. "Hmm. John Mosely's body has been discovered."

"About time someone took care of him. He was a loose fucking cannon. Not good for business. I tried to get her to see that but she wasn't listening. Always thinks she knows best."

"Yeah, someone needed to fix it." *Bonnie and Clyde* had nothing on Lola and Pierce. She was as good a loyal partner as it gets. She would prove it over and over, if that was what it took. Just ask her to bury the body in the back forty and see how quick it got done. She loved that about herself. Her trustworthiness. Once she hooked up with Pierce, she knew. He was her Clyde and they would go the distance together. She'd only been toying with Josh, enjoying upsetting Anna. She'd hated her forever. Her thinking she was better than everyone else. Her righteous nose always in the air. Well, it was about to end. Lola one, Anna zero.

Her partner in crime grabbed her by the arms and pulled her up onto him. She straddled his hips, enjoying the sensation immensely. "How about you ride me this time, cowgirl. You know how I love to watch those perky boobs bounce."

She gave her trademark laugh. "We'll have to be quick. I'll be late for work otherwise."

He grabbed a handful of her breast, rolling the nipple between his thumb and forefinger. "Soon this shit will be over, and no one can tell us what to do. No one ever again."

The idea heated her core like no other. "Now you're talking my language, cowboy."

THIRTY-THREE

Anna slipped back into her room; the diary hidden inside her parka. She shucked her outside clothing and curled up on the bed. Then pried off the lock and opened the book. The first entry was almost a year ago. The name of the writer, Sister Margaret, written on the first page. She quickly checked for the last one to know the date. Three weeks ago. Good, it should provide a snapshot of events at Ironwood this past year.

Back at the beginning, she began reading.

> *I arrived today to be greeted by my new friends. They all seem so happy to see me, content in their work of trying to make this world a better place. We all have the same purpose. To live off the land and share in the bounty of the earth. Mother is amazing!!! So beautiful and kind. She knows everything. She's unlike anyone I have ever met. I'll never meet anyone like her ever again.*

Yada, yada, yada.

It was nothing Anna had not heard before. She

skipped ahead, hoping to learn something new. If not, she'd check the last few entries and then give the entire journal a quick skim. She could go home now, of course, she had news for Kelly and she'd delivered her message to Faith, but she couldn't leave in good conscious if anyone was at risk here. The very fact the diary entries ended three weeks ago was ominous. She had to know why.

Today I helped fill over five hundred white doves with our special vitamin mix. A new record. For doing it I got a filled white dove to keep all to myself or to share as I see fit. I love how the vitamins make me feel. Full of energy and ready to take on the world. I know I should share them, but how do I do it fairly? There are not enough for everyone to have an extra one. I think I'll hold onto them for now. I've hid them where I keep my diary, that way no one can take them. Mother says allowing others to be tempted by opportunity you unknowingly provide to them, makes you guilty of the sin as well. I can't have that happen. I need to keep my soul clean.

Vitamins, right. Probably something laced with speed to create happy little drone bees. She needed to get her hands on a sample to prove her case. Selling drugs was a sure-fire way to make money to look after hundreds of people. Anna turned the page to the next entry.

Someone stole my vitamins last night. When I went to tell Brother Adam, the head of security about it he got really angry about my pettiness. He said I should have taken better care of them. That it was all my fault. I was so upset, I cried for hours. I needed those vitamins. They were mine. I won them fair and square. Shouldn't they replace them for me? I mean it's only right.

I decided to go back and confront him. Tell him he was wrong. I had hidden them well and used them sparingly and still had half of them left. But when I got there and knocked on his door he didn't answer. I saw the light was on and I crept up to a window.

What I saw was shocking. He and Mother were going at it on the bed. Doing the unthinkable. It disgusted me and broke my heart in two. Mother has told us she was chaste, unbothered by any sins of the flesh, that the Archangel Gabriel had spoken to her in the desert and told her she was the chosen leader. She swore she must abide by a life of being unburdened by lust or any needs of the flesh.

She looked different too. Her hair was not platinum but brown. It was all wrong and made me sick to my stomach. I knocked on the window, letting them know what they did had been seen. I was mad, so upset, feeling scammed.

I'm writing these words and putting them back in the hidey hole to keep them safe. I have to decide what to do next. I think I will have to leave here. I don't see any other choice. It breaks my heart, but I can't be where I'm being conned, taken advantage of.

I will go back to school, learn how to make something of my life. I can work hard. I'm young and strong. I don't need Circle of Friends to make it in this world. I've learned how to live off grid. How to construct a yurt. Winter camp. I won't let them win. They are not who they say they are. No different than the others. I must sleep now. I'm exhausted. Life sucks at the moment. Good night, world.

The entry was riveting. Anna's stomach rolled over. What had happened to Margaret three weeks ago to stop her writing in the journal? Had she simply left Ironwood? But why not take the diary? It would make more sense for her to keep it with her. Even if just some kind of souvenir of her time there. She needed to know more about this woman. She needed her real name. To check if anything showed up about her on social media. And if she could get a sample of the so-called vitamin pills, all the better. She read the next entry learning nothing new, but the last one made her heart lurch.

I went back to the main house tonight and peeked in the window. Maybe I had been dreaming it? After all I have an overactive imagination according to any foster parent I ever lived with.

I waited for a while, crouched by the back window, feeling more and more uncomfortable for spying. The cold began seeping into me and I was about to give it up when Mother and Brother Adam came into the room. They were wearing strange clothing, made of black material like grained-leather. Mother carried a whip and she handed it to Brother Adam. Her breasts were exposed, the nipples hard. She leaned over the bed and he began to whip her! I was so shocked, I let out a scream, then turned and ran for the woods.

I had to get out of here. I was going crazy. I ran for a long time through the trees until I came to an open meadow. In the light (it was a clear night with a full moon) I found a row of large rocks, so perfectly aligned someone had to have placed them there. I counted them as I walked down alongside them. Thirteen. At the end of the row, an open hole in the ground loomed, about four feet wide by six or seven feet long.

*What was it for? My worst thought was what if it is a
grave? Were all these thirteen rocks gravestones for people
who had died here? I was scared and so cold, yet my heart
was racing too fast. I had to get back to my bed. I had the
most awful feeling that if I was discovered standing over
the hole, it would be a bad thing. Was all this a hallucina-
tion? I didn't think so, but it didn't matter. I have to leave.
Tomorrow.*

Oh fuck! This was bad. Really bad. Was Margaret
killed because she'd seen Mary Jane Wattley and Mr.
Menace getting their jollies on? She had to find those
graves. She had the smoking gun in her hands that could
blast this place wide open. She quickly slid it into her
pants, suddenly worried about anyone finding out about
it from a causal word from Tabitha Owens. Someone
could come looking for it. No, it would be best to get the
hell out of here and bring back help. An investigation
would no doubt ensue. The graves, if indeed that was
what they were, would be easy enough to spot from the
air with the description from the journal. She had gotten
a bit too casual about this whole damn thing, thinking
nothing but the creepy unease she'd been experiencing
since she'd been here was caused by the blind loyalty so
many had for one woman. A woman who was as slick as
any grifter or conman and dangerous as a snake.

She decided to leave the electronic bugs behind. If
they were found, so be it. She'd be long gone. It was late
in the day, but she'd hike out to her truck and hit the
road anyway. She'd had a trickle charger placed on the
vehicle, solar powered, so it the engine should turn over
even in this freezing weather. She pulled on her parka
and zipped it up, tucked her hair under a knit cap and
tugged on warm gloves, then headed for the front door

where she'd left her boots. *Please don't let Wattley or Menace come in now and catch me.* Just a few more minutes and she'd be out of view and on her way. Time to take this place down.

Anna scanned the area before leaving the safety of the veranda. The wood pile had been abandoned for the day and the grounds appeared quiet. Perfect. She moved quickly, clamoring down the few stairs and across the wide expanse in the direction of her truck. The sun was setting in a glorious array of crimson and golden hues and would provide sufficient light if she hurried. She increased her pace and stayed on the roadway leading away from the compound. The fields were simply too deep with snow to navigate in a rush. She prayed that no one would need to use the road for the next few minutes. She'd prefer to avoid a confrontation, if possible, but if they insisted on knowing why she was leaving, she'd simply tell them it wasn't for her. That she'd had a dream Mother was a false prophet. Sure, they'd be angry, but what could they really do? They had to let her go, as they had to know people would come looking for her soon. Another day or two here and it was pretty much guaranteed Josh, Zoe, Tom, or Zeke would come. There was no way to explain it if she wasn't let go immediately upon requesting it, not to mention it would avoid legal charges against them for any interfering with her person. But still, a sense of unease lingered. The very air of this place was suffocating. Hidden secrets. Evil deeds. What was really going on?

Soon, she comforted herself, all would be revealed in the guaranteed upcoming investigation. She'd arrived at the gates to the property now and walked through them with a sense of relief. No one was on guard anywhere near them, and she made it to the perimeter road without being accosted. She hurried the last few hundred yards to her truck. When the shape of the GMC loomed in the growing darkness, she let out a relieved breath. She'd soon be on her way. Then she could bring help to stop whatever crimes were being perpetrated against this vulnerable flock of people just looking to live life a better way.

She went straight to the rear wheel well and yanked off the metal security device holding her spare keys to the inner fender before climbing inside the frigid box. She thrust the keys in the ignition, then turned the engine over. Nothing. How could that be? There had been sunny periods the past couple of days. Had someone tampered with her vehicle?

She clamored out and yanked up the hood. Damn it. Someone had gone to the trouble to remove her distributor cap, disabling the vehicle. Now there was nothing for it but to walk out for help. She had another backpack hidden in a secret compartment under the back seat of the crew cab. It would have to do. The pack held enough water and protein bars to keep her going, though the water would be frozen solid. She'd have to tuck it against her body to melt it. Not a pleasant suggestion, but the bag also held a very useful extra cell phone.

She pried up the floor compartment under the back seat with a special tool for the job, a six-inch thin metal rod she kept in the glove box and took out the small backpack. Then pulled out the bottle of water and slipped it in her pants pocket to start to thaw it. That was when she realized her Glock and phone had been taken from the pack. Her vehicle had been searched and her weapon and emergency phone stolen. Another charge she could add to the growing list of laws the leader of the cult would no doubt be charged with. She pushed her arms through the open straps, settling it in place. She had a long walk ahead of her. But if she was lucky, she'd make the main highway in a few hours. She could catch a ride there with one of the many truck drivers heading down to Anchor.

She had barely begun her journey when a single wolf howl pierced the black moonless night. Even the stars were obscured by thick cloud now. A storm was moving in.

She'd made it a few miles a couple of hours later, and snow was just beginning to fall. Suddenly headlights turned a curve up ahead, blinding her. She crouched down and rolled into the ditch. If it was one of the members coming back from a supply run, best to avoid them. Her lack of a weapon preyed on her mind. In the future, she'd hide another gun or two in her truck and fuck the consequences. In her line of work, better to be safe than sorry.

The vehicle slowed down. She cursed softly to herself. *Keep going.*

But her prayers were not answered when it came to a sudden halt and four men jumped from the truck. She recognized one of them. Mr. Menace. She scrambled to her feet and ran into the tree line. It was immediately hard to navigate. The snow was deep, over two feet in most places at this point of late winter. It sucked at her pant legs, trying its best to trip her up. Her breathing increased as she called upon her body to move at top speed. She ducked and dove around trees in the darkness, cursing the dark night. She could hear the men behind her crashing through the bushes. Fear pushed at her. She was alone out here. No one to call upon for help. What would they do with her? Haul her ass back to the compound? Put an end to her out here?

She kept slugging through the deep snow. It didn't get any easier. It got harder, her muscles depleted of oxygen in mere minutes. She had to be careful of not getting lost as well.

I must find a place to hide. Now. Before they catch up with me.

She spotted a huge fir tree ahead with overhanging branches. She could hide there. Climb up a ways and stay hidden until they gave up. A spotlight suddenly turned on behind her, blanketing the area around her.

"There she is!"

No time to waste. She forced her body to use the last of its resources to push ahead past the safety the large tree had promised a very short moment. *Just keep moving,* Anna, she told herself, refusing to believe it had come to this.

It felt like Custer's last stand when she realized her body was out of juice. No other way forward than confronting the situation straight on.

She stopped moving. Turned and faced her pursuers. "What the fuck are you doing chasing me?" she wheezed, her heart thudding wildly. She didn't add like most foolish celebrities, *don't you know who I am?* A steady roaring in her ears made it hard to hear. She tried to quiet her breathing.

"You need to come with us. Quietly or otherwise," Mr. Menace said, coming closer.

"What? Or you'll shoot me?"

"Take a good look. There are four of us and one of you. Who do you think has the upper hand in this situation? Even the great Anna Hale is not going anywhere without our say-so."

"Me. When the cavalry arrives at any moment."

"Fuck them. They'll be too late."

"What are you talking about?" But her words rang hollow in the dark of night. A wolf gave a single howl of warning, increasing her sense of dread. "What's going on?"

"You'll know soon enough. Coming?" He didn't even bother to tie her hands after he checked her for weapons and confiscated the diary, which was even more worrisome. Was he that sure of himself? She felt the loss of the journal keenly; it was proof of shady dealings with the cult, helpful in backing up a prosecutor's case.

She was marched like a prisoner by the four men who closely flanked her all the way back through the thick trees to their waiting vehicle. It seemed a greater distance then it had felt running through it and she was once more puffing when they reached the roadway, but then so were the four men. Good. But nothing could still the wild beating of her heart. What did he mean, she'd know soon enough?

THIRTY-FOUR

"What did he die of, Morgan?" Josh asked, though he knew she couldn't possibly know yet. Doctor Lisa Morgan was their new ME, taking over from the notorious Ripper wannabe, Cross, who'd never see the outside of a jail cell again in this lifetime. She was a welcome change, far friendlier, and good at her job as well. "One minute he was recovering, the next he's dead. Something's not right here." Josh moved closer to the autopsy table. It had been a hard blow to have the man he'd rescued, found lying in the middle of the road a few days ago, suddenly dying for no apparent reason.

"Perhaps he had a heart attack or a stroke? It would be only a guess at this point. I'm running toxicology test, but those take time." The victim lay prone on the table, a marble statue. Far too young to die. What life choices had brought him to this state? Or was it just genetics? And fate. He'd died because it was his time.

"Now this is interesting," Morgan said, turning the victim's head to one side, peering at the flesh of his neck through her lighted loupes. She wore them over her eyes, immersed in the first stages of the autopsy, checking the body's skin barrier. "Looks like a small puncture on the left side of his neck."

"Yes, I can just see it, meaning he might have been murdered?" Josh's pulse rate increased as he stared intently at the tiny needle mark.

"Possibly. Unless he injected it himself?"

"Strange place to inject yourself."

"I've seen stranger. But if nothing else becomes apparent, and the drug tests show up a substance in his blood that should not have been there, then yes, it is definitely suspicious. Was he a drug user? Did he seem depressed to you?"

"No. Well, he was obviously upset by whatever had happened to put him in the state I found him in. He was running from something. He had bad dreams. But his family had come and he seemed happy to see them. So no, I don't think he was ready to off himself or anything like that. But who knows what's in the mind of another." The memory of Anna being in a bad way after Tia, their sister, had been taken by the Black Rose Killer loomed front and center. What she had gone through until she rallied to help find Zoe had been so painful that she had admitted to being on the brink of despair during one moment of vulnerability with Josh. He still felt the guilt of that time. Not being here for his sisters and Anna. It had been a rough fucking go.

His cell phone rang and he stepped away from the table before going into Lisa's office to answer it. He had been expecting the call from his sister Zoe sooner or later.

"Yes, Zoe," he said. He scrubbed a hand through his short dark hair, tugging at the roots. This was going to be a dicey conversation.

"Have you heard from Anna lately?" Zoe was always direct, but today her voice was firmer than ever.

"No. Not since she went undercover at Ironwood." Perhaps he could avoid the trap of mentioning what had happened between them that no doubt had some bearing on why he hadn't been in touch with her?

"I don't like this. Something's wrong. Even undercover, she always manages to keep in touch. It's been three whole days since I've heard anything from her. Did you two have words or something? There's something you're not telling me. I can hear the strain in your voice, Josh. Tell me right now. What's going on? What happened?"

"Nothing that affects you. She was just feeling so elated to have been okay after the plane crash. Grateful to be alive like anyone would feel and we got to drinking, and well, things took a turn."

"What! Did you two finally fall into bed together?" Zoe gave out a loud hoot. "Well, I hope you both finally admitted the torch you two have shared since like—forever."

Josh felt heat rising uncomfortably in his body. "No. It was just a momentary lapse in judgment, okay? She admitted as much." If only it had meant more to her. He knew it had been life changing for him. His disappointment was still raw and ran deep from her leaving him so soon. "Then she got this new case and I think she wanted time alone. You know, to think about things. Probably got her feet up there chanting or something."

"Chanting? Anna? Are we talking about the same woman here? No way. I don't like this but at least it makes some sense now."

"If I don't hear from her in a day or two, I'll head up there. Does that satisfy you?" Last thing he wanted to do but Zoe was right. Anna shouldn't stay offline so long. Others were counting on her in Anchor. And she had lots of people who cared about her. It wasn't fair to make them worry.

"Fine. One day. But we head up there tomorrow. I'll go with you. I have the day off as it happens."

"Great." At least he wouldn't be looking quite so lame or needy if Zoe was with him. And now he had to admit, he was getting worried about Anna. It was unlike her to vanish for so long. "I'll pick you up first thing in the morning."

Josh dickered on whether to head back into the autopsy room or go to the station as he slid his phone back into his pocket, deciding in the moment to check in with Charlie. Thank goodness for Charlie. She was the mainstay of Wolf Pack Justice investigations.

"Have you heard anything from Anna?" Charlie asked before he could say anything.

"No. Zoe and I are heading there tomorrow to check up on her. Everything okay there? I thought I'd bring a report for her if you needed her input for something?"

"Tom's handling things at our end. I'll send you an email with the updates for her on our newest case. A missing teenager from Whitehorse. Her father, a minister, contacted us yesterday. Police think it's a runaway situation, but he swears it's more than that. He believes his daughter was kidnapped by traffickers. Very upset and demanding our help. Not to mention the custody battle case with the grandparents is heating up. We could use some help here. Tell her she's needed at home."

"Of course. Her phone's been turned off, so she'd be in the dark, about all this. I'll see she gets the intel ASAP."

"Thanks."

An uneasy sensation sluiced through him. What was

keeping Anna up at Ironwood? It wasn't like her to avoid going to see Kelly. Had the plane crash pushed her off her orbit more than he'd realized? Or was something else going on? Had John Mosely's nightmares had some substance to them more than just bad dreams? He'd mentioned holes in the ground. A fire and an explosion.

The need to know propelled him out to his vehicle. He'd go now. If Zoe wasn't available, than he'd go alone. But he wasn't going to be dissuaded from driving up there tonight. Something was wrong. He should have realized this sooner. If he hadn't been so angry and hurt about her rejection of him after they'd had one glorious, incredible night together, he would have come to his senses sooner.

THIRTY-FIVE

Anna sat wedged between the two men in the back seat of the half-ton. Both were burly bouncer types, only paying attention to what the boss wanted. No one spoke to her. She didn't expect real answers from these minions anyway. If this was Wattley's decision, than she was the only one she needed to challenge.

The driver pulled up near the veranda, and everyone jumped out. She was pulled out roughly from the door nearest the front stairs, then the four asshats escorted her up to the front door and inside. The supreme leader of the asshats wasn't anywhere in view. Must be off getting her hair done. Anna was given but a moment to look around at the deserted foyer before being hustled right down the hall to a closed door. The one she found locked when she planted the bugs days ago. Seconds later she was shoved forward down a flight of stairs, barely able to keep her feet by holding on to the railing. The distinctive odor of earth and mold rose up to greet her.

The door was slammed shut and she heard the

ominous sounds of a lock mechanism engaging. *Well that went well.* She wanted to scream her frustrations but saved her breath instead. One glance at her surroundings and she knew it was a waste of energy. Carved out of the tundra, the room was approximately twelve by fifteen feet with one window above her head that proved out of her reach when she jumped up to try to reach the ledge. The walls were gray cement blocks though the floor was earthen. A rolled-up sleeping bag, a plastic bucket and a few bottles of water was the extent of it. Dismal, but at least it wasn't filthy making it a step above some jail cells found in foreign countries. Though the bathroom facilities left something to be desired. One overhead lightbulb offered some light, enough to observe no obvious vermin or rats. A three-foot opening in the back wall appeared to be a crawl space she was reluctant to enter just yet.

Now what? Would someone come to negotiate with her? Disappointed by the turn of events and in herself for not foreseeing how dangerous this crew was having just committed a federal offense of kidnapping, she slumped down, using the rolled up sleeping bag as a stool to think. Surely someone would come soon to check on her? They couldn't just let her starve down here. She reassured herself that soon someone would come looking for her. At least there was water in the meantime.

Being locked in the basement brought back stark memories of finding her sister Zoe held prisoner for days on end under the hunting lodge once belonging to the town of Anchor's former mayor. The bastard who had killed his wife and her lover during the Black Rose serial killer case and tried to hide the crimes as a copycat abduction was long gone, dead at her hands in a blinding snowstorm. No loss there. Sargeant Carter came to mind and she winced. He'd not think much of her for getting herself entangled in such a dangerous situation. He'd once said she had more courage than common sense and at the moment, he appeared to know what he was speaking of. She'd walked into this trap with her eyes wide open.

No point in crucifying herself. She needed to save her resources for an opportunity to escape this hellhole. The reason she'd not seen this coming was her own belief that sane people don't lock others up for questioning their faith. Wattley might have talked a good game, all sweetness and light, but her follow-up sucked. But where would it get her? An abduction charge was hardly conducive to running an organization that prided itself on bettering the planet. Crap. What if she was planning on leaving this place? Meaning she didn't care if Anna was abandoned here? Someone would find her, of course, eventually, but the leader could be long gone, taking all the groups funds with her. Probably start again somewhere else and lead another flock astray. If she was that desperate, to leave all she had built up at Ironwood, it meant she was really hiding something bad. Something that could land her ass in jail big time. The diary's writer must have been correct in their surmising the open pit had been a grave, likely prepared for her. Other Circle of Friends members, through no fault of their own but a belief in a higher calling, could be laid to rest under the frigid tundra alongside her with no grave marker but a stone to ever said they'd been here.

A lump rose up in Anna's throat at the evilness that some do while professing themselves to be charismatic leaders deserving of respect and honor. Wattley was no more worthy of it than a scavenger hyena in the Sahara stealing food from a brave lioness. She was scum. And needed to be returned to the swamp. ASAFP.

They could steal the diary, burn it, but they couldn't hide the gravesites. Even if they unearthed all the bodies and took them somewhere else, tracker dogs would pick up the scent in the disturbed soil. Not to mention it wasn't practical to move a dozen or so dead people in winter. And she would personally follow the woman to the ends of the earth to hunt her down. She could never be allowed to live and destroy lives ever again.

There was one other thing she realized could be Wattley's end game, and it was an even more disturbing image. What if she was going to entrench herself here, not allow anyone else inside the compound, keep armed guards at the gates to turn law enforcement away, and threaten harm to the innocent cult members? Turn it around and say it would be their fault for intruding on the sanctity of Ironwood. An armed standoff could begin. Oh fuck, if that were to be the case, then it could go the way of Waco. Had no one learned anything from studying history?

One lone wolf howl pierced her brain, telling her the horrifying truth. A terrible trial lay ahead and Anna was dead center of the crosshairs.

THIRTY-SIX

Josh fueled up his police SUV for the trip north, then replaced the nozzle in the service pump holder. The arid odor of gasoline permeated the cold air, though not nearly as overpowering as summertime. Removing the old work gloves he always used to prevent contamination, he threw them in the back on the floor. He crossed the parking lot and headed inside the gas station to pay the charge. His mind was busy, dealing with getting up to Ironwood as soon as possible when his shoulder bumped another customer. Shit, Lola. Last person he wanted to talk to at the moment.

"Josh. Nice to see you."

"Yeah. How are you, Lola?"

"Good. I'm just heading up to Ironwood."

Her news was unsettling. "Really? Why are you headed there?"

"A cousin of mine, Jen Rohl, invited me to visit her."

"You're driving all the way up there tonight for a visit?"

Lola shrugged. "I got a couple of days off. What are you doing now?"

He hated to lie and the truth was easier. "Just headed there myself to check on Anna. We haven't heard anything from her in a couple of days."

"Hey, we could share the trip. Save money. Cost of gas these days." Lola faux shuddered. "Be nice to have some company. It's a long, lonely ride."

Last thing he wanted was to drag Lola along. How to politely get out of it? "I wasn't going to stay long. Just pick up Anna and leave. You'll need your vehicle to get back home."

"I can hitch a ride back with one of the members. Somebody's always coming to Anchor for supplies they can't grow or make. They have a big congregation there now. Over two hundred members. Very impressive."

"You visit there often? I thought it was hard to get into the camp?"

"They're careful of who visits, but it's not impossible, unless they figure you represent danger in their minds. And you don't mean them harm, right, Officer?"

Her words had a different edge to them, not flirty like before, but harder. Perhaps his rejection had hurt her, more than she'd let on? He felt a twinge of sympathy for her knowing how painful unreturned affections are, even if it was only the promise of something more. Nothing had happened between them in reality, so he had not hurt her intentionally, just turned down the offer.

"Okay, we can carpool. But you're on your own once we get there."

"Of course."

A sense he'd regret his decision just about made him

walk away then but he'd already accepted. Instead, he paid for his gas and bought some junk food for the trip. Lola was even quicker to be ready. She'd grabbed a carryall bag from her SUV's back seat and jumped inside his police cruiser by the time he'd exited the convenience store.

Sighing, he trudged over to his vehicle and tossed his snacks inside before getting in. He buckled up and drove away from the pumps, wishing fate had kept this particular woman out of his orbit today. He had his hands full worrying about Anna.

"Got any good music?" Lola asked, checking out his selection on the iPod connected to his dash. She was scrolling through it, a slight frown of concentration as she realized most of the music was country.

"What? Don't like listening to the heartaches of real life?"

"Not if I don't have to. Drinking. Running around. Cowboys. Ugh. Pop and hip-hop's more my style. Taylor Swift, Drake, The Weekend."

"Sorry, you're out of luck. Probably wished you'd known that before hitching a ride with a boot stomper. Not too late to take you back to your vehicle. It's a long trip if you don't like the music."

"You trying to get rid of me, Officer?" She gave a pretty pout and placed her booted feet on the dash. "Not going to be that easy. I can two-step with the best of them. Just always thought country music was more for a honky-tonk like the Boots & Lace than easy listening."

"Boots & Lace. Don't think I've heard of it."

"Nashville. I took my mom on a bucket list trip a few years back. She's a die-hard country fan which meant, of course, I couldn't be."

"Right. What did you listen to during your Goth period?" If nothing else, her honesty was refreshing. Maybe this trip wouldn't be the nightmare he envisioned.

"Nirvana, The Cure, The Banshees. Don't imagine you've ever heard any of those bands?" She gave him a smug smile.

"All nice and sufficiently gloomy. Certain to annoy any adult. I was sorry to hear about your mom."

"Thanks. I have no regrets. We said our goodbyes. Not like we didn't have plenty of notice."

"Not sure how much that helps. Watching someone die is no picnic." Another twinge of sympathy for Lola followed the first. Perhaps that was the time she had changed, grown up and rejoined the large human race. Before she'd been a fringe player, living life dark and edgy. He had no idea what she'd gotten up to exactly, but if any of the rumors were even partly true, some strange things had gone down in the legendary land of the midnight sun.

"No. But it does make you stronger. Made me realize how devastatingly short life is. It's a limited run and no getting out alive. Why not live it up when you get the chance? Have you ever wanted to win the lottery and live life like the rich?"

"Who hasn't dreamed of it. I buy tickets now and then. Never paid me as much back as I put into it. At least not yet."

"See, you have hopes of living high too. Everyone does. Question is, what would you do to make that happen, Officer?"

There was that devil again, surfacing through the outer charm. She intrigued him but it also repelled him. He liked that Anna was the same person through and through, no hidden lies in her nature. She was unafraid to say exactly who she was and what she stood for.

"Is this just rhetorical? Or for a fact if given a chance? Like finding a bag of money and keeping it?"

"It's just a game, Josh. Nothing more. I would imagine your sister Anna would never play it. She's far too righteous to even imagine taking money that didn't belong to her. But I see the bigger picture. Life is too serious to be taken seriously."

Her words rang a bell. One of his own personal sayings.

"No point in dreaming of what you can't have, Lola. I don't think life is about how much money you have, but learning to live it on terms that make you happy. Listening to your heart and letting others know what they mean to you. It's also the things you do every day that matter most. Being kind. Being there for someone in need. Having as many laughs as possible by trying to find the humor in human existence. It's there, believe me." He surprised even himself with his revelations. Maybe he just hadn't tried hard enough with Anna to let her know how he felt? It was never too late. *Not until you've closed your eyes for the last time.*

"Why do you have to be such a good guy?"

She looked more upset by his words than he would have expected.

"What's going on?"

"Nothing. Okay. I'm just tired of the human race today."

"I hear you. Sometimes I despair about the state of this world. Then I remember how passionate some people are about helping others. Anna's thirst for justice knows no bounds. I feel better for knowing it, knowing her. You're an unsung hero too in your own right. Taking care of others."

Lola muttered something he couldn't hear. But the expression on her face told the tale. Talking about Anna wasn't helping her one bit. He should be flattered by the jealousy but all he felt was an uneasy apprehension he couldn't place.

THIRTY-SEVEN

Anna stood up. She had to do something. And the crawl space in the back wall had yet to be checked. The very idea of actually going in there didn't exactly regulate her blood pressure any, but better now to know what she was up against than when she was sleeping and something went bump in the night. Josh would hate it even worse than she did. She comforted herself with the idea he'd be coming for her soon. This thing would come to an end sooner or later. What that would look like was anyone's guess at the moment. She just hoped she could push it in the right direction.

She got to her hands and knees at the low entryway, then took a deep breath before moving slowly into the space. It was black as pitch just past the opening. She'd have to feel around to check it out. *Please, please, don't let there be anything in here that could bite me.*

There was no bad odor like a body decomposing, which was somewhat reassuring. Her hand come across something sharp and she swore out loud as a sliver pierced her finger right through her gloves. She carefully felt her way around it and realized it was a wooden handle for something. She backed out of the tight hole, dragging whatever it was behind her. She was barely able to contain her excitement. Maybe it could be used as a weapon? But when a rusty old spade was revealed a few seconds later, she gave a short little prayer of thanks. Now she had exactly what she needed.

Find me.

The words came rushing in out of nowhere stopping her dead in her tracks. Who had spoken? She looked around but she was alone.

"Who are you?" she asked. It wasn't her sister Tia. This was a male voice with a low timbre.

Nothing else was said, and she began to feel foolish standing there and listening.

She set to work, digging at the hard-packed floor and throwing the dirt in front of the window. She stopped every so often to pack the earth down with the head of the spade. It would take some doing, but with enough hard labor, she'd built a small hill and break out of this prison if it was the last thing she ever did. No one should get away with the fucked-up-shit Wattley was up to. No one.

The sound of heavy footsteps on the ceiling stopped her mid-action. Now what? It would be impossible to hide what she was up to. She gave a brief prayer. *Don't come down here.* But if they did, she had no problem bonking whoever it was over the head.

She waited, listening, leaning on the shovel and breathing heavily. She had long abandoned her parka. She was drenched in sweat. Though the tool she was digging with was rusty, it had proven sturdy and she was making decent headway with her task. But it would be a considerable number of hours yet until she'd have a pile high enough to break the window glass and climb out. The question was if she would get the time necessary before someone checked on her? Or were they just going to abandon her? Maybe the entire congregation would pick up and move, like Jim Jones driving his doomed flock all the way to their tragic demise in Guyana. Shit. The damn unknowns in this case were killing her.

She climbed up the stairs even more worried when another sound like someone dragging something on the floor above made itself known. She held the spade at ready in both hands, a fairly decent weapon. First person through was going to get the surprise of their life, a face-plant on the back end of a shovel. Long minutes passed, but no one turned the doorhandle. Good decision.

Hearing nothing more after a few worrisome minutes, she descended the staircase and resumed her efforts. Another couple of hours passed and her arms began to ache, depleted of oxygen to the point of near exhaustion. She was rationing the precious water her body craved but succumbed to having a few sips to over-come the fatigue slowing her efforts. Picking up the tool once more, she had barely begun to dig again when she spotted something white. Not another damn rock. But when she leaned down to check it wasn't a rock but something far more ominous. A skull. Human. And looked to be very old.

Something crawled over her skin making her entire body tingle with a terrible sense of unease. How had they died? Had they been abandoned, left to rot in this pit, lonely and in extreme anguish for what some fellow human had done to them? It never failed to shock Anna what homo sapiens did to one other. And even though it broke her heart each and every time, losing a small part of herself in the process, she always comforted herself with other thoughts of the good people could do as well. How a mother can lift a car off her child if necessary or a fireman run into a burning building to save a life. So many lived lives of heroes, even if it was just the getting up each morning to go to a job they hated to be able to put bread on the table. To make certain their families were provided for.

She stopped using the spade and began to dig by hand, not wanting to damage any more of the bones. As each one was revealed, she set them carefully to one side until she had a complete skeleton. She'd found no clues to who they had been in life. Just the bones, nothing else.

She bowed her head and gave voice to her thoughts, "I'm sorry whatever happened to you that left your remains in an unmarked grave. But I swear I will see you properly buried. With DNA testing, we should be able to find out your name. And if you were murdered, I will see to it your murderer is brought to justice." If only the dead could carry on conversations. A reminder of her sister Tia sometimes coming to her since she had died made her rethink it. Realize it was entirely possible it could be happening again. Someone has said, *find me*. "And if there's anything more you want to tell me, I'm listening."

It seemed a strange thing to say, but it also comforted Anna. She bent to her task again. She needed to get the hell out of there and see justice done. Ignoring the pain in her hands, she doubled her efforts, wanting to escape before sunrise if possible.

THIRTY-EIGHT

"I don't think you should do it," Beatrix said. She took Sister Joan's hands in hers, something she could not have imagined doing a day ago. But now the fate of her new friend's future rested on her far too thin shoulders. "It's too dangerous. Something could happen to you, something bad. You could even drown."

Her new friend set down her hairbrush and glanced at her. They were sitting on her cot in the dormitory, having been given the last hour off to prepare for the ceremony. "Drown. No, that won't happen, silly. It's just a baptism. A representation of death and rebirth. You said so yourself. And it's almost time. I can't back out now. Plus, they won't let me stay if I don't join them." She gestured at her hair. "Will you braid it for me?"

Beatrix took up the task, deftly dividing the silky strands into three sections. "Why don't we go away together? We can go anywhere. Do whatever we want. We're young, in good shape. Think about how good it could be. Just you and me making our way together in the world." Beatrice pushed all the enthusiasm in her heart directly into her words. She had to persuade her new friend of the dangers of staying. She couldn't take a chance on losing her now. "We could become like angels. Go places and spread the good news, do good things for others. Like angel warriors or goddesses."

"Is this because of your mother? You want to see her?"

"What? No. That's not it at all. She didn't give a damn about me when I was there, except to use me. Why should I go back now?"

"If my mom had survived my birth..." She began to cry, the tears spilling down her cheeks. "I need to do this. I'm so guilty. It's the only way. After I'm baptized, maybe then we can think about it. Okay?"

Her heart and mind filled with a worry that made her entire body ache. A terrible thing was going to happen here today. She knew it to the very depths of her soul. Sister Joan would not survive First Call.

What can I do about it? She finished the simple braid and tied it off with an elastic hair band. She wasn't capable of fancy fish tail braids or anything fancy for that matter. But she could be a good friend. One thing she was good at. Loyalty beyond all common sense. Which explained her doing the horrible, vile things she had done for her family until they'd broken her and she had to leave or die. What would a good friend do in this situation? She racked her brain for an answer, even considered knocking her friend out and hiding her. But then she would be angry with her and might pull away, abandon Beatrix all together. No, she couldn't allow that to happen. If she did the wrong thing, she'd lose her and that was unacceptable on every level. She had opened her heart to Sister Joan, something she never thought possible. No matter how hard she pondered, no answer came to her, no route to leaving everything in her new life intact. Something would have to give. What was she willing to give up to save her new friend?

"Will you pray with me?" Sister Joan asked, giving her a tremendous smile. The vulnerability and beauty in her face and especially in her eyes touched Sister Beatrix on every level. *I never want this moment to end.*

"Of course." They clasped hands, bowed their heads, and closed their eyes.

"Thank you, dear Lord, for this glorious day. I ask you for the strength to do the right thing today. To help Sister Joan in becoming her best self. To rise from the water feeling your love and healing purpose. She's a good person, and I know you must know that. So please let her stay with me and together we can do good things in this world. Please don't take her away from me because she's too good for this world. I beg you. Keep her safe. Amen."

Sister Joan gave her a weird look but didn't say anything though added her own *Amen.*

The church bells began to ring out, signaling everyone was gathering in the dining hall.

"It's time." Sister Joan got to her feet and smoothed her long white gown down over her knees. Sister Beatrix did the same. It would be a sea of white today among the friends. A chance at a new beginning with all their numbers now accounted for. It was the only thing keeping Sister Beatrix from going completely mad. Mother needed Sister Joan's conversion if indeed she wanted every slot filled for the congregation to move forward to the next stage, whatever that would look like. But still a thorn lodged in her heart, digging ever deeper as she worried about the outcome. And if she pulled it out, no doubt it would bleed all over everything she had accomplished here at Ironwood.

Reluctantly, Beatrix pushed herself off the thin mattress. She tried to give her new friend a smile of comfort and support but must have failed miserably, because Sister Joan took her into her arms and hugged her for a few seconds, patting her back as if she were a small child in need of comfort.

"It will be okay, I promise," Sister Joan said, gently pushing her away even though she tried to hang on and blessing her with a tremendous smile. "We'll be celebrating and feasting in no time. I hope we have chicken and dumplings today. I love those!"

"Yeah, they're good." Her mouth filled with the taste of ashes and her eyes filled with tears she worked hard to suppress. She linked arms with her sister. "Okay, let's get this done."

Instead of elation as they walked out of the women's dormitory, all she felt was a dread akin to be asked to ascend a scaffolding for their own beheading or hanging. She'd far rather be the one to undergo the test again than Sister Joan. Be the one likely to end up dead. Show them how loyal and true she was. But then she'd have to leave her friend anyway and that would suck. With no clear way forward, she began to pray with an intensity she'd never experienced before. *Dear God, save my friend. She's too young to die. Please tell me what to do.* She said the words over and over and over, like a mantra in her mind until she had closed herself off from the outside world.

She didn't see the large metal tank of water brought in for the occasion. The security detail standing guard near the staircase. The flock of members praying like a hive of worker bees on their knees. Or the cage of butterflies ready to be released at the moment of decision. All she saw was Mother as she raised her arms high, praying to God. She tried to project her inner mantra onto her, willing her to make certain Sister Joan would rise up from the baptism to become one of them. Was it working? Mother looked straight at her; they're eyes even locking for a couple of seconds. But she couldn't be certain. Mother's expression was closed off this morning, her face and body like marble. Where was the warmth? The tenderness and caring she'd shown Beatrix when she'd joined with them in Holy Communion.

Something was wrong. Fear instantly dogged her. She felt herself unsteady, the sensation growing stronger, as if she were walking on spongy ground, not the solid wood flooring of the hall. The distinct odors of the breakfast feast prepared and waiting in the community kitchen turned her stomach queasy. Why had she not tried harder to convince her new friend to leave with her? Her brain whirled, wanting to find another way, another rout to saving her. There had to be a way!

But by then it was too late for ideas. No time for a diversion as Sister Joan quietly and with an elated expression on her lovely face kissed her one final time. She then regally ascended the steps to the top of the tank to await her fate, abandoning her.

Mother stood at the top, smiling down at her. *Fake. Fake. Fake.* For the first time she could see right through the woman. She was a charlatan. A pretender. Suddenly, all was clear as if blinders had been ripped away.

But she stood there, unable to move, frozen in place as her dearest friend in all the world gave herself over to the woman, her very life hanging precariously in the balance. She watched as Sister Joan stepped into the water, her white gown billowing around her, her face so beautiful it made her heart ache. When Mother gave her usual spiel, she could only watch in horror, unable to breathe.

"Are you willing to accept First Call, Sister Joan?" Mother asked.

"I am willing to offer myself to God's plan," Sister Joan said, her voice gentle yet determined.

"You must die. If you come back, then you share with all of us what you learn. If you don't, you've been chosen to move on from this plane. Reincarnation will be your route to salvation."

She saw the fear and indecision cloud her friend's eyes for a moment and she closed her eyes. When she reopened them, they were filled with fresh resolve.

"I am ready, Mother."

The entire congregation hushed. A moment of complete silence descended. Now was the time for decision. One out of their hands, or so Mother always said. A decision that affected everyone present for all eternity.

The woman took Sister Joan by her crossed arms and bent her backward into the cold water, ducking her head beneath the surface. She held her firmly, her expression cold and devoid of human compassion. The seconds ticked by, each one too long and yet not long enough. Was Sister Joan doing okay? How long could she hold her breath? She'd not thought to ask her. Were her lungs even now filling up with deadly water? The spell was broken when she imagined her drowning, becoming one of the chosen asked to move on. That couldn't be right. Sister Joan wasn't done with being on earth yet. She had conflicts, worries, and things to work out, like everyone else within the Circle of Friends.

"No!" She rushed toward the stairs, but she was grabbed just as swiftly by the two men standing guard at the bottom of the tank.

She heard the loud gasps of members as she was shunted aside, her limbs flailing in an effort to get away. She kicked one of the men in the shin and he let out a curse. "Let me go! She's not the Mother! She's fake! She's going to kill Sister Joan!"

A hand was clasped over her mouth and she bit it without a second's hesitation. A red haze descended over her eyes. Her anger increased. Roared. They were like all men. Vile and only using or abusing women. She wished she had a gun or a knife. Why had she not thought to arm herself? A slap across her face stunned her for a moment, then she renewed her efforts.

"Satan has entered our kingdom and must be driven out!" Mother shouted from above. She barely heard her over the ringing in her ears, though the words only served to make her triple her efforts. Her survival training kicked in full force. She'd lived in one of the poorest sections of New York City and knew a few things about self-protection. She managed to use one knee to slam one of the guards in the nuts and he broke his hold on her, grabbing for his precious jewels. The second guard immediately put her in a chokehold.

This one was harder to escape. She fell to her knees as the man held on to her neck like a python, increasing the pressure painfully. Darkness narrowed her vision. Her oxygen deprived brain began to shut down, pinpoints of light piercing her brain. Then the room vanished entirely as she was rendered unconscious.

THIRTY-NINE

Anna leaned heavily on the spade. Even though she was in the best shape of her life, the endless shoveling was taking its toll. It was nearly dawn and she'd hoped to escape before daylight. She picked up the water bottle from the ground and took a last sip of water, realizing it was now empty. And still she was thirsty. She'd never take having plenty to drink for granted ever again. She tossed it aside and resumed her digging. She was close to being able to reach the window, the mountain of dirt nearly high enough.

A few minutes later she finished the job. She climbed up to the top of the packed earth holding onto the spade and her parka, then used the tool to bust out the glass from the window frame. She prayed no one was going by and would hear the noise. But everything remained quiet since she'd heard the bells ringing a bit ago. The space wasn't as large as she would have liked, but if she was careful, she should be able to squeeze her way through.

She tossed out her jacket, then ducked her head into

227

the hole, enjoying the fresh air even if it was damn frigid. It instantly chilled her, the sweat on her body allowing the cold to pierce her flesh more easily. Her clothing caught on the wooden frame and she yanked it free, hearing the material tear. She balanced precariously on the windowsill and then she was free, falling forward into the snow piled up around the building.

She got to her feet and yanked on her parka, zipping it up. Dawn had arrived, but the compound appeared deserted. Everyone was most likely either still in their dormitories preparing for their day or already in the dining hall. She prayed for just enough time to put her plan in place. She quickly slipped around to the front door and went inside. She headed for the kitchen first. She washed her hands at the sink, then grabbed a water bottle out of the fridge and a hunk of cheese. She opened the bread box to remove half a loaf of bread. She slipped the items along with a butcher knife into her parka pockets and headed toward the bedroom area.

At the cult leader's room, she went inside and closed the door behind her. She would eat fast and hide. Ambush the woman when she came into her room. No doubt she'd enter it at some point today. Evidence of her leaving in a hurry this morning appeared everywhere. Her dressing table was in disarray, cosmetics strewn about. A white gown lay haphazardly on the bed, tossed aside in favor of another no doubt. *Vanity, my name is Mary Jane Wattley.*

She quickly consumed the food, listening intently for any sounds of anyone entering the house. Her glance flicked around the room, checking for the best way to surprise the monster. A large wardrobe looked a likely spot. She clamored inside and left the door ajar a crack to be able to keep a check on things.

Her stomach settled down to the business of digestion and her muscles eased up on their screaming protest. She was no doubt exhausted, but she couldn't afford to fall sleep, not with so much at stake. Not like she hadn't had practice during her time spent in the sandbox or long stakeouts in her current profession, but generally not preceded with so much intensive, physical labor.

FORTY

"Who are you so busy texting?" Josh asked. For the past half hour Lola had been on her phone constantly.

"Just a friend with a problem," she said without bothering to look up from the device.

"We're almost there. If it's your friend at Ironwood with the problem, you'll soon be able to talk it out in person."

"Maybe it's best we don't go in together," Lola said. "You could drop me off nearby and I can walk in."

"Why would you say that?" The request didn't sit right.

"They don't take kindly to outsiders. Okay? Especially law enforcement. They'll get their backs up when they see us together, and I might not get to help my friend. She's got woman troubles and really needs to see me."

She didn't specify the kind of "woman troubles" and he wasn't about to ask.

Something occurred to him right away. "I thought

electronic devices like cell phones were banned. Who are you really talking to, Lola?" The woman had been all over the place during the ride. Strange topics being raised and ending with an odd request. What was really going on?

Suspicion only grew as she continued not to look him in the face but fiddled with her phone.

"There are a few cell phones given to the security guards. She took one, okay? Now she's worried someone might find out and she'll be excommunicated. I think she's considering leaving."

"All the more reason you need my help. I can offer protection to her if she decides to go."

"Yeah, I guess." Lola's knees were jiggling up and down. "I think it would be a mistake. She's been happy there. They do good work and use few resources that are not renewable. Sometimes I wonder if that wouldn't be a better way myself."

"Really? I never saw you as a willing member of a group like that." But then she had belonged to a group in her teens. But this was a huge leap in another different direction. He thought she enjoyed being a paramedic and helping others with her medical assistance.

"What? I can't care about the planet as much as the next person?"

There was that angry, emotional Lola back again. Thank goodness they hadn't gotten involved any further than a half date. She was far too volatile for him. Too easily riled.

"Okay. I'll drop you where you want." Couldn't happen soon enough in his opinion. To think he had found her attractive and fun to flirt with. Where had *that* Lola gone?

A few more long minutes passed.

"Pull up there." Lola pointed out a spot on the side of the road. There were within a quarter mile of their destination now.

He quickly did as she asked, and she gave a decidedly unenthusiastic thank you as she disembarked.

"Nice to see you too," he muttered as he spun away in his vehicle.

At the gate leading into the road to the compound, he pulled up and got out of the cruiser. The iron bar was effectively barring anyone from entering the grounds.

Dawn was at least an hour away. Would there even be a security detail available to let him in? If not, he'd climb over the fence and walk in. No way was he leaving without seeing Anna. No way in hell.

"Anyone there?" he shouted, holding his hands together like a megaphone in efforts to make his voice carry further in the breeze. He had noted the small guard hut about forty feet from the entrance, new since the last time he'd visited more than two years ago. There was a dim light on inside visible through a window.

A few seconds later, a head popped out, followed by a large body. The man was dressed all in black with a balaclava pulled down over his face. He walked aggressively toward where Josh was standing.

"What do you want, Officer?" the man asked, stopping about six feet away. He crossed his arms over his chest, stance wide to increase his body's size. "It's the middle of the fucking night."

"I'm here to see Anna Hale. I'm her brother." He was so much more than her brother but now was not the time to admit it.

"Come back in a couple of hours. Everyone's asleep."

"No can do. I need to see her now. It's a wellness

check." It was a bit extreme, but he had no other recourse. And not likely they could check up on it or report it anytime soon anyway. They were in the middle of nowhere where most anything goes. Which only served to double his worries about Anna.

"You got a court order or document that gives you the right?"

"Not necessary. I'm family. I have the moral obligation to make certain she'd well and staying here of her own accord."

"I'll have to check with my boss. Wait here."

"You do that."

Another ten minutes dragged by while he cooled his jets waiting to get inside the compound. And where was Lola? She should have been able to walk that short distance by now. Maybe she had slipped the fence, knowing how hard it was to get inside Ironwood? He filled with regret for not doing the same. He could be inside now, reunited with Anna.

Just when he was about to leap over the gate, the man came lumbering back to speak with him.

"Mother says you have to wait. I have fresh coffee available. She'll be by soon as she can to speak with you. She's at prayer."

Josh frowned. Was it better to keep their cooperation? Or storm the gates?

He didn't want to look the fool. Or make these people even more leery of law enforcement. And Anna would be pissed if he woke everyone up and it all turned out to be for not, that she was fine and planned to return home today.

"Okay. I'll have a coffee." He could use the caffeine. "But I'm not waiting around forever."

"Wait here. I'll be right back."

He drank the coffee sitting in his own vehicle and watching the road into the compound for any movement, drilling his fingers on the steering wheel. The gates would remain closed until the leader agreed for him to enter and she appeared to be dragging her heels. How long did prayers last in this place?

FORTY-ONE

Anna was fighting sleep, her body protesting every single second, her eyes drooping. She was about to give it up and head outside. Take her chances with being spotted. They wouldn't really harm her as that would unleash hell on their safe little world when it became known. However, they had raised the stakes with keeping her captive and that was worrisome.

The muffled sounds of voices and footsteps in the hallway stopped her from stepping out of the wardrobe. Her tiredness vanished. Maybe she could finally have her say and find out more about what was going on at Ironwood?

The door opened, and she was immediately a witness to Wattley's tirade.

"It was totally unacceptable! To think she confronted me like that. Calling me a fake in front of all our members! She has to go. I want her out of here. Today. That little traitor is history. She almost ruined everything. I even had to change my plans for Sister Joan at the end there. Let the dimwit live."

"Of course, I'll see to it. I'll drive her into town right away."

The so-called Mother was speaking with her subordinate and bedmate, Mr. Menace. He didn't sound quite so menacing now, more like a boy being chastised. But the statement about letting Sister Joan live was beyond chilling. She was casually admitting to murder. The woman was diabolical.

"I need to meet with someone today as well in Anchor. At least our plan is going well and on schedule. Brother Mathew says we almost have enough vaccine now to finish the job. I just need to change and I'll be on my way. Drop that Stubbs bitch off at the bus station with just enough money to get home and no more."

"Who are you meeting with?"

Anna recognized the jealousy barely hidden behind the question. The idea of a vaccine being produced on site was a surprise. A vaccine for what?

"It doesn't concern you. And be warned. There's some asshole at the gate wanting in. Take care of it."

"Of course."

The door closed and she watched the woman pace the room, opening drawers and pulling out items. Crap. Would she open the wardrobe? Anna didn't need to confront her at the moment. She wanted to speak with Faith Stubbs first and find out what the hell had happened. Get her take on this place. She could be vital for making a case against Wattley if she objected to what she had planned for this Sister Joan.

The woman shed her white gown and pulled on slim-fitting pants, a blouse with a sweater over it, all in shades of cream. It screamed rich-bitch. Huh. While she gave the young girl just enough pocket money to travel home and no more.

236

After she left the room without bothering to straighten it up, Anna clamored from the wardrobe and went into the ensuite bathroom. She used the facilities and cleaned her hands and face. A shower would have to wait, badly as she needed one. Even she could smell herself after digging in the earth all night, but time was of the essence. She wondered who the leader was meeting with. If only she had her phone, she could alert Josh or another Wolf Pack Justice member to keep an eye out for her in town. She made a thorough search of the rooms but had found no cell phones. They were most likely kept in a safe somewhere.

When she was certain enough time had passed to allow her to navigate the grounds without being spotted by the wrong people, she left the main house and headed toward the large barnlike building everyone seemed to be entering and coming from during the day. It must be their work area. Inside, she was disappointed to see stalls that would have housed animals back in the day and no activity. The room was chilly, unheated. They had to be working underground then. Where was the entrance? Anna began to carefully study the layout, walking around in a grid pattern looking for the way in.

The sounds of footsteps alerted her to company and she slipped inside a stall to observe, crouching down in efforts not to be seen. Who was the person Wattley's partner in crime mentioned was at the gate? What if it was one of her own people wanting answers for why she hadn't been in contact for such a long period? Entirely possible. She'd do the same for one of them. If it was the case, perfect, she could catch a ride out of here today.

"I've never seen such a thing happen. Have you?"

Two members were talking, and it sounded like it was about Wattley's public defeat.

"No. It was horrible. Sister Beatrix should be shunned. Saying those horrible things about the Mother. Terrible. Absolutely vile."

"She deserves everything that happens to her. Go into the world and see how it treats you. Then you'll be sorry. She'll never have it so good again."

The sounds of a trapdoor opening followed by muffled conversation gave away the game. Anna moved quickly from her spot and pulled up the wire ring holding the wooden structure in place. Time to see what over two hundred busy bees were up to.

She descended the staircase, surprised at the sheer size of the underground bunker as it came into view. It appeared to have a number of rooms, partitioned off with partial walls, fans blowing down warm air from above. Probably outside fire boxes kept the structure warm which was one of the reasons they cut so much firewood.

About three dozen people were busy talking and packing white doves with some pills. Right. Drugs. An easy way to make ready cash anywhere in the world and entirely illegal. Try to slip out of this noose, Wattley. The making of drugs disgusted Anna on every level. And the fact they used a religious enterprise to cover them made it all the worse.

She didn't garner much attention, everyone seemed to be too busy discussing and gossiping about the morning's events. Anna would have loved to have been there and seen the look on Wattley's face when she was called out, certain it would have proven priceless.

She moved past the buzzing hive and into the next room, impressed in spite of herself with the vast walls housing lettuce, tomatoes and cucumbers in nutrient rich water. Modern and easy to maintain. A few workers, dressed all in white suits, were tending the plants. One looked at her curiously and she smiled back, continued walking with confidence like she had a specific destination in mind. She did. She needed to know what else was going on here. She'd had suspicions about Ironwood for months now, since the outbreak of food poisoning during the Ripper case. It just seemed too convenient. There was precedent to such a thing happening. Another cult group had taken to poisoning the residents of their nearest town with salmonella when they wanted voters unable to make it to the polls on Election Day. It could have been a test to observe the outcome. But why they needed to create a vaccine was even more a curiosity.

She walked past a section filled with bunk beds that could house most of the members, shelves loaded with dry goods, and most chilling, an impressive array of weaponry. Siege mentally was alive and well in Ironwood. She continued on into the back area, taking the route down the alley between the row of beds. The final room looked different than the rest. More secure, the walls enclosing it entirely to the ceiling. What were they hiding in there? This had to be the lab.

She tried the door put found it locked. At the side of it was a buzzer and she pressed it. No time like the present to give it a try. Nothing happened. She held her finger pressed on the buzzer continuously without letting up. It should annoy anyone sufficiently enough to answer.

The door opened and a man in a white hazard suit greeted her.

"What do you want?" he growled. His head gear was off which allowed her to see his dark eyes and stoic expression.

"Mother wants an update." She made a stab in the dark.

"I just told her things are on schedule. We'll be ready by the deadline."

Anna shrugged. She tried to see around the guy to see what they were up to but he filled the space. "What can I say? She's upset about events this morning. Asked me to have a quick look around."

"What?" Suspicion darkened his eyes. "That's not right. No one comes in here without her express say so. She always calls first. Who are you?"

Anna pulled the knife from her pocket and held it next to his ribs, letting him know she'd use it if she had to. "Someone who wants to know what the fuck's going on?"

He put up both hands and backed away, stumbling in fear. Anna got a glimpse of the lab. Far more advanced than she'd expected. It looked to be a high-security containment lab capable of handling earth's most deadly viruses. Or manufacture their own. The development of a supervirus had always loomed large in the back of her mind. Since the Wuhan disaster. Three white-suited workers were using extreme precaution handling vials through a glass wall using long-sleeved protective gloves through the protective shield. All wore special breathing apparatus. They were all situated behind an outer wall also made of thick glass and facing away from Anna.

She moved quickly, grabbing the man around the neck and pressing the knife to his side. "Now, walk nice slow and show me." Sure, they could charge her for her actions. But quid pro quo, doctor. She could charge them for the kidnapping and obstruction. She figured she was still ahead in the game.

"You don't want to go in there. Trust me. It's too

dangerous without suiting up." He pointed at the row of biohazard equipment lined up nearby.

"I don't need to go inside. Tell me what they're working on."

"Are you one of the inner circle?"

"Thinking of joining up but I won't without knowing exactly what I'm getting myself in for. So spill it. You said you'd be ready on time. For what?"

"Why don't you suit up and see for yourself." His one hundred and eighty degree shift was worrisome. What did he intend to pull?

"But you'll need to leave your knife out here. Too dangerous inside. One small hole, well, it could lead to disaster. Exposure. And we are more than prepared here to do what we must to protect ourselves."

"What are you talking about and working on? You got to the count of ten to spill or I swear I'm going to test the sharpness of my new knife."

One of the people in the biohazard suits got to their feet at that moment, turned and caught sight of Anna with a knife pressed to the side of one of their members. Even through the clear plastic shield covering their face she could read the overriding fear and concern.

She used her knife hand to gesture at them to join her in the outer area. The person hesitated for a long moment, then sat down abruptly and thrust their hands back through the protective rubber sleeves. They picked up the vial they had been working on so diligently and carefully. But their next actions struck fear deep into Anna's own heart. They threw the glass vial onto the floor where it exploded into tiny glass shards, allowing whatever was inside to escape. Then they hit a button on the console and the air duct exchange system roared to life, sending whatever had just been unleashed into the entire underground building. It was the actions of a madman. She knew it to the very depths of her soul. They had been planning something so vile that destroying what they had built was preferable to exposure. It defied reason. But then they were wearing a safety suit and Anna and her hostage were not.

A red pulsing light began flashing inside the containment room. A loud siren began to scream overhead, short bursts of noise meant to annoy humans into action.

"What did they do?" Anna shouted over the dim though she already knew.

"What he was told to in the event of a breech. It's already too late. Everyone out there is already affected. It's scattering through the air ducts even as we speak." The man slummed forward. She let him pull away from her. The knife she held dropped to her side.

"How deadly is it?"

But the man was too far gone to answer. She took him by the arms and shook him so hard his teeth rattled. "Tell me. What's the survival rate?" He rallied at her wake-up call, focused on answering her.

He ignored her question though and just began to spill the facts. "It's airborne, a super flu. We named it COFAR. Stands for Circle of Friends, Alaskan Region. We took the newly emerged H5N1, and generating a mixed or 'reassortant' virus, created a brand-new bioterrorism WMD. Far worse than the world has ever seen. Overwhelms the immune system and can kill within hours. Days if you're stronger. The most fit and a lucky few will survive as have done since humans began inhabiting this planet."

"Why the fuck were you making it then?" It was diabolical to create such a monster and unleash it on an unsuspecting public. Bioterrorism. A weapon of mass destruction. What the hell were these people thinking creating an apocalyptic event like this?

"Too many people are killing this planet. Hell, killing each other over differences in ideologies. People ignoring the law and storming borders. Not enough resources to go around. It's time to start over. Past time to reduce the human population." His eyes were glassy now, his thoughts turned inward. "Just didn't think it would be my friends affected first."

"Is there a vaccine?"

"Yes, but we haven't vaccinated everyone here yet. You're a few days too early." He was blaming her? She wanted to knock some sense into him but held onto her temper. She needed information more than satisfaction for letting him know what she thought of him.

"Are you vaccinated?"

"Yeah, all the lab workers are. Mother, the messenger, and Brother Adam, of course. About half of our brothers and sisters." A slight noise made Anna glance over at the containment room. There was chaos ensuing inside the lab now. The other workers were confronting the man who had tossed the vial on the floor. Time was running out for Anna to get essential answers as to the disaster's proportions.

"How far will it spread?"

"Each person will infect as many as a dozen others. It's a mutation, an antigenic shift with no known immunity among humans. It's a brilliant work of art. It's degree of sustained transmission—well, let's just say this is the Big One. The worst mix of the possible one hundred and forty-four combinations possible. The very one, most lethal, that scares the World Health Organization and the Centers of Disease Control and Prevention to the core. A toxic mix of influenza A and B no one has any immunity against anywhere in the world yet. It will kill millions upon millions, ridding our planet of its invasive species. An opportunity exists now to start again and do it right."

She wanted to slap the look of pride right from his face. "How much vaccine do you have stockpiled?"

"Not much. We were only going to protect the chosen. Begin the human race all over again here at the New Eden. A chance to do things differently this time. Respect nature. Respect others. Make a better world."

She ignored his pitiful excuses. This had to be contained. "No one can leave here. That's a given. Does anyone outside the compound have the virus available to them?" What if it was already too late? Where others out there just waiting to unleash this horror on the world?

Before he could answer, the door between the glass alley opened. The lab workers flooded out.

"We have to warn Mother," one of the workers said.

"I'll take care of it," a second worker spoke up. He went over to a shelf on the outer wall and picked up a cell phone.

The others gave her a cursory, almost pitying glance. Like they knew she wasn't going to be a problem for long. But this wasn't just about her, this was about all the vulnerable people in the compound and beyond. Guilt hit hard. Has she caused this with her actions today? No, this was pre-planned. She had just found out about it now and would do her best to halt it. Keep the virus contained at Ironwood. If it was even possible?

"We'd better prepare for a lot of sick people. Damn it! If only we'd had time to vaccinate everyone."

"We have to warn the town." Anna rushed the man holding the cell phone and yanked it away from him.

He was stunned, giving her a few precious seconds to end his call and key in new numbers.

"Pick up! Pick up!" Josh's phone rang for the third time before his voice came through loud and clear.

"Anna. Are you okay? What's going on there? I'm at the gate."

"No! Don't come in! Stay the fuck away! A super flu bug concoction, COFAR, has been unleashed. Airborne. You need to warn the town. Keep everyone inside the compound. Surround it with full security. Don't let anyone out, including me. We have to keep this thing contained. It could kill millions. It's a bioterrorism weapon of mass destruction."

"What are you talking about?"

"Now, Josh! Stay. The. Fuck. Away. Warn everyone and don't let anyone in. Understood? I don't have time to explain further. Things are in flux." She remembered then about their sacred number, knowing in the moment its importance to keeping it contained. "There are approximately two hundred and twenty-two people affected, far as I know. And they're well-armed." She rattled off the number of the cell phone she held and took a deep breath, realizing that this might be the last time she ever got to speak with him. "I love you, Josh. Always and forever. Please tell Zoe, Charlie, Tom, Friday, and Diva, I love them to the moon and back." Thoughts of her wolfdog, so loyal and always steadfast by her side, made her choke up. She couldn't imagine never seeing his wise mug ever again when they went for long walks on the land she'd purchased on the edge of Anchor. Most of her most indelible memories were actually of the every day. Simple pleasures were the best.

Another worker grabbed the phone before Josh could say anything more. She could only pray he heeded her words of caution and did what needed to be done. His quick actions now were Anchor's only hope.

"Did you have anything to do with the salmonella outbreak in Anchor?" She could feel the doomsday clock spring to life in her mind, one second closer to midnight.

No one answered her question, but the looks passing between the lab workers bore no good tidings. She might be fucked, but she could damn well save others.

FORTY-TWO

Josh stood there stunned. What the fuck had just happened? It took a few seconds to rally his thoughts, to stop himself from charging through the gates to get to Anna. Her words of love, *always and forever*, caused a flash of bittersweetness, and he swallowed against the lump in his throat. Regret for the lost chance to say it back. Some asshole had grabbed the phone. But then it dawned on him it wasn't just the woman he loved in danger, but a whole host of people were counting on him to do the right thing now. The image of millions of infected and dying people scorched his brain, made it hard to think clearly.

The security guy at the gate watched him intently. He knew something big was up. Josh's expression must have given him away. He was certain it was one of equal parts horror and terror. The guard's curiosity got the better of him and he sauntered over to speak with Josh.

"Everything all right?" he asked.

"No. It's not. If I were you, I'd get the hell out of here. Something just happened inside the compound. I got information that a killer virus has been deliberately leaked. We're going to have to quarantine anyone inside. If you don't leave now, you'll be made to stay once law enforcement arrives." Including his beautiful Anna. That hurt worst of all. Even as he spoke his words of warning to the guy he was hitting send on the call to Chief Lloyd Davis. The new mayor, John Wells, would have to be informed as well.

"Chief. Bad news, I'm afraid." He went on to give what few facts he knew about COFAR to his boss. The security guy just stood there, staring at Josh. So be it. He'd soon be locked in with the others. They only had a short window to contain this thing.

"Shit. That is bad. I'll send reinforcements immediately. Declare a state of emergency. Choppers should be there first. I'll need to call the mayor and request backup from surrounding towns as well. State officials for military backup. ASDF. Everyone right up to the White House needs to be alerted. But right now, our immediate goal, we need enough officers to prevent *anyone* from leaving in the moment. How large does the perimeter need to be?"

"The fence encompasses a half-square mile. The compound's dead center of it. The building themselves cover over an acre alone." It was going to be a huge challenge to contain everyone but the stakes had never been higher. Without one hundred percent containment, a deadly plague of biblical proportions, would be unleashed on mankind that would blow COVID right out of the water.

"That's a lot of land to cover. Three hundred and twenty acres. That's over thirteen thousand feet of fencing, a man positioned every twenty-five to thirty feet to prevent anyone slipping through the net. About four hundred positions to cover at least. That's a staggering number of people we're going to have to send right the fuck now. And everyone will need full protective gear. If this thing ever escapes..."

Josh said nothing, knowing the chief was thinking aloud. He watched the security moron walk back to his shack. Then head inside and close the door. Guess he made his decision. Bad one.

"If anyone tries to leave, Detective, you have to stop them by whatever means necessary. You understand my meaning? We got one chance at containing this thing. No one can leave. *No one.*"

"I do. But I can only see those coming down the main road in and out." The whole world was vulnerable right now. For these next few precious minutes until the calvary arrived. Only he stood between life and death. The weight of it pressed down on his shoulders strong as he knew them to be having endured two deployments in Iraq and Afghanistan. He couldn't think beyond it. His worry for Anna would encompass him entirely, making him useless. No, he had to use his military training to stay focused. Block out everything else until all protections possible were in place to prevent a worldwide disaster. And pray Anna would come out of this nightmare alive. As if the chief could read his mind, he turned back at that moment.

"I'm sorry about your sister, Josh. But my bet's on her. If anyone can survive this thing, it's Anna Hale."

Josh could only nod, forgetting the chief couldn't see him, too choked up to speak.

FORTY-THREE

"Pack your shit. You're leaving. Now!" Brother Adam accosted Beatrix a few minutes after the fiasco in the dining hall back in the women's dormitory. She'd gone there to hide and get a grip on things. When she'd seen her friend rise from the waters alive, she'd been stunned, beyond thankful their leader hadn't decided to drown her like the other rich people in the past. She knew she was in the wrong with her fellow members. They'd turn on her for this. But she hadn't expected to be thrown out. Not now when Sister Joan was still here. Why hadn't they run away together when they had the chance? They could both be clear of this mess. Would her new sister hate her forever for interrupting her big moment? She needed to talk to her. How to make this right? She'd fucked up bad, calling Mother all those vile things. Maybe the devil had really gotten a grip on her? How else could she explain this?

"I have to see Mother. I didn't mean it. I was possessed. Maybe I need an exorcism or something?" She looked at the head of their security force with hope riding high in her eyes. "You can't just throw me out. I have nowhere to go. Please, let me talk to her. I can make this right. I'll go before the community and beg for everyone's forgiveness. Get down on my hands and knees. Please, Brother Adam, I've done a lot of good here. I deserve a second chance. Doesn't everyone?"

He shook his head, his eyes cold as black obsidian glass, his arms crossed over his massive chest. Even his scar stood out more, a white ridge of hardened flesh against his weather-damaged skin. Her heart sunk.

"Pack. You got five minutes. Or you'll go without it."

Beatrix worked to gather her scant things in a complete daze. What did anything matter now. She was being separated from the only existence that had given her life any meaning. No one would trust her now. She'd never see her best friend ever again.

"Could I just say goodbye to Sister Joan? Beg her forgiveness for ruining things for her?"

Brother Adam didn't bother to answer, just gestured with a curt head to continue.

A loud bang of the outside door alerted them to company. Sister Joan came dashing across the dormitory to where the pair of them stood, her expression one of concern.

"Are you okay, sister?"

Beatrix could only shake her head.

Sister Joan pulled her into her arms and hugged her tightly. "I'm sorry you got scared."

"I had a vision of you dying and I couldn't bear it." Beatrix let the tears flow down her face unchecked. Her friend didn't hate her. She'd come to her to let her know things were okay. She wasn't going to shun her after all.

"As touching as this scene is, Beatrix has been given the order to leave," Brother Adam said.

"Leave? You can't make her leave. That's not right. She belongs here. She's sorry for what she said, right sister?" Sister Joan gave the security guy a quizzical glance then looked back at her.

"Yes, I'm truly sorry, and I will do anything to make it right. Anything. Please, I just need a second chance."

Brother Adam shook his head. "Sentence has already been passed. She has to go. Now. If you don't want to be asked to leave with her, then I suggest you step aside, sister."

"I will not! My friend deserves to stay as much as anyone. She was just protecting me." Sister Joan stood in front of her now, her expression firm. She had never felt more valued or cared for in her life than at that moment. Just knowing Joan would stand up to Brother Adam in her defense was enough. She couldn't allow her to mess up her life within the chosen like she had.

"No. It's okay. I can go now, knowing how much I mean to you. I don't want you to mess up your chances here because of me. I couldn't live with it." The self-sacrifice came at a heavy cost, but it felt right. One day the pain would dim. Time fixes everything, right?

"If you're sure?" She caught just a glimpse of relief in Sister Joan's eyes. She cared about her no doubt, but she did want to stay.

"I'm sure." *No, I'm not.* But there was nothing else for it. She had made her bed and lying in it in misery now would be her fate.

They hugged one last time. Then they both finished gathering her few possessions.

"I want you to have this." Her friend held up a simple gold chain with a small guardian angel charm hanging from it she pulled from her jacket pocket. Her hair was still damp from being emerged in the water tank, but she'd changed her clothes and put on a warm winter parka. She fastened it around her neck, then kissed her cheek. "I have no way to keep in touch with you, but I hope we meet up again one day. Maybe in heaven."

"Yes, maybe in heaven." Beatrix swallowed the lump in her throat and straightened her spine. "Okay, I'm ready."

The sound of a shrieking alarm suddenly going off took everyone's immediate attention. Now what?

"Stay here!" Brother Adam shouted over the blaring din and raced for the door.

"What's going on?"

Sister Beatrix shook her head. "I have no idea." But for some reason she'd been given a reprieve on having to leave immediately. Was this God's way of giving her a second chance?

Less than thirty seconds later their fellow sisters began to rush into the dormitory, shocked and worried looks on all the faces as they milled around in small groups.

"What happened?" Beatrix hurried to confront a fellow member scurrying past her, reaching out to grab her by the shoulder. It was Sister Erbin.

"What? Oh, it's you." The woman gave her a strange look. "Were you vaccinated recently?"

She nodded. The memory of how very ill it had made her, far worse than any shot she'd ever endured before, was still fresh in her mind. If that was how the vaccine made her feel she couldn't begin to imagine how ill the real virus could make someone.

"Then consider yourself one of the lucky ones. If it even works. Now let me go!" Sister Erbin pulled away from her and was quickly swallowed up by another small group of sisters.

"What's going on?" Sister Joan worked to grab her attention, tugging at her sleeve.

"I'm not sure, but I think there must have been an accident in the lab," she half-shouted back. Would this horrible din never quit? A migraine threatened at the edges of her vision, pinpoints and flashes of light that heralded her usual debilitating headaches. She'd not had as many here, at the Circle of Friends, but they still plagued her on occasion when stress reared its ugly head. And today had to be one of the most stressful days she had endured and it was not even lunchtime yet.

FORTY-FOUR

Anna had to keep busy. If she thought about what was coming in the next hours and days, she'd go stark-raving mad. How many would even survive this deadly super flu? All she could do in the meantime was prepare. Set up a quarantine area for the sick and try to keep those still uninfected apart.

"What's the plan?" she asked the man she'd threatened with the knife. He stared at her blankly. Exasperated, she took him by the shoulders and got right in his face. "What's the plan for looking after those affected? Where are we setting up?"

He shook his head back and forth slowly, obviously in a daze. "It wasn't supposed to be us. It was meant for the outside world. This shouldn't be happening."

"But it is! Surely there's some plan of action for a lab accident?"

"We have plenty of cots and space down here. We can set up a mini-hospital in short order. Now, while everyone's still well enough," one of the other workers chimed in. "Only use the friends already down here. It might help slow the rate of infection to those on ground level."

"Who are you?" Anna asked. This guy at least had his head on straight.

"Brother Thomas."

"I'm Anna, and I need your help to get this thing up and running. How much medical equipment do you have?"

"We're decently stocked. Especially of PPE equipment like masks and gloves. IVs and respirators for the afflicted. We weren't planning on a contagion like this among our members."

"Right. Just everyone else in the outside world." She couldn't keep the disgust from edging her tone.

A darkness slid over his expression, like something had just dawned on him. Something vile and bad. He turned away from Anna to approach another of the lab workers and pulled them aside, whispering in their ear. The second person nodded, their mouth firming into a flat line, their eyes grim.

"No one is allowed to leave here. The military and law enforcement are on their way. Anyone who leaves will be shot on sight," she said, raising her voice to make certain everyone understood the perils of even attempting such an evil endeavor. If what she suspected was true, these idiots were still planning to infect the outside world with real people now, instead of vials of the contagion.

"You don't know that. And they aren't here yet." The handful of workers went to push past her, obviously bent on a new plan of destruction—getting out before lockdown hit and spreading the pathogen around the world.

Anna was stunned, but not too stunned not to act to stop it from happening. She was the only thing standing between the infected cult members and an innocent population. COVID19 had been bad enough, emptying old folks' homes and killing the vulnerable. But this thing would be far worse, a plague of biblical proportions. She would do what she had to, no matter how difficult. She'd had nightmares of such a thing happening, but never thought she'd be enmeshed in such a nefarious plot to purposely inflict it on their fellow humans.

"No." She pulled out the knife again and grabbed the nearest member of the cult, Brother Thomas, pressing it to his neck. "No one leaves. Or he dies."

The other lab personnel stopped dead in their tracks. One appeared to be weighing their options of rushing her. Sure, some would get away from her. She couldn't take out them all out. But no one wanted to be the one to die here today. She hoped her ploy worked. She didn't want to have to kill anyone. Surely sanity would surface? She just had to hold onto things until the reinforcements arrived for Josh. By now they had to be on their way. Choppers would come first, spilling out their well-armed response teams. She just had to hang on. Every second she prevented these people from leaving meant help was getting one step closer. Soon, an armed militia would surround all of Ironwood. Problem was, Anna was going to be on the wrong side of the fence.

"What are the first symptoms?" She needed more information and to keep them talking, diffusing the situation as best she could.

"Headache, fever, sore throat, a rash, vomiting, and diarrhea. Then your lungs fill up with fluid, and you essentially drown in your own mucus. Expect to get very ill very soon, Anna Hale."

"You think we don't know who you are?" another

worker scoffed at her raised eyebrows. "You're notorious for sticking your nose into other people's business."

"If you mean my sleuthing out murderers and serial killers is 'sticking my nose into other people's business,' then yes, I'm proud to say that's my mission. Looks like I've ended up in a nest of the worst kind imaginable this time. Diabolical assholes who think their ideology isn't covering a blatant hatred for their fellow humans. What makes you the judge of who's chosen to live and who's not? All of you disgust me." She couldn't keep the words back, her anger nearly overcoming her common sense. Baiting them wouldn't help anything, but damn it, it felt good to let them know what she thought of them.

"Be that as it may, it's a little late to be discussing the why of it. I'd be more concerned about focusing on helping those people right here that you have now exposed to the virus with your reckless disregard for human life in storming our lab," another worker said, twisting the truth. But isn't that what psychopaths do? Everything is always someone else's fault.

She ignored the idiocy and asked, "How many medical personnel do you have on site?"

"Enough. We'll lose some, that can't be helped, but enough are vaccinated to prevent a total collapse."

What would happen when she got sick? Would anyone help or would she be thrown out into the cold to die alone? She wouldn't put it past these vile monsters.

"How long are you going to hold us hostage?"

"Just until I hear safeguards are in place to make damn sure no one leaves Ironwood." How long would it be? She nodded curtly at a worker who was trying to circle around and attack from her flank. She kept the knife pressed to the cult member's neck. "Stay where you are."

"You think you can contain this thing?" Another lab worker shook their head slowly back and forth, his beady eyes focused on her knife. "Not going to happen. People will be rushing the exits even as you hold us here. No way can law enforcement or the state militia get here in time."

She couldn't let them destroy her faith. Help had to arrive in time. Decency had to prevail.

FORTY-FIVE

The sound of choppers was the sweetest sound in all the world. It signaled the calvary. Josh scanned the open sky looking for the blackbirds. He counted fourteen, meaning other jurisdictions had already been contacted and answered the call. A good mix since Anchor only had access to three. One very well-equipped recently procured Airbus H125 which can fit six passengers plus one pilot, or six passengers. The pride of Alaska, the helicopter was equipped with advanced imaging equipment, communications systems, and specialized search and rescue gear. They also had two S-92 SARs. Coastal Helicopters had a fleet and had sent seven of their Airbus AS350 and the Coast Guard their H-65 Dauphins filled up the remaining numbers. Four landed on the road outside the compound, not far from where he stood guarding the gate. Men and women in black tactical gear and armed with rifles and handguns swarmed out of the bodies of the aircraft and onto the road. The other aircraft swept right on by and flew into position on the other three roads surrounding the acreage, dropping out of sight.

But it still only gave them approximately one hundred people to do the job of four hundred. Resources would be stretched thin until the trucks could arrive filled with military personnel, the state's National Guard and anyone else they could round up. He prayed they'd be pushing the speed limit all the way to Ironwood. They had only one chance at this and the window was closing fast.

Chief Lloyd Davis strode right up to Josh, his expression grim.

"Chief," Josh said with a nod of respect. A decent boss as bosses go, Davis could be counted on to get on with things in an emergency. He'd come through today, never doubting his detective's word for a second. Of course, the intel came from Anna, a woman the whole town mostly respected now after nabbing the Ripper wannabee. He didn't like to think of what she had endured when their sister Tia went missing, the deplorable recriminations and suspicions thrown her way. By one of their own. A shameful moment in Anchor PD.

"Anything happening, Detective? Any word from inside?"

"Nothing, dead quiet, and as far as I know, no one's escaped. At least not down the main route in. Can't speak beyond that."

"I'm establishing a second perimeter, ten miles out, in case anyone slipped out the back way. And the towns around have been alerted to be on lockdown, not to allow anyone into their homes or businesses until we have confirmation that it has been contained. Any idea of numbers inside?"

"Anna said about two hundred and twenty-two."

"We need to establish a connection with the person responsible for this disaster. Who's running the show in there?"

"Mary Jane Wattley calls herself Mother, former Vegas entertainer who found the 'light' in the desert. She's a survivalist, stockpiling supplies and living off the grid. They grow most of their own food and medicines by the sound of things." Tom Jackson had filled him in on the extra details.

"Weapons?"

"Yeah, Anna said they're well-armed."

"Just great." Chief Davis rubbed at his jawline. "Got a phone number?"

"Yes, sir." He'd been trying to get someone back on the line without success since Anna called.

The chief keyed in the digits and gave him a quizzical glance. "What are they calling this thing?"

"COFAR."

The phone rang and rang, but no one picked up.

"Keep trying," Davis instructed.

Josh glanced down the roadway. The tactical crews had dispersed themselves at regular intervals down the snow-covered route. Big gaps between them. Come nightfall it would be easy to slip by in the darkness. And being winter, the threat was looming.

"Soon as the trucks arrive with reinforcements, I'll be flying back on the next chopper. Can't trust the mayor to handle all this on his lonesome."

Josh cracked a smile. The long-standing rivalry between the mayor and the chief of police was holding firm. At least some things never changed.

"How the hell could this be happening in Alaska?" Chief Davis said, shaking his head while staring off into the distance. "To think of the planning this took, the specialists buying into this so-called Mother's message, and to what end? What earthly purpose does this serve? Inflicting such pain on others."

"They think of themselves as the chosen. Apparently, no one else matters." Josh felt sick to his stomach thinking of the pure arrogance of such a position. "A wise woman once told me people carry both good and evil inside them. Darkness and light. Violence and peace. Mercy and justice. The key is making sure your cause is righteousness, to keep the darkness from taking over. The leader of this group allowed the darkness to take over. They had a choice and chose wrong."

"Sounds like it might have come from our Anna Hale."

Josh nodded. "Yeah, her cause is finding justice for others, same as ours. She just has a bit more freedom to bend the rules."

"Sometimes I envy her. Because right about now, at this moment, I'd like to nuke the hell out of this place. Make certain the possibility of a biblical plague is turned to cinders before anything can happen to the outside population. People count on us for safety, detective, for being able to sleep in their own beds at night. Having my hands tied on following the letter of the law slows down reaction time. Allows a higher risk." He shook his head even as Josh felt a rush of fear with Anna locked inside, unable to escape even though he knew Davis would never do such a thing. "Well, it can't be helped. Maybe it's time for a little prayer."

"It can't hurt, Chief."

"Let me know when you get an answer. I want to talk with this *Wattley* firsthand."

Chief Davis strode away to check in with his crew,

going from person to person on the firing line and bolstering morale. It was early yet, later, standing around in the freezing cold would come at a higher cost. But soon warming buses should show up with supplies, food, and water.

It was then that Josh remembered that Lola was also somewhere inside the compound. Now she was most likely infected as well. How many would die? *Please God, keep Anna safe. She's my whole life.* Memories of their recent tryst came to the forefront of his mind. If only he could go back in time, somehow, he would persuade her to stay with him, never to come here to this hell hole in the middle of nowhere. Now they were on opposite sides of an impossible-to-scale fence and his precious Anna might die. Alone. It was almost unbearable. The quicksand of worry opening up beneath his feet could trap him immediately if he let it. He had to fight this. Fight to get her home. Problem was they were all at the mercy of this thing, this deadly pathogen rising up and preparing to strike vulnerable humans. Nothing was known about it, but soon that would change. The Petri dish that was Ironwood would soon suffer all the consequences, demonstrating in real time exactly what path the virus would take. A terrifying experiment.

FORTY-SIX

Anna breathed a small sigh of relief. Someone had finally turned off the sirens. Now she could at least hear herself think.

"How long are you going to keep us here like this? We need to start setting up, prepping for the sick. We don't have much time. And holding a knife to our chief virologist's neck is not going to endear you to anyone looking after you once you come down with COFAR, Miss Hale. And you *will* come down with it. Very few will be lucky enough to escape its clutches. It's just a matter of hours before it's going to strike."

She ignored his dire warnings, more concerned with the present situation. Had enough time passed now to have tactical teams in place? She couldn't hear anything of the outside world buried down in the ground such as they were. Frustrating didn't half cover it.

Another thought struck. "You mentioned someone—the messenger? Who is that?"

Furtive looks passed between the lab workers but no answers were forthcoming. And what about Wattley?

She was on the outside looking in now, if she had really left the compound. And no reason to believe otherwise, or she's already right there like the pain in the ass she was, causing even more grief.

"We really do need to get moving."

The phone rang again. She had stopped them from answering before. She couldn't afford to lose control of the situation, at least not yet, but this time she needed intel. She gave a curt head gesture. "Answer it. Find out what they want."

"Circle of Friends," the worker said. She snorted. Huh, friends, more like fiends.

"Yes, Detective Pace, she's right here." The man held out the phone toward her with a pained glance.

"Ask him if reinforcements have arrived?"

"He says yes. The chief of police and a hundred reinforcements. Fourteen choppers."

"What kind of choppers?" She wasn't taking any chances. These people had already proved themselves villains.

"Airbuses H125 and H350 plus H-65 Dauphins. A couple of Sar helicopters."

The intel seemed specific enough.

"Okay. Give it over." She dropped the knife away from the doctor's throat. "You can get to work now."

He glared at her but ended up walking away and grumbling to his cohorts.

"Josh."

"Anna. Everything okay?" The sound of his worried voice softened something inside her. Just a short while ago she had thought she might never hear it again.

"Yeah. So far. No sign of Wattley. I did overhear her say she was leaving the compound this morning."

"That was going to be my next question. Have you learned anything else?"

"There's mention of someone called the messenger. And this virus, you basically drown when your lungs fill with fluid. Tell medical to bring breathing apparatus and oxygen tanks and whatever else that kind of equipment a disease like a super flu requires. Sounds something like COVID but deadlier and quicker to strike." What if they wouldn't let doctors and nurses in? Or would they even try to arrange for volunteers? They had to worry about being taken hostage by a group of misguided cult members.

"I'll do my best. The decision about medical intervention is out of my hands. Fuck. I wish you hadn't gone in there, Anna."

"It is what it is." A part of her felt the same, the human survivor within screaming about taking insane risks and putting their life on the line. But another part knew she was exactly where she needed to be to help these misguided idiots. If she hadn't been there, they would soon be spreading this thing into the world unchecked, and then what would happen? She didn't want to die, but she was still standing now. She had to believe she'd come out of this mess stronger for it. She knew she had an altruistic streak a mile wide. Didn't mean she was anybody's fool, just someone wanting to do good in this world during the brief time she had. All human lifetimes were over in a blink of the eye. Hell, less than that. She'd read somewhere that if all the time since the earth began 13.8 billion years ago was compressed to a Universal Year, you'd have to live four hundred and thirty-seven years to even live one full second, meaning a hundred-year-old person only lived 0.23 of a second.

Shocked her to the core, how infinitesimal human lives are. Made her far humbler.

"I'll be calling often. Chief wants to speak with Wattley at first opportunity."

"I'll keep you informed long as I can." She refused to feel sorry for herself. She'd walked into this situation eyes wide open. "There's something else you need to know about." She went on to fill him in about the diary and the bodies. And about her overnight ordeal, much as she knew it would upset him, he needed the full picture.

"So those that survive this thing are likely headed to jail." Josh's voice was strained to the breaking point. She wanted to hug him in the worst way and clutched the phone so tightly her hand ached.

"Do you think they'll even let medical personnel in? That's if we can find any volunteers willing to risk their lives?"

"I'll ask around. When they get overwhelmed with the sick, I would imagine they will." She had her doubts though. They weren't dealing with the mentally most sound, what with their hive-like activity, not if they for one second thought their plan was in any way a choice for decent human beings to make.

"Be well, love."

His honest, raw tone about did her in. She swallowed against the rush of tears.

"Stay safe, Josh."

They hung up again, and she felt overcome knowing each time in the coming hours she'd worry it would be the last time.

FORTY-SEVEN

Mother paced the back and forth in the safe room. The messenger sat in an aerodynamic chair, ignoring her, caught up in the apocalypse unfolding in real time. They were observing the array of screens from the security cameras intently, bringing in some views closer to get a better look. It was obvious they were displeased, their expression dark and disturbing. Much as she was getting paid for this gig, much as she felt compelled to spread the word of Gabriel, still, she couldn't say she'd ever been comfortable around them. Hell, they didn't even recognize they had a gender, calling themselves *they* instead of *she*. Maybe she was getting old, not understanding the new pronoun situation. Yeah, today she was feeling every single year of her life. This was not how she saw this thing unfolding.

"Has anyone made it through yet?" she stopped pacing to ask, biting a thumbnail to the quick. She'd been praying for that outcome for the last ten minutes, ever since that busybody Anna Hale had put things in motion by attacking the lab before they were ready. Now they were rushing to catch up. Damn her for interfering in God's business.

"No." One barked word said it all.

She slumped down on the daybed. The room, hidden underground and self-contained under the main house, held all the supplies necessary to live for weeks on end. Two of the now dead members' inheritances had paid for it. And more as well, before they were chosen to move on to the next world by Gabriel himself during First Call.

"You need to fix this thing, Mother. Gather up your ducklings and lead them to the promised land. Now. We clear?"

Mother felt the room spin around her. "What if they try to stop us? They'll shoot to kill, right?"

"Perhaps." The messenger shrugged, like it didn't mean much to them. "Just be smart and slip through the back door like ninjas. The planet, Mother Earth, is counting on you. Go."

But still she hesitated. "I don't want to die. Please, we can go somewhere else, start again. It's not too late."

"It's too late for all that. This is our last hope to reset the human race. Do as I ask or prepare to face the consequences." The messenger pulled a gun from their pocket. "Now go and spread the faith." They grinned wickedly, showing teeth that appeared almost canine.

"I'm going." She stumbled to her feet.

"There's a group in the women's dorm. They're less likely to shoot females. Use them. And only about half of them are immunized. And take this vial with you."

The callousness of the idea made her pause, stripping away some of her recent ideology. What had she been thinking? How had it come to this?

She pulled open the heavy steel door and heard it

whoosh shut as she climbed to the main floor of the house. She dressed warmly, then left the building, heading for the women's dormitory.

Soon as she was recognized when she stepped through the doorway, the female members flocked around her. A sea of worried faces surrounded her. Thirteen members. Enough to do some real damage in the outside world. It would spread like wildfire.

"What are we supposed to do?" Sister Beatrix asked. What the hell was she still doing here? She didn't let her displeasure show but hung on to her anger.

"Get dressed. I'm leading you out."

"But we've been exposed. Shouldn't we stay here, Mother?" Sister Joan asked. "I don't want to risk giving this to anyone outside the compound."

She had to think, find the words to make them do her bidding. She'd never prepared for this scenario. "It's safer to leave now. Medical personnel will meet us. They'll be wearing protective gear. No worries."

Faces cleared. Good. She was holding her own, barely. There could be no missteps now. Not with the messenger threatening to end her reign. She checked her pocket for the vial she'd been given by the messenger, wondering if she'd even get the chance to use it.

The women quickly dressed in their warm parkas and footwear. One woman she didn't recognize. "Who are you?"

"Lola Marcom. Brother Adam's friend."

She narrowed her eyes at the woman. "What are you doing here?"

"Just visiting." Lola gave her a challenging look. She decided to ignore it. Not like she didn't have a much bigger problem on her hands.

"Let's go. We'll head out the back way, single file."

Like the obedient little circle members they were, they followed her instructions to the letter. Soon everyone was struggling through the deep snow leading to the tree line, grunts of frustration at the slow process could be heard, though no one complained out loud.

Her pulse raced, any second she expected to be shot at. If not by law enforcement, then maybe by one of their own. She'd never felt more exposed, more vulnerable, and she hated the sensation with every fiber of her being. She was the one designated to be in control of things, meant for others to bend their knee to.

FORTY-EIGHT

A scratchy, painful sensation in the back of her throat. Anna gave a bark of a cough. Sharp eyes met hers. She was working with one of the lab workers. Brother Job, he called himself. They were busy setting up cots for the soon-to-be-afflicted in the underground bunker.

"Were you vaccinated?" she asked.

He nodded. "First group. We did it in order of joining. I've been here the longest. Guess you didn't get your chance. I'm sorry."

"Do you agree with what's happening here? Do you want to see millions die for your cause? Do you think playing God with people's lives makes you a bigger person?"

He gave her a dark, haunted look. "People have brought this plague down on themselves. If only they'd listen to the warnings, the world would not be in this dire strait. Wars, broken borders, economic chaos, plague, a planet strewn with filth and garbage."

"You sound like a damn parrot."

He blushed deep red. "Look. I just found out about

this recently. I don't think its widespread knowledge what the full plan is, in fact, I'm fairly certain it's not known by anyone other than the lab personnel and the leadership what's really going on here."

"But now you agree with it? The killing of innocent men, women and children?"

He ignored her question, his lips tightening into a thin line.

An urgent need to breathe fresh air overcame her. She left the man to finish up alone. On the way past the weapons cache, she picked up a loaded handgun and slipped it in her pocket, praying not to be seen. But no one was paying her any attention, everyone busy dealing with the new reality. Still, she held her breath as she kept moving. She hurried through the rest of the underground chambers before scrambling up the steep staircase to arrive topside in the chilly barn. She barked another cough, feeling strange chills race along her limbs. Crap, this thing did hit quick. She zipped up her coat against the growing wind chill. Another winter storm was on its way, the clouds heavy and gray when she emerged into the open. It was the great wilderness view, pristine and snow-ruffled, the fir trees and distant mountains jutting from the frozen tundra.

She scanned the area closer in carefully and caught some movement near the women's dormitory. She watched a group of females struggling single file across the deep snow and toward the tree line, recognizing Wattley and Beatrix. Fuck! Was that Lola Marcom? How in the hell had she landed in this mess? No time to dwell on it. They were going to escape and spread the pandemic. She had to stop it.

She checked the knife was still safely in her other pocket, then began to follow the cult members, being careful not to draw attention to herself. She'd intercept them after they made it into the trees.

The grounds were nearly deserted in all directions. Most people were likely hunkered down inside, shocked and wondering what to do next. She had to believe that most of them had no idea of the diabolical end game decided on by someone else. Just who was that someone? Wattley didn't seem to have the wherewithal to create such a plan. To recruit the necessary medical people to carry out the deed. No, there had to be a mastermind. There was mention of an individual called the messenger. She'd look into it if she ever got the chance. The clock in her mind was ticking far louder now, screaming its red alert. Risk assessment: beyond extreme.

She made the tree line just as snowflakes began falling heavily, obscuring the landscape. A hush had fallen over things, even Mother Nature held her breath. Anna worked hard to control a stronger urge to cough, covering her mouth with her gloved hand to keep from giving away her location, her eyes instantly filling with tears. She blinked them away in an effort to see clearly. It was darker in the forest, the sun pale in the sky. She wanted to get to the one leading the pack. Outflank them. There was still time. The knee-deep snow was holding up progress for the cult members. Anna was fitter than most, having worked hard to keep up her physical strength with proper training. Right about now she'd love to be hitting the gym, slamming the heavy bag. But instead, she'd have to make do taking down a madwoman.

A more serious frigid chill hit, making her shiver uncontrollably. It was soon replaced by an over-whelming bout of feverish heat with sweat pouring down her face and body. Her neck burned the worst, the long-ago scars sustained during the raging inferno that had taken her mom once more feeling like they were on fire. This onslaught of disease was unlike anything that had come before in her experience. Never had an illness come on so fast. She knew her immune system was top of the line. Damn, she had to keep it together and do this final deed. Then the world could manage without her for a few days. Maybe forever. She lay her hand against her chest thinking of the wolf medallion she wore always, taking strength from the symbol of courage and resilience.

Anna worked her way through the thick growth of trees, finally moving ahead of the group by sheer force of will. She leaned against a tree trunk and waited for her chance to intercept Wattley. She clutched the gun in one hand held behind her back, hoping to negotiate with the cult leader first.

Thankfully it didn't take long before the woman came into view, her face a study in annoyance as she worked her way through the deep snow banks, blinking away the frozen snowflakes.

Anna moved from beside the tree and into Wattley's direct path.

"What are you doing here?" Wattley demanded.

"I thought it was time we had an honest conversation."

The other females came closer, half-circling the leader as if to protect her.

"You might want to step back while Mary Jane Wattley and I have a chance to discuss business."

The women looked taken aback for the most part, no doubt wondering who Mary Jane was.

"How are you, Sister Anna? I was worried about you. Were you also exposed to this terrible virus?"

"You know damn well I was. Same as everyone else here who wasn't vaccinated. Same as you want to do to the world. That's your end game, right? Yours and this so-called messenger. Who is that, by the way? What kind of monster kills off millions in some kind of sick ploy to challenge the status quo?"

"What is she talking about, Mother?" one of the women asked, her face gone white as the snow she stood in.

"She's obviously deranged, maybe delirious from the illness. Give her no mind. We need to keep going and make it to the highway. And to answer your question, since it doesn't matter anymore anyway. The messenger is someone you know well enough, sister. Dr. Molly. It was probably her beef with you that started this whole thing. So lay the blame at the proper doorstep."

The name came with a deadly shock attached. But Anna had to ignore the terrible blow, sickened as it made her. She had to stay focused. Not let a psychopath deter her from what had to be done and done right now. Later there would be plenty of time for guilt to strike its heavy hand. "You're not going anywhere and spreading it to innocent people. I can't let that happen."

"But someone is supposed to meet us and put us in quarantine, right, Mother?"

"That's right. Now, step aside so we can get these sick women to medical aid."

"I'm sorry, but that's not in the game plan. I've talked with the authorities. No one is meeting you. At least not medical personnel. This whole area is on lockdown to keep COFAR from spreading. My job is to make certain you don't leave." Anna gave it one more try, hoping to persuade the group of the importance of turning back.

"That can't be right?" Lola Marcom chimed in,

moving away from the group to confront Anna. "You can't possibly think you are going to keep us from leaving. It's unconstitutional. So, step aside, Anna Hale. You don't look so good anyway. I doubt any of this is going to matter to you in a few short hours." Lola gave her a scathing look, her eyes darkened by rage.

"I see the old Lola is back, just like I warned Josh about. No wonder he dropped you like a hot potato."

"You don't know anything. I don't need Josh. I got my own guy and he beats your brother all to hell. Now move it."

She had to make one final appeal. "Are the rest of you really going to allow a plague of biblical proportions be visited on your mothers and fathers, sisters and brothers, out in the real world? You must all have families you still care about, even if you haven't been in touch for years. Do you really want them to die? For the world to find out how evil this group truly was, hiding behind a smoke screen of doing good in the world only to unleash the worst of horrors on mankind? History will write you all up as mass murderers. You should know that. You need to wake up." A bout of harsh coughing overcame her and she had to stop speaking to allow it to pass. The sound of her wheezing breath startled her and she had to work hard not to give in to maudlin thoughts. The here and now was too important. She was but one unimportant person in the wheel. *Stand your ground.*

"There are far too many people in the world. You of all people should know that." Wattley scoffed. "Who are you to talk, anyway? Always going after people. A lot of them die by your hand."

"They are the guilty ones, the murderers. What you're talking about here are innocent men, women, and children. There's a world of difference, Wattley. If you can't see that, than you are a true psychopath and need to be locked up and never be set free."

Anna felt the world tilt sideways. She didn't have long. She needed to cut the head of the snake now, or at least one branch of the gorgon. She backed away from Lola and pulled the gun out from behind her, holding it braced in her two hands. "Now, all of you. Turn around and march right back to camp."

Some women hesitated, holding tight to their leader's side, but others appeared to get the message and began to walk back the way they had come. Sister Beatrix or Faith Stubbs, whichever she preferred to be called, gave her a look of resignation and turned back as well. Good. Voluntary was the way to go.

"We're all leaving now. You can shoot me if you want, but I'm getting these women necessary medical help." A fake and pious answer. She had only the intention of spreading the misery, inflicting a plague on the world. The woman who called herself Mother began to stride toward the roadway, her expression determined.

"Stop or I'll shoot!" Anna blinked through the sweat streaming down her face again. She kept herself from swiping at it, the salt stinging her eyes, every second an eternity. The woman ignored her edit, kept marching through the snow, giving her no choice. Damn it. Another stain was going to be enacted on her mortal soul.

She sighted the handgun carefully on the retreating figure, then pulled the trigger. The noise resounded in the woods, deafening. Wattley stopped walking and slumped into the snow. Someone knocked into Anna and she was thrown to the ground, landing hard on her right shoulder, the gun going off a second time by accident. It was Lola. The woman half fell on her before rolling away.

Bang. She felt something burn a hole in her side. *Who shot me?* She lay in the embrace of the snow, the sounds of silence around her comforting. Everyone must have left her now. She prayed they were headed back into Ironwood. Was Wattley still alive? The sharp odor of gun smoke filled her nostrils, her ears still ringing. She had to get up, make sure no one escaped. She had to protect them. Save humanity at all costs.

She crawled across the freezing snow toward the fallen woman, her body barely feeling connected to her brain, each movement awkward and clumsy. She found Wattley's body, the woman's sightless eyes turned toward the skies. It only seemed right and proper to close them and offer a brief prayer.

She slowly managed to get to her feet then, so dizzy she was uncertain if she would be able to stay upright for long. She looked at the snow prints, trying to determine if anyone had escaped. Most had turned back. But one set led toward the highway. Lola. It had to be her. Drops of blood littered her trail, meaning she'd been hit as well. Good, it would slow her down.

I have to stop her. She lurched toward a tree and used her knife to cut a long, sturdy branch to act as a crutch. Then began to follow the tracks toward the highway. She felt the blood flowing down her side under her parka. At least no vital organs could have been hit if she was still functioning, she reasoned, praying it was true. The truth was she could be bleeding out and not know it. No time to check now.

The road was only fifty feet away when Anna caught sight of Lola. The woman was moving slowly, obviously hindered by being shot as well.

"Stop." Anna spoke as loud as she could but it only came out weak and pathetic.

Lola turned around, cradling her arm. She gave her a look of pure hatred. "Give it up. You're a walking dead woman. Anyone can see that."

Anna dropped the crutch and pointed the gun, trying to hold it as steady as possible. *Body don't fail me now.* Her steely resolution must have shown because Lola's smirk dropped from her face. When she reached into her pocket and the glint of a gun winked at Anna, she fired twice to make sure. Lola dropped just as she heard shouts. The shots must have alerted authorities. She'd done her job. Anna let go of the gun, her body following it as if in slow motion to the ground. Her vision narrowed as she stared up at the snow-filled skies, feeling the icy cold on her skin and her eyelashes. The sounds of shouts muffled now as if from a great distance.

Then everything went black.

FORTY-NINE

Bang. Bang. Josh ran all out down the road. Who was shooting? One of the soldiers raced behind him, rifle at the ready. The heavily falling snow was obscuring his vision, and he swiped at it angrily.

An SUV was lumbering toward them, coming from the opposite direction, bouncing its way through the accumulated snow drifts swirling beneath its winter tires. He recognized Zoe's vehicle and put up a hand to stop her.

"Go back!" he shouted at her. He continually scanned the area, looking for the cause of the gunshots. It was then he saw the bodies. Two women lying twenty feet or so apart, both near the ditch on the edge of the treeline.

The soldier had overcome him now. "Stay back," he shouted. "Don't go near them! They could be contaminated."

"The hell I will! That's Anna Hale lying there. She risked her life for ours—for humanity. We can't just let her bleed out in the snow."

Zoe joined them, breathless. "What's going on, Josh?"

282

It was then she noticed the bodies lying close by. "Is that Anna? And Lola Marcom?"

"Yes. I'm going to get Anna and put her into your vehicle. I want you to leave with this soldier right now. She's likely carrying a deadly pathogen we can't allow to be spread."

"But Josh, you'll be infected." Zoe looked stricken, her eyes filling with tears.

"Nothing to be done about it. Just call ahead and ask for a quarantine room at the hospital to be prepared. We have to do this, Zoe. I have to save her. Now, please, go back and stay safe. Can you do that for me at least?"

Zoe looked like she was about to protest again but finally nodded and stepped back, allowing Josh to hurry through the deep drifts to Anna.

"I'll see about getting a chopper to save time. One with a prepared crew to deal with this kind of thing. I'll call you soon as I have something arranged."

Josh waved to let her know he'd heard her, then kneeled down at Anna's side in the deep snow. He checked her pulse first, two fingers to her neck. *Yes.* "Hang in there, sweetheart, I'll get you some help. You're going to be okay. I promise. Just stay with me. Fight like you've never fought before." He opened her jacket, noticing the hole in the thick fabric. Her shirt was soaked with blood. He lifted her shirt and breathed a sigh of relief. The bullet had only grazed her side.

He checked Lola next and found her deceased. Was it Anna who had shot her? It looked like that from the lack of any other human prints in the surrounding snow. But why? What had been going on behind closed doors? The only person with answers was Anna herself. And what did it matter? Anna would only do what she was called upon to do and no more, no question about it.

He got to his feet and hurried back to Anna. He bent down and picked her up in his arms, then worked his way carefully through the deep drifts toward Zoe's SUV. Opening the back door, he slowly eased her down onto the seat, covering her with a spare blanket. She was unconscious, her skin pale and concerning. "I'm going to drive you back to Anchor, sweetheart, if you can hear me?" He kissed her forehead tenderly, uncaring of germs, only knowing his Anna needed him. He was the one person standing between her and the grim reaper holding the deadly scythe above her head. He'd fight the bastard tooth and nail if it came to that. Josh moved into the driver's seat and pressed his foot flat to the gas pedal, then eased up when it began to fishtail on the icy road. Much as he wanted to go above the speed limit, it would do no good if they ended up in a ditch.

He kept an eye on Anna in the rearview mirror. "Not long now, love. You're going to be okay. You just have to believe it." He said the words over and over, not certain who he was truly reassuring. Him or Anna.

About a half hour out of Anchor, he began to cough, feeling unwell. He shivered and then sweated and he knew. The man in black might be coming for them both.

His cell phone rang and he answered it.

"How's Anna?" his sister Zoe asked abruptly.

He glanced into the rearview mirror for the umpteenth time, checking for any movement on Anna's chest, always relieved when he saw the rise and fall, no matter how slight. "Holding her own. Is the hospital ready for us?"

"Just about. How far are you out?"

"About twenty minutes."

"Pull up on the north side and honk three times. Someone will meet you. I'm already here, helping them to prepare. Chief Davis arranged a chopper for me. Sorry I couldn't do that for you, Josh. There just wasn't time to prepare a crew and everything that entailed."

"No worries." Even though he was a bundle of worries, concerned that any delay was too long, he couldn't hang this on his sister. Thank goodness Zoe knew the hospital system well. She worked with them with her outreach social programs for young at-risk youth and had plenty of training, always taking courses well beyond her pay grade. She was a nurse by training. She would most likely be involved with helping keep Anna alive.

"Almost there, sweetheart. Just got to believe you're going to be okay, right? You look good. Are you dreaming? You'd better be dreaming of me. That was some night we had. Seems a lifetime ago. You and me. Who would have thought it? Well, me actually. I've loved you so long, Anna, I don't even remember when I didn't, it's been that long."

It seemed forever, but finally the H for hospital sign flew by and he was on the outskirts of Anchor. He turned into the driveway and drove around to the right door. He honked three times and jumped out. He opened the back door and leaned inside. Anna's eyes opened as he reached down to grab hold of her.

"There you are. We're at the hospital, sweetheart. I'm going to carry you inside. Grab hold of me."

"The messenger…"

Her voice trailed off and she licked her lips and tried again. "The messenger is Doctor Molly. Don't let her get away from Ironwood."

"I won't, I promise." He gently pulled her into his arms and she gave a little gasp but then shut her lips firmly together.

He carried her across the short distance to the door and held her tight to his chest, waiting for someone to open it. Each second he waited, he worried he would drop her if they didn't hurry up. Sweat was pouring off both of them now. He felt the world spin dizzily; his immune system was under attack like never before. His knees were about to give way when suddenly the door flew open and two people outfitted in full protective white safety gear came out pushing a gurney.

He laid Anna on the narrow bed and followed the two workers into the hospital. The wing of the hospital was cut off from the rest of the building by a temporary wall he imagined Zoe had helped with. He watched as they wheeled Anna into a hospital room as he followed closely behind them. There were two beds set up in the large room. Other medical personnel milled around, all in proper safety gear. He spotted Zoe even with the full hood on soon as she approached him.

"You need to take off those clothes and climb into the other bed, Josh. You look like hell." Her voice was muffled through the layers of the mask.

"Yeah, I know. But I'm in way better shape than Anna is. She was shot as well."

Now that Anna was being taken care of, he could stand down once he told the chief about Dr. Molly being the messenger. "I just need to make a call first."

"No time. Get undressed and put this on." She held up a faded blue hospital shift.

"Then you have to call Chief Davis and warn him that Anna said the messenger is Doctor Molly. Right now, before she escapes Ironwood. I think she's the mastermind behind this whole thing. She's looking to harm the world, same as her family did helping the Nazis in World War II. Same as her brother, Elvis Strobel did."

Zoe's eyes widened with alarm. "The Black Rose Killer. Our sister Tia's murderer. I'll take care of it."

She rushed from the room and Josh went about getting undressed and into the flimsy gown. Much as he hated being sick, or worse yet have to be in a hospital, today he knew there was nothing else for it. *Please, let my Anna live.* He watched the crew working on her as he climbed onto the hospital bed. She was half alert, her eyes dull with the virus and raging fever, and it pained him to the core.

A nurse came to join him and she immediately took his temperature. When she saw the numbers, she shook her head, her face grim through the mask. "You've only been exposed for two or three hours, right?"

He nodded. "That's about as long as it takes to drive from Ironwood to Anchor, so yeah, I'd say so."

She turned away to confer with a colleague and he lay back to assess his condition. His body ached all over, and his breathing felt a bit more difficult with each breath he took. How could it strike so quick and so hard?

He found himself praying, not only for Anna, but for the world beyond. *Please don't let this thing spread. There are lots of good people in this world. No one deserves this. We need more resources, sure, to help people do better. To help keep them on the right path. But killing innocents blindly is not the way. I'll do my part, work to make this world a better place, but please, save the world.*

"Amen, brother."

He hadn't realized he'd been speaking out loud until one of the medical people gave him a look of understanding.

The room began spinning again, and he closed his eyes.

FIFTY

A sensation of waves lapping at the shore rose in her mind bringing with it the urge to see the water. Her mom had always wanted to take her to see the ocean. Never enough time or money, but the wish had been there. Maybe now they could be together and do it? But when she tried to move, she found she couldn't. Then her mom was walking toward her, a smile as wide as the day was long on her sweet one-of-a kind face. She felt her mom embrace her, the love filling her up, but still, she couldn't move.

Her mother's arms dropped away and she was instantly upset. She wanted to hold onto her mom and never let her go. "It's not your time, Anna. You have to go back. The world needs you yet."

"But I've done so much. Surely, it's enough," she begged. She hated herself for sounding so whiny, but she couldn't understand why she had to stay, a woman who had killed others, while her good mom, who never wished anyone any harm, was going away again.

"You have much more to do. You have other roles to play."

Her mom faded from view, and she let out a scream of anguish. And then she was suddenly back in the world, looking at a hospital room and breathing in the sharp scent of disinfectant.

"Aw, you're back." A female medical person dressed in full gear loomed over her. "You gave me a startle there. Bad dream?"

"Yeah, no, not really. I saw my mom...but...she's gone. How long have I been here?" Her throat was dry and painful, her voice raspy, like it had been years since she'd used her vocal cords.

"Seven days."

She tried to sit up but found herself too weak. She looked at the other bed in the room, noting Josh was in it and hooked up to a breathing apparatus. She recognized the rhythm of the machine was what she had thought to be waves resounding at the shoreline in her dream. Her heart lurched with worry.

"Josh, is he going to be okay?" He had come to save her. If he hadn't, she knew she would have died in the ditch. He couldn't die now, not for doing such a good deed. The universe just could not be that unfair. Even though it had never been much to favor her, surely a good man like Josh should be allowed one miracle.

"He's fighting the good fight. He needs help to breathe right now, but he's strong and still young."

"Is anyone else sick from the hospital staff?"

The woman shook her head. "Rest assured. No one else came down with it on staff. We took every precaution and it paid off."

"What about Ironwood? Did they bring in any other patients?" Instant worry for Tabitha Owens, Kelly's friend, rose up. She'd just joined the cult, meaning she probably had zero protection against the virus.

"A couple, two young women. One called Faith Stubbs and her friend Crystal Vanderbilt. Sorry to say she died soon after she arrived. They waited too long. But Faith's okay, she was vaccinated. Most wouldn't come. You should be resting, Anna. Lots of time for answers."

What had been happening while she was out of commission for ten days? Who has survived this plague?

"There is one thing I should share with you, being your doctor. I'm Dr. Naomi Holland, by the way. Did you know you were pregnant?"

"What?" The shock of the words she never thought to hear emptied her brain of anything else.

"It's fine. It's early days so the baby shouldn't be affected in any way. It's just a clump of vital cells right now, but it's growing. In about eight and one-half months, you'll be a mother."

Anna could only stare at the doctor. She wasn't sure how she should feel. Obviously, the world had some surprises to pull on her of late, but this one, going to have a baby, she'd never seen coming. She looked over at Josh. He didn't know, not yet. *You have to get well, Josh, for me and for the baby. We're both going to need you.*

"Who's the father?" the doctor asked. "I can see this comes as a shock to you."

"He's lying in the hospital bed next to me." In her shock, she found complete honesty was the only route she could handle.

"Then he has even more reason to get well. Now rest, I'll see you later."

"Wait. Does my sister Zoe know?"

The doctor shook her head. "I'll leave you to tell her."

Anna took a deep breath, then another. How could this have happened? Well, the usual way, of course. But it wasn't like they hadn't taken precautions. Just not enough, by the look of it, remembering Josh had said the condom was old.

She wanted to get out of bed, go over, and join Josh in his. Whisper the news in his ear, make him come back to her. To them. She laid an exhausted limb over her tummy. *It's okay, little one. I'll make sure he lives.* She prayed it was a promise she could keep.

FIFTY-ONE

Anna woke sometime later, groggy. She took in her surroundings and discovered Josh's bed empty. She struggled to sit up. *Where is he? Is he okay?* The questions chased around in her head, scary and riveting. An impending sense of doom drove her. She managed with monumental effort to throw her legs over the side of the bed and rise to her feet. The damn IV was in the way and she contemplated pulling it out. She was about to do just that when the door to the room opened.

"What are you doing up, Anna?" The accusatory voice belonged to another caregiver. Not the doctor she'd spoken with earlier.

"Where's Josh?" She held on to the side of the bed rails in an effort to steady herself. The damn room was spinning, but she'd never admit it out loud.

"He's doing better. They're taking out his breathing tube."

Sweeter words were never spoken. She had envisioned a completely different scenario.

"Now let's get you back into bed. You don't want to

be pulling out your IV. Your hand already looks like a pincushion from us having to reinsert it every time it blocks up."

The door opened again and Josh was wheeled in on a gurney, then transported into his hospital bed by a couple of sturdy orderlies. He was awake, pale, but alive and breathing.

Anna lay back against the pillows and watched him being administered to. When everyone was satisfied everything was back in place, the room emptied leaving the pair of them alone.

He glanced over at her and attempted a smile.

"Hey...sweetheart." His voice sounded like hers yesterday, rough and raspy, only in a much lower timbre. He licked his lips as if they were dry.

"Hey, handsome."

She watched his expression shift at her words. A good shift, one filled with speculation at why she had said something she'd never said before and in such a different tone.

"What's up?"

"Just lying here beside my hero, thankful to be alive." Truer words were never spoken. If Josh hadn't come for her, insisted on the hospital taking her in, she'd be long dead.

"Thankful looks...good on you."

"Go to sleep. You're exhausted." They had lots of time to talk. Later, when he was recovered.

"I sense some...something you're not telling...me."

Josh had always known her best. Well, maybe he'd recover quickly if he knew.

"Promise me you'll stay calm, but yeah, turns out, we're going to be parents."

Dead quiet. She knew the shock he would undergo

and his continued silence didn't bother her. Now she'd slept on it, the idea wasn't so far out there. If she had a son, she'd name him Cole Alexander Hale, after the man who had adopted her so readily, and if a girl, Cindy Helen after her two mothers.

"I'm scared, but also happy. You?"

"Yes, I think I am."

"Scared or happy?"

"Both. But I know you'll be a good father." For the first time in many years, she did indeed feel something good happening inside. A sense of peace she hadn't had since, well, she couldn't remember. Maybe the universe was going to give her a break after decades of fucking with her, having those she loved torn away.

———

"Anna, Josh, you're both looking good!" Zoe came sailing into the room, her smile wide like the mom she'd shared with Anna had been over the years. Anna couldn't have asked for a better second mother than Cindy Pace.

"You need your eyes examined, sis. My hair needs a good wash and this gown sucks ducks, as Charlie would say," Anna said. She was bored out of her tree, sitting around waiting for her body to recover. She needed a case, something to involve her entire being, give her a new focus. It had been two whole days since Josh had come around. Surely it was time to go home.

Zoe was followed by Charlie, Tom, and Kelly. Word had come through official channels today that her friend Tabitha has survived the virus, making it a nice reunion. Anna wished they could have brought her wolfdog along, but it was a stretch for the hospital to allow. Another reason to get the hell out of here. Talking to

Friday on the phone wasn't nearly enough. He needed to see her in person to be certain she was okay. Even over the phone, she could sense his unease. Thank goodness he had a friend in Diva, the beautiful husky that had joined their small family last summer during the Ripper investigation.

Charlie and Kelly were all smiles, but Tom seemed subdued. They'd got the messenger, found Doctor Molly hiding in an underground bunker like the rat she was. All the bodies had been recovered from the graves mentioned in the diary. And the virus had been destroyed. Everyone at Ironwood was still under a strict quarantine. What else could be wrong?

"You got something on your mind, Tom?"

He shook his head. "It can wait."

"Spill." She gave him a look to get on with things. "I'm well enough to help again. At least share any insights. Plus, I need something to occupy my mind more than this." She gestured at the expanse of the room.

"That case I told you about? The woman and grandparents fighting over custody? Husband died in an accident."

"I remember. It's why I told you not to go to Ironwood with me."

"I wish I could have been there for you, Anna." His anguished expression shared he'd been as upset as anyone with everything that had happened to her.

"Thanks, but it doesn't matter now." She knew Tom had a thing for her in the past. She'd have to be careful about how things unfolded now with the simple fact her life had undergone vast changes in a matter of days. Things would be different going forward. How different, she didn't exactly know at the moment, but it was inevitable. A child would change her life. Her mind felt wrapped in cotton wool just trying to see her way through the labyrinth that awaited her.

"The case has taken a twist. The daughter-in-law's been arrested on suspicion of murder in her husband's death."

"And you don't think she did it?"

"Not certain. Are there red flags in her background? Yes. But the family dynamics, they're so convoluted, I need more time. I think the police jumped the gun on this one, needing to pin it on someone. The evidence is entirely circumstantial. I mean no offense, Josh."

"None taken." Josh was frowning, listening intently to Tom. "It's not my jurisdiction anyway. This all happened in Green River, right?"

"Yes. The victim comes from a very wealthy family."

"We all need to work on this," Anna said. "When can we kick this joint?" And just like that, she was back. No more wool gathering. Now was the time for action. Make a difference in the world and everything else would fall into place.

The wolf, *pathfinder*, let loose a howl, a strong reminder of who she was and where she had come from. A member of the outlier pack, unafraid of doing what had to be done to save others and bring them justice by whatever means possible, as necessary as any other, and part of something bigger than she was. Yes. Her guiding light had never steered her wrong.

ACKNOWLEDGMENTS

I want to thank everyone at Rough Edges Press for their wonderful support, especially Mike Bray, Jake Bray, Rachel Del Grosso, Amy Briggs, Jason Bates, Patience Bramlett, John Buck, Brent Towns, Thonie Hevron, Darrel Sparkman, and all the other authors who blessed me with not only a warm welcome, but a wealth of wonderful stories to read and enjoy!

And to you, dear reader, thanks for taking the time to read and perhaps review with thoughts of sharing my work with others. Absolutely nothing beats word of mouth! And if my story gave you some entertainment or respite while captivating you to another world or touched your heart, that's the best an author can hope for.

A LOOK AT: CITY OF LIES
A HARDBOILED MYSTERY

A Gripping Tale of Identity, Crime, and Survival...

Claire Preston, a script reader for a Hollywood movie studio, has recently lost her mother. Discovering she was adopted as a baby, she goes on a perilous quest for her true identity.

Assisted by her mentor, the seasoned private investigator, Jake Sterling, Claire delves deeper into her past, only to unearth a labyrinth of secrets more daunting than she ever envisioned. Soon, she finds herself in the crosshairs of a ruthless serial killer—an ex-Nazi fugitive evading justice for decades.

As Claire confronts her heritage, grapples with danger, and races against time to evade the clutches of a deadly predator, she finds herself wondering: Is uncovering the truth in a city of lies even possible?

AVAILABLE NOW

ABOUT THE AUTHOR

January Bain is an award-winning author who firmly believes that stories unite us, that good stories help us to discover the commonality of the human experience by supporting values, empathy and understanding. She has had the pleasure of select novels being turned into games, and her work is also available in different languages.

She and her husband live in rural Canada on peaceful acreage where a variety of wildlife comes to visit regularly and expect to be fed and paid attention to.